Eternal Dominion
Book 19
Trials

By Bern Dean

Eternal Dominion Book 19 Trials

Eternal Dominion Book 19 Trials

Contents

Eternal Dominion Book 19 Trials

Books in Review.

As always, I like to do these every three books, but I also don't want 20 pages of review, so if you need to refresh your memory on books 1-12 book 13 has got you covered. Now as always these are not complete and if they are all you are reading of my prior books you are going to be lost at points. They are meant to simply jog your memory before you sit down to enjoy the latest of my works.

Book 13.

Book 13 sees Xeal/Alex and his companions dealing with both issues in reality and the world of Eternal Dominion. First, they finally complete locating the last of the phoenixes and obtaining their marks as they learn a bit more about the lore of them. Alongside that we have the first group of dwarves arriving as they begin to take up residence in the kobold-infested mines they call Ginlodur. With that handled, time passes as they celebrate a few birthdays while each of Xeal's four NPC wives get closer and closer to their due date.

Meanwhile in reality, Anna and Dan are starting to get serious about each other as it comes out that life as a celebrity's little sister isn't as fun as one might think. Especially when it seems everyone wants to get closer to her to get to Alex and she wants to avoid it all after the year ends. So, a deal is made where the school will allow Anna and her friend Lauren to complete their senior year remotely. However, this also requires FAE to present multiple times a year on the various aspects of ED, with the first one being before the current school year was set to end.

During said presentation it becomes clear that not all those in attendance are willing to ignore Alex's relationship choices as one student, Brianna Anderson, takes it upon herself to confront him during the Q&A. While her actions are handled as best as they can be, it becomes clear that some movements are occurring behind the scenes as they prep for an exposition the following day for all high school students 16 and up. Ignoring the protests in the front and the questions from the press that are clearly out to make Alex look bad if given a chance, the event proceeds as smoothly as can be expected. With his role fulfilled, Alex takes a moment to visit Mr. Carter, who is still trying to sell his home before Sam's due date as they enjoy a bit of relaxation before it is time to leave once more. While there, Ava, Mia and Kate decide that they should at least say hi to the Juns, even if they expect a poor reception. Once there what follows is a bit of a surprise for Alex, especially as Ava and Mia seemingly make Mrs. Jun short circuit by hugging her before they leave.

Once back in Colorado, Alex is surprised to receive a call from the school as Brianna Anderson is essentially forced to apologize to him. During this Alex can tell that she is in a bit of distress and among other things learns of her father, a local preacher, having fathered more than one child out of wedlock behind her mother's back. Feeling slightly guilty over his role in exposing her father, due to him pushing her and others to cause Alex issues, Alex attempts to comfort her and offers to help her discover who her siblings are if she so wishes. With the call over and many things on his mind, Alex returns to the never-ending grind of reaching the top of Eternal Dominion.

Book 14.

The time has come and Alex/Xeal's children come one after another, as Xander, Maki, Xin and Ellis are born to Enye, Mari, Lingxin and Dyllis in Eternal Dominion. Following these events, Xeal finds himself needing to quickly complete his tier-6 ordeal. Only as he works to complete the task of rescuing the princess from the grasp of an evil noble, Xeal finds himself being confronted by the main system's AI through the very princess he needs to rescue. Through these interactions, Xeal receives several revelations as well as questions that he may never get an answer to, as he puts them to the side and focuses on completing his ordeal. Upon reaching the conclusion of his ordeal, Xeal finds himself receiving a quest that would involve himself returning to the world in which his tier-6 ordeal took place. While the exact details are unknown, Xeal knows that he can't simply ignore this quest as if he does, it could have ramifications beyond what he saw as acceptable due to the nature of it.

Still, Alex/Xeal was able to put the quest to the side as it would be a while before the rest of the participants would be selected. So, after the announcement of the start of the arena leagues, he returns his focus to his family, both in reality and in ED. This includes the family and friends who have arrived to celebrate the upcoming births of Sam's and Nicole's daughters. This sees Alex interacting with those whom he barely remembers from his last life, whom he has no real desire to reconnect with, but accepts that Sam, Nicole, Dan, Fred and Amanda still have connections to them. As such he does his best to be a gracious host while still keeping his distance as much as practical, even if he still ends up snapping at a few of them.

Finally, Alex finds himself with Sam and Nicole as they go into labor and deliver their daughters within hours of each other, but still separated by the stroke of midnight. As they are resting and recovering, the biotech nanite-enhanced stem cells are administered to babies Ahsa and Moyra as all three parents receive a booster for theirs. Alex just smiles as he knew that it was these cells that were responsible for allowing people to interface with many technologies, to include the VR equipment that makes Eternal Dominion possible.

Book 15.

Home from the hospital and all the visitors gone, Alex/Xeal and company return to daily life as they adjust to dealing with the new arrivals. This includes the start of the first arena league, his first anniversaries of being married in ED, the preparations for the marriage meeting between Nium's nobles and the beast-men tribes and more. All of which kept them all busy as they focused on advancing deeper into the Vault of Ucnuc as they begin to encounter vampires and begin to discover how their society is organized.

Life continues like this as Alex/Xeal begins to find himself truly opening himself to Ava, Mia and Kate as he watches them interact with his daughters. As he begins to take the next steps with Ava and Mia, his birthday arrives and with it a visit from Kate's father, Jasper, and mother, Catherine, as they inform Kate's parents of their desire to have Kate removed from the Astor family before marrying Alex. Jasper agrees far too easily for Alex's liking as he wonders if, being the habitual plotter that the man is, Jasper doesn't have some other intent behind his actions.

Still, life moves on as Alex's mom delivers her son, Alex's younger brother Andy, and the beast-men and nobles' marriage meeting occurs. Following the completion of the marriage meeting, Xeal's NPC wives all return to their training as they work to reach tier-7 before war grips the continent. As they do so, the dwarven Princess Dafasli joins them, having reached tier-5 since arriving in the mines beneath Darefret's forge.

With Cielo city's return fast approaching, the rest of ED's players seem to be focused on securing the slots that are being distributed through a guild-only competition. Meanwhile, FAE, Salty Dogs, Fire Oath and Dragon Legion all simply need to select the members they wish to become dragonoids from their own ranks. As such when the time arrives and Cielo city returns to being accessible to the few players selected, Xeal aids in guiding the super guilds' players there.

Finally with that complete, Xeal finds himself negotiating a deal with both Habia and Paidhia concerning the situation with the inevitable war. As Xeal works to secure a deal that ensures certain lines will not be crossed, he finds himself being saddled with two more princesses. Only he just smiles as he hands them over to Enye's master, Zylah Novy, for a year of training as he puts off the mandatory time he must spend with each until they return.

Book 16.

With Princess Lorena and Princess Bianca off with Enye's master, Zylah Novy, Alex/Xeal settles back into life as usual. At least for a short moment as life seems to fly by, as Ava and Mia declare that they are pregnant and Kate's family is making things difficult. Frustratingly for Xeal, the issues with Kate's family make it so that it is no longer possible for FAE and Fire Oath to remain on friendly terms and the ending of their deals becomes rather more messy than he would like. At the same time, FAE has begun to recruit wealthy players who wish to obtain the dragonoid race for themselves to replace part of the revenue lost from their dealings with Fire Oath as Cielo city returns once again. Though each of these players will need to wait a full year in ED as they will be trained to succeed by FAE's members during that time.

Following this, Xeal continues his push to clear the Vault of Ucnuc. All the while keeping tabs on the countdown as one player after another is selected for the Quest for Godhood that Xeal received upon completing his tier-6 ordeal. This quest will have Xeal facing off against 64 other players to gain complete control of this other world. For this it appears as if each player will be based out of a city that has yet to fall to the demonic swarm that has infected the world as a whole. Thereby causing Xeal to find himself reunited with Princess Tsega and Austru once again, as Austru makes her desires towards Xeal known.

Thus, with a whole new world to focus his efforts on, Xeal finds his focus split between his efforts in the main ED world, and the struggle in this new quest world and reality. Culminating in Xeal's first victory over another player in the quest world and the assimilation of a second city-state, Xeal finally officially proposes to Kate and Thanksgiving comes. With the arrival of Ava and Mia's estranged mother, mixed in with all the other guests, one thing is certain, Alex/Xeal's life is always interesting.

Book 17.

With Thanksgiving morning handled, Alex and company find themselves navigating the rocky family relationships that seems to come with dating five women at once, in reality at least. Thankfully all of them have long since learned to grin and bear it, at least for the most part as Ava and Mia's wounds towards their mother are still fresh. Though it is clear that they still care, even if they are unsure if they wish for her to be back in their lives in any meaningful way.

Meanwhile, in ED Xeal is dealing with the return of Princesses Bianca and Lorena as he finds them vastly changed by their time away with Zylah. Still, tension is the nicest word that Xeal can use to describe the relationship between them and Enye, as the time has come for Xeal to start making good on his required time spent with each of the princesses.

Back in reality and with Christmas quickly approaching, Alex and most of those who live with him in Colorado once more find themselves in California as they prepare for Amanda and Fred's wedding. Though before that, Alex has a Christmas gift for Ava and Mia as he asks them to wear a ring from him and become his fourth and fifth fiancées in reality. With their happy acceptance mixed in with a bit of teasing, all that remains is to see the legislation, that Kate has been pushing behind the scenes, passed for Alex to marry all five of them. Though there are a few weddings to take care of before that, the first of which is the aforementioned one between Fred and Amanda that happens just days after Christmas.

Following that New Year's comes and goes with Alex and Kate celebrating officially knowing each other in reality for a full year in a rather intimate manner. Shortly after the new year, it was once more time for Alex and his group to visit his old high school for another of the FAE presentations on finding success in the VR gaming industry. Once that is complete, Alex and company happily return to Colorado and resume their focus on clearing the Vault of Ucnuc.

With the prep work complete and everything as ready as

Xeal can make it, he leads the massive force of players into the Vault of Ucnuc and against the vampires within. They advance through one floor after another and seal each as they get closer and closer to their goal, while suffering heavy losses as they reach floors well above their current levels. As the struggle continues, Xeal eventually finds his party facing off against a corpse demon as he fights to seal the last floor while vampires threaten to overwhelm the remainder of his other forces. Thankfully with the trump cards that Taya brings from her connection with Eba the nature phoenix and Lucida brings with her connection to Brangwen the shadow phoenix, they are able to overcome the challenge.

At least that is what they thought as Xeal calls on Queen Alia Lorafir and hands her a drop of Brangwen's blood for a bit of insurance, as they dive into the area beneath the Vault of Ucnuc. It is there that they learn of the dark secret that lies behind not only the Vault of Ucnuc, but Bula's line and access to the sight as well, as they meet one of the sources of vampirism, the undying orc Ucnuc himself. As tensions build, words of anger are exchanged as Bula unloads her pent-up anger at her ancestor and the source of it all, the demonic god of predictions, Laplace himself, shows up. Tensions build as Xeal tries to figure out a way to overcome the circumstances without triggering an end game quest, but coming up empty as he focuses on talking his way out if the situation.

As things look like they will end up going a terrible direction, Daryu, the ED developer who has been tasked with monitoring Xeal, arrives. Claiming that to go any farther would threaten to create a situation that ED is not equipped to handle at the current time, he anticlimactically ends the situation in a way that leaves none of those involved happy. Though Kate is able to secure a path for

Bula to go from accessing the sight through Laplace to doing so through Freya, if the goddess is willing to accept her. Thus ending the struggles in the Vault of Ucnuc with Ucnuc escaping to threaten them another day, but Xeal still manages to collect the last of the shards of the shattered blade. Although, until he finds an adamantium-level smith to repair it, it will do him little good.

Finally, Xeal finds himself preparing to make the final push to reach tier-7 as he breaks away from the rest of the team that he had cleared the Vault of Ucnuc with and forms a much smaller party. Included in this party is Eira, who is more than happy to once more get a chance to catch him as her birthday arrives once again. This time, unlike the times before, Xeal finds it a true struggle and fails to avoid her as she succeeds and they are married directly after in a small and intimate ceremony.

Book 18.

With the Vault of Ucnuc firmly in the rearview mirror, Xeal and company are firmly focused on reaching tier-7 before war comes to Nium. Though before that, they find themselves having to deal with the fallout from the revelations of Bula's access to the sight and the fact that Durz and Chief Xuk seem unwilling to accept change. As Bula accepts Freya, a battle breaks out which is only contained due to Queen Aila Lorafir's assistance. Following this, to pacify the horde of orcs, Bula declares Xeal to be the future orc chief and her their seer in a manner that makes it seem as if Xeal will take her as a wife.

While this succeeds in salvaging Nium's current alliance with the orcs, it causes a whole host of other issues. Along with the revelation that the cleric Lucy, who has joined his party, is the divine scion of Aceso, Xeal finds his time filled with headaches as he tries to balance everything at once, only to feel overwhelmed. Upon learning that the women he loves have been trying to overload him, Xeal retreats to the quest world to clear his head. While he understood the why, it still hurt as he finds himself spending time with Austru as that relationship moves forward and Xeal decides to mark her. With that Xeal returns to Nium to add Austru's blood to the revival point there, only to find Gale waiting for him as Freya summons Xeal to her.

A rather tense exchange later and Xeal uses his ability to transfer between worlds to make his way back to the quest world despite Freya not being done with him. With that Xeal spends a bit more time with Austru as they fight some demons together and eventually part ways as Xeal retunes to clear the air with those he loves. A productive meeting later and Xeal is feeling much better about things, but still has a few extra headaches to deal with before he can say that everything is handled. Still, time moves on as Xeal preps for another battle in the quest world.

Meanwhile, in reality, life has been continuing as normal as Ava and Mia get ever closer to their due date, but before that Alex has a meeting with Eternal Dominion's lead developer, Ellayina Walsh. All to try and gain a quantum-entangled server for the FAE guild city that is planned for Wyoming. Through a bit of luck Alex is able to secure a second meeting with more of those who would need to be involved in any such decision, clearing the first hurdle. Though there will be several more before Alex will rest easy on the notion.

Back in the quest world, the time has come for Xeal to face off against the second player that he will need to vanquish to gain complete control over that world. This time it is personal though, as Xeal discovered that it is his backstabbing guild leader from his prior life, Frozen Sky.

Unable to hold in his malice at being given such an opportunity, Xeal fights Frozen Sky with the sole goal of utterly demoralizing him and succeeds. With Frozen Sky fleeing the match by forfeiting, Xeal claims two more of the 64 shards of divinity that he needs to gain complete control of the quest world, bringing his total to four.

However, Xeal's actions creates ripples as it triggers the beginning of the wars in Nium far too soon, as no player in all of ED has reached tier-7. With the dwarven kingdom of Dhurnrim under siege, it falls to Xeal to ensure that they are given a bit of relief before Nium is ready to invade Habia and Paidhia. However, before that, it is time for Xeal to face Freya once more as Xeal works to mend the fence that has been damaged. Thankfully he is able to do so by offering her access to the quest world for her and the new pantheon that she is creating. Though not before she forces Xeal to feel the intensity and reality of Bula's feelings for him, causing him to become even more torn on how to handle that particular situation.

Finally, the time has come and Xeal takes Daisy and Violet with him as he makes use of their illusion magic to trick both Habia's and Paidhia's armies into thinking the other was attacking them. This causes the two sides to react and engage in war with each other, forcing some of the resources being focused on Dhurnrim away from it on both fronts.

(*****)

.

Morning March 31 to Evening April 3, 2268 & ED Year 6, Days 43-54.

Alex took a deep breath as he stepped out of his VR pod on the morning of Tuesday, March 31st, as he saw Kate, Sam and Nicole do the same. Still, he was already missing getting to see Ava and Mia first thing after each logout, as both were already with their four new little ones. Neither of them were logging on for more than an hour here or there, save for two three-hour blocks each day that were only for sleep. Becoming mothers had taken over their lives and they were offline for over 10 hours a day currently, all of which was spent with their little ones. The roughly seven to eight hours that they were online that wasn't focused on sleep, was being split between grinding and training with mirror shards. Doing this was allowing them to keep pace, just barely, with where they needed to be to reach tier-7 at the same time as Enye's group, assuming that they passed on their first try. That said, Alex and the others knew that they would likely sit at level 199 for a while, as even Sam and Nicole still were having concerns about being online so much, rather than spending time with Ahsa and Moyra. They all knew that at just over nine months old, both Ahsa and Moyra would be fine with just the normal four hours a day that they would all be logged out for during the tier-7 tribulations, but emotions and logic rarely agreed.

Alex found his thoughts being interrupted as Kate claimed her morning kiss and he put his arms around her as he just enjoyed the moment, before turning his attention to Sam and Nicole in the same way. Once they had all exchanged morning kisses and hugs, the four of them made their way down one floor of their private area and into the room where all of the babies were currently being watched. Once there, Alex smiled at seeing Ava and Mia sitting as they each were nursing in tandem, with the Carters and Alex's maternal grandparents on hand as well. While they had set up two of the rooms in this area for watching the kids, Ava and Mia had decided that they preferred feeding while seeing Ahsa, Moyra, Andy and Evelyn. The four older babies seemed to be curious about the new additions as well, though Ahsa and Moyra were still adjusting to not being the center of Ava's and Mia's attention. As such, when they saw Sam, Nicole and Kate, they were quick to reach out for them and giggle and it wasn't long before both Sam and Nicole were nursing as well.

As Alex sat in the space that Ava and Mia had left open on the sectional that had been temporarily relocated to this room while the new nap room was built, he just smiled while rubbing both of their backs. This was followed by a few slightly awkward kisses as they worked to not disturb any of the four babies as they nursed. Alex just enjoyed the moment, which was only occurring due to the fact that the prep for Dan and Anna's wedding on Saturday was in full swing and all morning classes had been canceled until the following week. Even so, he knew that he would need to head down soon to get breakfast and take care of making sure that his portion of the prep was being handled. Today that was the suit fittings that involved a tailor making the trip out to them, as Alex was paying for every convenience he could due to the pressing nature of events in ED. Just thinking about how busy it was going to be between now and his own wedding, that Kate was still insisting happen on the 16th of July, which was also his birthday, made Alex internally groan.

Still, he loved his life as even with the headaches that

trying to fit everything on his schedule brought with it, he was almost drowning in love and affection. At times it could be a little much, but nothing relieved the stress in his life better than simply enjoying some time with one of the 12 ladies that he was currently in love with. He only wished that the seven that only existed in ED could join them in reality as well. Sadly, laws were such that any AI that could be considered sapient, like all those in Eternal Dominion, were not allowed to interact with humans outside of a virtual space. The fact that the main system's AI seemed to have a way to upload his brain into the game itself was already pushing what was legal, especially as it would come at the cost of his life in reality. However, after he had let Kate and the others know of this offer, Kate had provided the documentation that made it legal, though it was still dangerous.

It had been established that the right to upload your brain and transition to a digital life was a personal choice and not considered suicide. This had been codified into law with a bill that had been passed when full-dive VR games had gained major popularity and many started pushing for more research to make it possible. The issue was that the process of doing it had been in the experimental phase for an extended amount of time, and most who signed up in the early days had died and their digital selves had been extremely flawed with major holes in their memory. This led to the subject falling out of popularity as fewer and fewer people signed up to be test subjects and it became something only those who were about to die would do. Still, according to Kate they had eventually perfected it, only to run into the next issue of being able to store the amount of data that a human brain contained. With two and a half petabytes of data needing to be uploaded, even at six terabytes a second that was a seven-minute process that had to go smoothly and it couldn't be broken up into sections like other data.

While technology had made storage devices that were reliable enough and large enough to do just that available, they were still expensive to make and required a decent amount of power to keep online. Then there was the legal issues with whether or not to consider them human or AI at that point. This dealt with things like if they were even the same person and if they were, if they could be considered alive, as well as many other nuances that surrounded such things. Currently such entities were classified as not being alive and having barely more rights than the AIs in ED did. As such, the common practice for those that had chosen that route was to set up a trust around ensuring that they weren't turned off and had some legal standing beyond it being illegal to delete them. Still, accidents did happen and more than one digitized individual had been lost due to a hardware failure that may, or may not, have been an accident.

It was due to all these issues, as well as the costs that it took to set up and maintain the system that you would live in and more, that made it a rare thing for anyone to choose to do so in modern times. Even families like the Astors never did so in a manner that was known to anyone. Kate had said that there had been an attempt to create a digital world for all those who were near death to use, but it had become a mess in the first five years of operations. As digital entities, the now-deceased members of the family would demand to be treated the same as when they were alive and those who were expecting to be uploaded soon had sided with them. Meanwhile, the younger generation rebelled at this due to them seeing it as placing them as disposable pawns in the grand scheme of things, without any real possibility of ever leading. While Kate didn't know much of what happened, it was enough to know that the system had been shut down and any family members who still uploaded their minds did so secretly. This was why no one asked many questions when an Astor family member of advanced age suddenly vanished without even leaving a note.

Alex knew that overturning the established order in regard to AI-human interactions was among the top goals of ED's main system's AI. The question for Alex was just what ramifications would doing so have, and if it was even possible with every simulation and apocalypse story that had come out surrounding such scenarios. Once you added in the past attempts to do just that, that had resulted in disaster and Alex couldn't see it as a possibility, even if he would love to have all his wives and children with him in both worlds. While Alex was pondering all of this, Ava and Mia finished nursing Aidan, Nadia, Evan and Nova and started to talk, pulling Alex out of his thoughts.

"Time to go to Daddy."

"Yep, have to make sure he gets plenty of time with you."

Just like that, Alex had Nadia and Nova in his arms as they looked at him with the blank expressions that newborns always seemed to have as they took in the world. At the same time, Ava and Mia were working to burp Aidan and Evan as Kate came over and grabbed Nova to burp her as Alex started burping Nadia. Once they were all burped, Alex found himself with both girls back in his arms as Ava and Mia snuggled into him while holding their sons.

"Aren't they just perfect?" cooed Ava.

"Yeah, exhausting, but perfect," agreed Mia.

"I think we all might be a bit biased," quipped Alex. "But yes, they are perfect to me, at least until they start thinking that they can rule the world, or decide that they start liking boys, or girls."

"What, you don't think that they will pick well?"

"Yeah, I mean they are going to have us as an example."

"And we picked very well."

"Perhaps too well."

"It's not who they pick in the end, it is any that they pick in between that worries me," replied Alex.

"Is that right," interjected Sam. "Alex, which one of us had a boyfriend before you?"

"Umm-"

"And don't count anyone that we went out with once and moved on," added Sam. "I mean, if they didn't even get to the point of us kissing it doesn't count, as we decided not to pick them after investigating in that case."

"Got it. For you the dozen guys who didn't even get a call back from you in high school don't count," commented Nicole. "What about what's his name in middle school? I think you were with him for like two months."

"Oh, god, no, middle school doesn't count for anything," retorted Sam in disgust.

"Ha, let's see, I think if we only count those I kissed I am at zero like the rest of you," interjected Kate. "But if it is only two dates, then I would be at 50 or so, as my family had been trying to find me a match since I turned 16."

"Hold on, you turned down over 50 guys?" questioned Ava.

"Were they all just stuck up, or something?" inquired Mia.

"No, they all just saw my family and not me. Alex is the only man that I have ever been involved with that hasn't just seen me as a means to an end. I didn't even realize just how attractive that was to me until I got to know him and now I think that it's what is wrong with the entire Astor family."

"Kate, we all know your ex-family is messed up," commented Sam. "Still, 50 huh? You really never kissed any of them, I mean not even on the cheek?"

"Sam, that's not a kiss, that is a greeting. This is a kiss."

As Kate said that, she moved back to where Alex was seated and leaned over to give him a deep kiss, before standing up with a smile on her face as she continued.

"Now I think that it is time for us to head down to breakfast."

With that Kate just walked out while Alex held in a chuckle as he, Ava, Mia and Alex's maternal grandparents took the four newborns to the other room that was set up for them. As they were still sleeping almost all of the time that they weren't feeding, this room just had a couch and two bassinets set up. With it still being before any of the four newborns were moving around too much, it was safe to let them sleep with their twin, which Ava and Mia insisted on. Alex knew this went to the heart of their own issues, as they had still not attempted to make any real progress on being able to be separated. Though they both insisted that if they had to for some reason, they would be fine if it was with Sam, Nicole, Kate or Alex. However, Alex still worried as they had yet to try it due to the issue not being forced as of yet. Even though it was all just based on their feelings and Alex was hesitant on forcing the issue if they didn't absolutely have to. He also felt that having them talk with a psychologist first might be a better way to handle the issue if needed, but he wasn't going to rush things on that end either. After all, he believed that it needed to be something they wanted first and they seemed to not even mind it.

After they dropped off the four babies and left Alex's grandparents with them, it was a few more kisses before

Ava and Mia hurried back upstairs to log into ED as the rest of them headed to breakfast. When breakfast ended, it was time for making sure that none of them had gained or lost weight since Fred and Amanda's wedding, as the team of tailors showed up to take care of the fitting for their suits and dresses. Just like that, time passed as every logout was split between a bit of family time and wedding prep, as Alex didn't even get his normal dates, or personal time in. Though he was happy when he woke up on Friday night and had been able to see the nap area that would be ready to use as soon as the paint dried. The room itself had just required two new walls and a bit of electrical work for lighting, as the ventilation had been worked around. That was really all it was to Alex, as the cribs and bassinets would be removable and the room could be converted into storage, or knocked out completely once they no longer needed it. Though that would likely be sooner rather than later, if they moved to Wyoming when the guild city that Kate and Tara (Taya) were hard at work to make sure stayed on track.

Xeal found himself dealing with many things, both good and bad, as he handled things in-between his grinding sessions in ED. The first of these was the return of the five ex-pirate captains after Queen Aila Lorafir had taken care of getting them set up to attempt to create their own legacy. While Xeal didn't know the exact details of this process, he did know that it was a unique experience every time. While many legacies could be similar, they could never be identical. That was unless it was a shared legacy like what the five captains had been attempting to create. As Xeal received the summons to come and see the results of their attempt, he laughed at the fact that it had failed to mention if they had succeeded, or failed to ascend to tier-8.

Still, he figured that Queen Aila Lorafir was just having a bit of fun as he made his way there on day 44 with Eira in tow.

When he arrived, he was greeted by Queen Aila Lorafir's guards and let in as if he was more of a resident than a guest. This was something that Xeal was still getting used to as while he was no longer escorted out by guards at Nium's royal palace, he was still guided to King Victor each time. Though he knew it was due to the fact that he was in a relationship with Queen Aila Lorafir, even if it was a measured one that wouldn't be consummated until her daughter Alea took over the duties of ruling. Still, as Xeal made his way around on his way to the room that Queen Aila Lorafir had instructed him to head to in her summons, he wondered just what the five illusionists' new legacy would be like. Though as he stepped into the room, he was met with a scene that was not what he expected. Sitting there were the five ex-pirate captains looking exhausted and jittery like you would expect from someone who had been thoroughly traumatized by something, and even after escaping didn't believe they had. Each of them was surrounded by a blue dome made of force magic that Queen Aila Lorafir was maintaining as she looked at Xeal with a frown as she started to speak.

"I am sorry, but it appears that they failed and each of them was essentially scared to death during their attempt at ascending. I wish that my summons had been good news, but it seems that their minds are beyond my ability to recover. As such, I am recommending that we simply put them each out of their misery."

Xeal frowned as he looked at the five women that had once seemed so sure of themselves and defiant and sighed, resting his hand on the hilts of his swords as he spoke.

"It seems that I was mistaken in believing that they

could-"

Xeal quickly flung his sword at Odelia who was the closest and watched as the blade bounced off the shield and clattered to the ground. Queen Aila Lorafir was just about to speak when Xeal held out his hand as he recalled the tiny bit of electricity that he had left in the blade after activating his elemental blades skill. Instead of coming from the sword on the ground, it came from off in the distance as he spoke.

"I have to say that you almost got me. Honestly, you should have had one or two of you still be sane if you wanted me to believe it. Would have also made a much better scene for you all to act out."

"It seems that they will need to do a bit more work," replied Queen Aila Lorafir from Xeal's right as the scene before him dissolved. "Still, I wish you would have touched something before ruining my fun. Now here, try this apple."

"I order that all illusions being cast by Odelia, Saphielle, Sylmare, Cremia and Itylara are to be dropped right now!"

As Xeal finished speaking, he smiled as Queen Aila Lorafir became Odelia holding a lemon and the other four could be seen in the four corners of the room. Queen Aila Lorafir could be seen seated along the far wall from where Xeal entered looking smug as she spoke.

"You could have at least played along and eaten the apple."

"Aila, I didn't believe the scene, so sorry, but I doubt that it would have tasted like an apple. You would have kissed me before offering me the apple."

"True, now let them turn that lemon back into an apple and see if that is true," replied Queen Aila Lorafir.

"Don't tell me that they can alter reality with their illusions now. That would break more than a few rules from what I understand."

"We don't alter reality, we alter your perception of it," retorted Odelia. "You were the only one who saw anything. I did nothing to shift my voice, yet you heard me as if it was Aila speaking, even after you stopped believing I was."

"While there is still more testing to do, they each have the ability to completely fool one of the five main senses even if you know it's a lie," commented Queen Aila Lorafir. "The only drawback is that it requires all five of them to work together if they wish to fool all five senses."

"Which is why we wish to be placed on the same ship for this war," added Odelia. "That way we can truly rule the seas. Just imagine what will happen when we put an entire fleet under such an illusion."

Xeal instantly thought of sailors seeing a massive fleet of hundreds of ships emerging from a fog and thinking that thousands of attacks were headed for them. Add the results of them believing that their perfectly intact ship was sinking, and the ability to capture vessels with no fight became insane and too easy. Xeal frowned as he thought about this and replied.

"What is the drawback? Anything that broken must be balanced by something."

"It costs an insane amount of MP," replied Odelia. "While the five of us could trap an individual in such a world for days, we expect that around 5,000 will be our limit and that would only be for about two minutes. Normal illusions affect everyone in range equally unless the caster purposely excluded them, which increases the drain on them, while our new abilities are pretty much the opposite."

"So, you won't be able to defeat a fleet of warships without any trouble, but you could create a fair bit of chaos. What happens if you make me believe that I just died?"

At Xeal's words, Odelia and the other four ex-pirate captains frowned as they looked at each other in a way that spoke of some recent trauma as Queen Aila Lorafir spoke.

"That was what they all experienced at the end of their ascension. After hearing it myself, I can say that it surprises me that they didn't actually die."

"We had to keep saying that it wasn't real over and over in our heads while fighting the pain," added Sylmare quietly. "I will say that if given the choice between going through that again and dying for real, I might just choose to die."

"It is actually part of what I wish to discuss with you as I know you are not one for torture, but I wish to allow them to test their abilities on Durz and Xuk."

"No! Aila, if it involves pain I will not allow it. Tricking them into-"

Xeal paused as he realized something that might be possible as he looked at the five and frowned as he continued speaking.

"I forbid any use of your ability to trick others into doing anything that would violate, or nullify a contract under normal circumstances. That said, you will be working to test just what is possible using your abilities to nullify such deals without triggering the consequences, quite extensively."

Xeal could see the realization hit each of those in the room as Queen Aila Lorafir smiled while the other five all frowned and started to sulk slightly as Xeal continued.

"The five of you will be staying here and training under Aila's watch and I am fine with you seeing what you can do to both Durz and Xuk. While I will not allow you to actually torture them, you can cause minor pain occasionally and try to trick them all you want. I will also be having Kate joining you all from time to time to test things with contract breaking and you are all to follow her orders as if they are mine."

"We may have been pirates, but sometimes I wonder if you are not something far more sinister," commented Odelia.

"I am. Not by choice, but by the necessity of being a noble and guild leader with a war to win. On that note, if there is nothing else to discuss I need to return my focus to that."

"Really," scoffed Eira, finally breaking her silence as she observed the situation. "You discover that you have five new tier-8 assets at your disposal and you act like it is a trivial matter. Xeal, I doubt that the beast-man tribes have any but Chiharu and that is still one more than the orcs have."

"Eira, I only have them until this war ends and can only use them to control the sea and raid ports. They should allow Nium to easily gain the naval advantage, but their ships can't jump from place to place. Even if we only wanted to transport them at will, garrison portals function terribly at sea, much like they do for travel to Cielo City."

"We would be willing to do more if you were as well," interrupted Sylmare.

"Got it, you don't want to give them that so you don't expect much," retorted Eira. "I agree, they would be poor choices for you to even give an inch to."

Xeal just smiled as the five ex-pirate captains frowned and he made his way over to Queen Aila Lorafir and after a few kisses and hugs and sending a few messages, returned to his normal routine. The fact that he did so with a rather potent weapon for the near future was enough to keep a smile on his face as he did so. Even though they were still stuck on the level 200 monsters and he was watching his experience from grinding diminish each time they leveled up. Thankfully, he was seeing progress and when the night of day 46 arrived, Xeal believed that they might be able to attempt to face level 201 monsters once he reached level 193 after a few more grinding sessions. With this thought on his mind, Xeal made his way to the quest world, where he was greeted by Austru as she smiled at him as she spoke.

"It seems that you didn't need to cancel on me like you had feared."

"Ha, yah, almost did with everything that is going on, but that would have seen me fail at one of my most important responsibilities."

"Oh, and what is that?"

"Placing the ladies in my life ahead of all trivial matters that can be done later. Even with the war in Nium ramping up, I am not on the frontlines and things in my reality can be handled by others for a single evening."

"Am I a lady in your life, or just a fling? I mean I still feel a bit like the other woman with how little of you I get. Though I also understand it, I just wish that I could be on the same level as the others who already hold a piece of your heart."

Xeal just smiled as he pulled Austru into a kiss before replying.

"Austru, I promise you that you are not the other lady. If it weren't for the fact that Aalin, Gale, Luna, Selene and Kate were all busier than I like, I would be happy to have them join us tonight. Though if you wish for that to happen in the future, I can see that it is arranged. I just thought that you wished to have me to yourself on these nights."

"I do want these nights to myself, so maybe just once every third night like this, or so, would be fine."

With that Austru pulled Xeal onto her bed where she

initiated another kiss and Xeal just laughed to himself as he enjoyed the moment for what it was. Once more he limited things to just kissing and snuggling that night and he just enjoyed the time he had available to spend like this. When morning came, it was once more time to return to the daily minutiae as he gave Austru a kiss goodbye and returned to Nium.

Time passed slowly as more and more information came streaming in on the situation on the frontlines of the war. None of it was good in Xeal's eyes, even if it was about what he had been expecting to occur at these stages of the war. Paidhia's advancement into Habia had stalled out as new battle lines were established there, while the assaults on both border forts that were along Nium's borders with the two kingdoms had begun. Xeal had placed Casmir and Caleb in charge of the fight on the Paidhia front, and Takeshi and Asa were handling the Habia front. With the town that FAE had built between the two wall forts on the Habia border, it was the one that Xeal and Kate had agreed needed the stronger defense. While Takeshi was rarely there, he would drop anything that he needed to if a major attack was imminent and Xeal would likely find his way there as well. Thankfully, the facilities there had also served to make it an attractive location to defend for all those who had gained access to it since it had been established, even if it was still only halfway built. Still, that was enough to act as a great forward operating base and as a result, Habia seemed to be looking for an alternative route of attack while Paidhia had already started a full assault on the forces guarding the forts there.

All told, casualties had already reached around 25,000 NPCs and 200,000 players across all fronts and no real change in battle lines had occurred as of yet. Still, rumors were everywhere and with all of the members of Fire Oath,

Salty Dogs and Dragon Legion arriving to head to Cielo city on day 50 as scheduled, Xeal found himself being asked even more questions. Many of these were related to how long he expected that Nium would be at war, or if there was a workaround to avoid the need for traveling by ship. In the end, Xeal just stuck to saying that they needed to secure their own passage to either Dragon's Heart city, or Anelqua, regardless of circumstances. While he knew that it was possible to facilitate them traveling through the Muthia Empire, Xeal also knew that would essentially reveal too many other cards.

With the direct questionings over, Xeal was happy when he had dropped all of the players from the three super guilds and his own off. At the same time, he was happy that Enye, Dyllis, Lingxin and Mari had at least consented to visiting the now completed area of Xeal's estate on Cielo city, where Queen Nora and Prince Vicenc were currently staying. With that handled, Xeal had met with the four rulers of the dragonoids before he allowed their daughters to spend a few days with them. This meeting had been mostly the formalities of the current situation on the ground and how Xeal wanted them to handle the exile situation of Durz and Xuk. Though neither had been transferred just yet, it was only a matter of waiting for the right time to do so quietly. While neither was tier-8, Xeal had been insistent that they be guarded by at least two tier-8 dragonoids at all times and that they were not to be killed.

When Xeal had escaped from that meeting, he made his way over to his estate to see how his wives and Queen Nora were doing. Especially as both Princesses Lorena and Bianca were currently staying there as well and he expected that there was going to be a scene when he arrived. That thought, however, didn't play out nearly how Xeal had expected it to when he arrived, as while there was a scene before him, it wasn't any of the ones that he had expected. Standing to greet him were both princesses dressed as maids as they bowed and spoke in unison.

""Welcome home, my lord.""

"No, just no."

That was all Xeal could say as he took in the scene of both of them bowing to him and addressing him as their lord, as Princess Bianca spoke while both of them still held their bows.

"My lord, we are at your service. Please don't hesitate to give us any order you deem appropriate."

"My lord, we have come to accept our role in your house and are ready to do what we must to gain any favor we can," added Princes Lorena.

"Who put you up to this?" asked Xeal as he tried to hold in his annoyance.

"Why would someone need to put us up to this?" replied Princess Bianca.

"We assure you that we made this decision completely free of any coercion."

At Princess Lorena's words, Xeal just walked past them feeling like he would be better off speaking with Queen Nora about the situation. As he passed them, they both stood straight and turned to follow him and Xeal spoke again.

"Don't follow me."

"If that is your will, my lord," replied Princess Bianca.

"Stop calling me that."

"Would you prefer master?" asked Princess Lorena.

"I would prefer you both acting like the princesses you are!"

"But that got us nowhere, my lord," commented Princess Bianca with a slight smile. "So, we decided to throw our status away and truly serve your house every moment outside of our designated alone time with you."

"I can just order you away if you are in service to me."

"But you won't, my lord," continued Princess Bianca. "For the same reason that we are up here in the first place. It would simply go against who you are. It is the same reason Princesses Mari and Lingxin found their way beside you, as well as Eira, Luna and Selene. While you are becoming more resistant, I believe that Daisy, Violet, Bula and Dafasli are more of whens and not ifs on becoming your brides one day. That just leaves the four dragonoid ladies that serve you and us, of those who currently want in and you have a chance of escaping from to consider. We can't train with any of you. You are only required to spend another 100 hours alone with each of us and outside of that time we will likely be ostracized by everyone. So, we have chosen to discard our pride completely and accept possibly being looked down on just to have even the slightest of chances!"

Xeal found himself locking eyes with Princess Bianca in a battle of wills as she looked like she dared him to deny her logic. The longer this continued the worse it would be and Xeal knew it as he finally responded while maintaining the staring contest.

"I will admit that I have underestimated your resolve, but it won't work. I am confident that I will not fall for either of you, even if I must offer you a chance to change my mind."

"That is fine, my lord," interjected Princess Lorena. "Our goal isn't your mind at all. It is simply to not be shut out by your wives. Now, can we please stop fighting over this and just accept that it is the current state of affairs and move on?"

"Fine, but under one condition. You both must live just like any other maid would the entire time."

"Did you think that we weren't?" retorted Princess Bianca. "How else could we expect for them to allow us to learn from them?"

Xeal sighed as he realized that both of them were serious about their decision, as he turned and continued to walk until he came to the room where his wives were gathered. As Xeal entered, he took in the room and took note of Queen Nora's presence as Xeal's children and Prince Vicenc played as if they had never been apart. Xeal could see the frown on Enye's face as she took note of Princesses Bianca and Lorena behind Xeal as she spoke.

"I take it that they actually swayed you to allow them to maintain this ruse?"

"Unfortunately. However, the first time that they seek to be treated as anything but maids outside the time that I must spend with them they have to give it up."

"Is that so? Very well. Bianca, I wish to bathe. Could you draw the water for me and Lorena? I like to be clean before entering the bath, so please prepare the supplies needed for you to clean my body."

"As you wish, my lady," responded Princess Bianca. "Do you have a preferred method for determining if the temperature of your bath is correct?"

"Also, do you have a preferred scent for the soap that is used, my lady?" added Princess Lorena.

"Today, I simply wish to see what you two choose. I am sure that it will be at least palatable as I am sure that you both are used to being pampered in such ways. Dear, I believe that I will go ahead and see if they are ready to serve in a Duke's house over the next few days."

As Enye said that, she stood and gave Xeal a kiss and both Princess Lorena and Princess Bianca left the room as Queen Nora spoke.

"Enye, don't be too harsh on them, for your own good.

After all, the last thing you need is to feel guilty over your actions towards them and find yourself letting them step closer to Xeal in a moment of weakness."

"I think Nora has a point," commented Dyllis. "So, I will join you, and I for one say that none of us should interact with either of them alone."

"You can just leave me out of whatever comes of those two," interjected Mari. "I will just accept yours and Enye's opinion when the time comes to either shut them out for good, or allow them in."

"I will join Mari on that as I find it too easy to see myself in them and wish to give them a real chance," added Lingxin. "Xeal, know that I love you and accept the why behind how you are treating them, but I don't like it and I for one will not blame you if they become mistresses for you."

"Lingxin!" shouted Enye. "How is that staying out of it?"

"I am joining her on leaving the decision to you, not staying out of it," quipped Lingxin. "I already said that I see a bit of my own situation in the one they find themselves in. There is a real chance that they will watch as everything they love is ripped from this world, just like you could, were it not for Xeal standing in the way of it."

"I think we all need to just let them feel like they are at least not alone during this time," interjected Xeal. "Lingxin, I have no intention to ever take a mistress of any kind. I only wish to show my affection to those who I think may become a wife one day. That said, 200 years is a long time and who knows what situations could arise between now and then. Now, in the meantime, you all need to make up your mind on Bula before anything else, as thanks to Freya I feel that my will to keep her from joining you is far too weak at this point."

At Xeal's words the room got silent for a long second as they all started to frown and he could tell that they were considering the issue. Xeal thought that it would take a minute before anyone responded when Eira broke the silence.

"Bula will likely join us as none of us hate her, especially after you shared what you did with us, but only after we all have reached tier-7 and you will never become the ruler of the orcs in anything but name. At least that is where I stand on the matter, though part of me wants to say that you should make her suffer through you embracing Daisy and Violet before you accept any affection from her. However, that is the petty part of me and it should never be allowed to decide anything."

"Eira is likely right," admitted Enye. "It is just too soon still for us to forgive her, but she should be well aware of that now that she has a better handle on her visions."

One after another, all of Xeal's NPC wives voiced their agreement as Xeal just shifted to enjoying the short break that they all had. As he did so, day 50 passed and became day 51, then 52 and so on. During this time, they all got used to interacting with the maid versions of Princess Bianca and Princess Lorena, as they diligently acted as his wives' personal attendants. It almost went without saying that Enye couldn't help but smile as they took care of her needs and Xeal actually worried that their plans might succeed in some strange way. Even so, he just let it be as he returned to focusing on increasing his level as the war raged and was happy to reach level 193 before logging out on day 54, as he prepared for a long day in reality.

(*****)

Morning April 4 to Evening April 19, 2268 & ED Year 6 Days 56-102.

Alex awoke on Saturday with a smile as he quickly took care of his morning routine before he joined everyone else in the preparations for Dan and Anna's wedding. While the pair had discussed several options for the venue over the past few months, they had decided to just have it at an indoor venue that had a great view of the mountains from its balcony. Though, there was all of the setup that still needed to be done, as well as getting to the venue for the late morning ceremony that would lead into the early afternoon lunch. For Alex this mainly consisted of the logistics of fitting everyone in four SUVs and one Corvette in a way that made sense. Thankfully, this didn't include any of the grandparents who were living out of the house, but it was a tight fit as Alex's and Sam's parents ended up riding with Alex's grandparents in their two cars to make space. Alex ended up finding himself sitting up front, with Ava and Mia sitting between their babies in the back two rows as Stacy took driving duties for them.

As they drove, Alex couldn't help but think about how they would need to buy a bus if they ever wanted to go on a road trip as a family. This led him to thinking of the nightmare of camping and what life would be like if he really did end up with 15, or more, kids in reality. Even going anywhere locally as a family was quickly becoming a major undertaking as today was proving. However, Alex also couldn't help smiling as he watched Ava and Mia play with their children in his visor's mirror as they drove.

When they were at the venue, Alex found himself busy

with one little thing after another as he and Fred handled the tasks that a best man was meant to. Once more a few dozen of their friends from high school had been flown in, as well as extended families of both Anna and Dan as the venue held the roughly 100 guests. The highlight of this was the fact that all of their senseis and instructors from California and Colorado had been included and were able to meet each other. Though as much as Alex had wanted to, he didn't have the time to do more than say hi as he made sure everything was on schedule that needed to arrive, while Fred made sure everything was set up properly. Once they had finished with that, it was on to the final stretch as Alex and the rest of the wedding party got dressed.

After that was done, it was time for the main show as Alex and the rest of the wedding party took their places. When it was time for them to enter, Alex found himself walking with Lauren as Fred waited with Jessica as they entered the room where the wedding would occur. At the far end of this room was a balcony that had large window doors that allowed for a picturesque view of Pikes Peak. While the doors could be opened such that the bride and groom would be outside while the guests were still inside as they watched, they had decided against it as it was still under 60 degrees outside. Alex was grateful that they had done so as while that wasn't that cold, it would still just add to Ava's and Mia's stress levels as they worked to keep Evan, Nova, Aidan and Nadia warm. Alex also smiled at seeing them sitting beside Sam with Moyra, and Nicole holding Ahsa and Kate as they sat together while wearing smiles. He was also thankful for Nana Quinn and Kate's mom, Catherine, helping out with the babies by sitting with them.

These thoughts were short lived though as Alex and the

rest of the wedding party arrived at their locations beside the arbor, where Anna and Dan would say their vows. When they were settled, Dan entered and stood with the priest as the music shifted and Anna made her entrance. As she did so, Alex caught the smile on Dan's face as he took in the sight of his bride, who was dressed in a white trumpet-style wedding dress and holding a bouquet of red roses with green foliage as accents. Her brown hair was done up in an elaborate bun and her smile matched the one on Dan's face as she slowly made her way to the arbor with Mr. Bell walking next to her. From there the actual ceremony was rather uneventful as the priest officiated the wedding and it wasn't long before they sealed their vows with a kiss.

From there, Alex was on auto pilot as he and Fred got to split a best man speech that they had crafted in the few moments they had in ED, and Lauren and Jessica did the same for Anna while they ate lunch. As the catered lunch came to a close, the white chocolate raspberry cake that Sofie had made became the center of attention. It stood a full five tiers high, despite four being enough to feed the room, as the four-inch one at the top would be saved for Anna and Dan to enjoy on their first anniversary. Still, they had fun with the spectacle that was the cutting of the cake and serving each other the first slice. While Dan ended up with a bit on his nose, Anna came out clean from the experience as the rest of the guests started to get their own pieces. As always, Sofie had outdone herself with the cake and the bottom four tiers that were meant to serve 135 people didn't last long as more than one guest returned for a second piece.

As the first guests finished their cake, the mingling and dancing portion of the reception got into full swing as Alex found that his dance card was rather full. After the first dance that had him paired with Lauren finished it was Sam's turn, followed by Nicole, Ava, Kate and Mia, before he finally got to sit out one song. After that it was back to rotating between his five ladies until it was time to leave as he focused on them. As the reception came to a close, they all bid Anna and Dan farewell as Dan drove the Corvette away with "Just Married" written on the back windshield. Once more Alex couldn't help but think about a scene of him needing a van, or SUV, to pull off the same scene for his own wedding as it was currently planned.

Still, as Anna and Dan had left, it was time for him and his family to do the same as Fred had already agreed to make sure everything was taken care of from this point on. As Alex drove back with Sam, Nicole, Kate, Ahsa and Moyra, the conversation focused around the wedding and what they liked and didn't like with their own in mind. Alex could already tell that the next three and a half months were going to be long as he was sure that his own wedding would be the main topic of discussion.

As they pulled into the garage, Alex had to hold in a laugh at seeing the Corvette parked as he knew that Anna and Dan wouldn't be heading away on their honeymoon until Monday. This was mainly due to Easter being the following morning and them being expected to participate in the major event that would be held at Alex's home. It was with this on his mind that Alex logged in to ED, after helping Ava and Mia, who were both exhausted from the day, get inside with their babies and a quick meal.

Sunday the 5th was another busy day in reality, as Alex played host to a morning Easter egg hunt, only he had had Jacob hide prizes that adults would want inside plastic eggs. These included all-paid spa days and one even had a note that Alex would trade for getting them their own VR pod. Though the VR pod was the top prize and was worth half of the total prize pool of the roughly 200 eggs that had been hidden, most of which had things that cost ten to 20 credits in them. In the end, it was one of Dan's cousins that got the VR pod and after Gido got his information, it was set to be shipped and the event came to a close for the morning.

That evening they gathered for dinner with the egg decoration that they had made the prior year sitting in the center of the table that Alex was seated at. They had once more set up all the spare furniture in the gym to accommodate all the guests. Alex couldn't help but smile at the decoration, despite the tackiness he felt from it when he looked at it in the setting, as he remembered making it. Memories like that were one of the things that he treasured in this life as they were lacking in his last and he couldn't wait to make more of them as his kids grew up.

As Easter ended, Alex officially started his 22-hour a day schedule where he logged off for two one-hour breaks each day to eat meals. While this allowed him to get in a bit of time with everyone, it was extremely limited as he focused on eating quickly before spending time with any of his kids that just happened to be awake. Alex knew that the adults understood his reduced presence, but he didn't want to become a complete stranger to his kids, even if he couldn't spend near enough time with them. Having delegated everything else to the others, time passed as he didn't even know what the seventh presentation of the year at his old high school was about. Though he did note the difference between Anna and Dan that had developed after they returned from their honeymoon with broad smiles on their faces.

Xeal's time in ED was simply nonstop as every second of his time had a purpose, even if that purpose was having an hour with the ladies in his life. All of whom were operating out of Cielo city as they continued to focus on reaching tier-7 with the same dedication that Xeal and all the players that were currently being trained by FAE were. This led to many long days for all of them, to include Queen Aila Lorafir, who after transferring custody of Durz and Xuk to Cielo city's care, was focused on aiding the five ex-pirate captains in their own training. The results of which had been mixed so far as Xuk had been completely helpless against their magic, but Durz had resisted it all through her access to the sight, which had only strengthened since her imprisonment. Queen Aila Lorafir warned that if Durz was left alone, she might truly tap into the true potential of the sight as it was obvious that Laplace was favoring her at this point.

Among all of this was the continued rise in the level of conflict that was occurring, as Habia focused on gaining control of the seas that bordered the lands that the beast-man tribes had fought in before the war. As Nium had nothing to act as a port in this area, it was a rather difficult battle for it to win and instead had shifted its focus to defending the few points that were vulnerable. While this wouldn't stop an invasion at the other points, it would make one much harder as those other points required traversing areas that were full of tier-7 monsters. Still, from the reports that FAE had, it seemed that Habia was focusing on building a harbor fort in the area for when enough players on their side had reached tier-7 and could clear a path for an invasion.

Paidhia, on the other hand, had already started to push into the elven lands that bordered them south of Nium's borders. While the elves were ensuring that it was a slow advance through the marshy terrain, it was an area that only had lower-level tier-7 monsters to contend with and had been long since used as a minor trade route. As such it was the main location where players were unable to offer any meaningful assistance in defending and if left alone it could prove a fatal weakness for Nium. Still, with the pace that things were moving there, it was such that Xeal didn't see it opening a viable invasion route before he reached tier-7. This didn't mean that the situation wasn't concerning, especially with the fact that the location of the conflict was such that Xeal couldn't affect the situation, which just made things worse.

All of this became more fuel for Xeal, as he continued to level as his party finally started to be able to push deeper in the Mist Woods dungeon as they leveled up. This allowed Xeal to maintain fighting against monsters at least 7 levels above him as he reached level 194, 195 and 196 during this time. He could see the finish line as the top players in FAE were beginning to enter their final stage of prepping to reach tier-7 as well.

All of this had been accented with Xeal spending several hours simply expanding his dominion in the quest world, as he reclaimed more and more land. During each of these visits, Austru had been happy to receive her kisses as she continued to exchange letters with Xeal's other ladies. This included the sudden addition of ones to Daisy, Violet, Dafasli and Bula. She had explained the others wished for her to exchange letters with them as they wished to include her opinion on the possibility of them courting Xeal one day. Xeal had needed to hold in a sigh at this as he worried that Princess Bianca was right on it being when, not if, for those four. He also just counted his blessings on the fact that the four dragonoid women and Princesses Bianca and Lorena had not been included. Still, the night that he spent with Austru on day 79 had been another one of relaxation for Xeal as he just enjoyed the comfort of spending the night with her.

As the Cielo city event for the year came to a close on day 100 as the city prepared to return to its normal altitude, Xeal and his family bid Queen Nora and Prince Vicenc farewell. At the same time, Princesses Bianca and Lorena, who had managed to maintain their role as maids while caring for the needs of Xeal's wives during this time, bowed as they wished them all well. At this Xeal could tell that Enye was torn on how to respond, as she had gone out of her way to ensure that the pair had proven their resolve during the 50 days that they were serving her and the others. This had included duties such as bathing all of them when they returned from fighting monsters, ensuring their equipment was maintained, cleaning up while they were away and more. In the end they handled it all with a smile and started to become a facet of daily life outside caring for Xeal's children, as they had been expressly forbidden from doing so. That said, Midnight had taken to the pair rather well and seemed to enjoy seeing them curtsy whenever he came near.

However, Xeal had needed to cut the farewells short as he received word of a full-out assault on both border forts that was utilizing a human wave tactic with adventurers. Were this being carried out by NPCs, Xeal would have been appalled as it was a sure way to see a country ruined, even if it won the war. The losses that would be sustained were such that if it were a million tier-5 attackers versus 10,000 tier-6 and few dozen tier-7 defenders, that the million would be lucky to have 100,000 left. However, at the same time it would lead to the death of all the defenders and the toppling of the fort and in three days they would be ready to do it again. While the losses would be heavy for the players involved, the fact that they would revive and be ready to do it again in three days made this tactic highly effective.

Xeal frowned as he knew that the only real counter to this tactic was to overwhelm it to the point that it was seen as pointless. It was with this thought that Xeal sent out his orders as he sent every spare FAE player to the Nium and Paidhia border. At the same time, he requested Queen Aila Lorafir to accompany him while bringing a contingent of high elf sorcerers that specialized in electrical spells like she did. Xeal was going to send a message to those behind this assault that it wasn't going to work, despite the fact that this exact tactic had proven extremely effective in his last life.

As Xeal arrived in the fort town, he was greeted by a quest notification.

(Quest: "Defend Nium's border from the assault from Habia." Rewards: Greatly increased favor and renown with the people of Nium and unknown. Warning: failing the quest will have negative repercussions on your account. Accept? Yes, or No)

After that, he quickly found Takeshi and Asa, who quickly got him up to speed on the latest developments. At the same time, Queen Aila Lorafir and the high elf spellcasters met up with ones that Nium and the beast-man tribes had sent. While they did so, the flashes of spells hitting the force shields that the tier-7 NPCs were casting seemed to never end. At the same time, ballistae and other defensive weapons were being fired as players continually cycled through being on top of the wall to attack from the gaps between these battlements. Most of these were average players who were armed with stones and other heavy materials that they threw as hard as they could at the players attacking the force shields at the bottom of the walls. It was only thanks to these shields that had the advanced feature of being one directional that only tier-7 spellcasters could achieve through the advanced force magic skill, that the walls had any chance in these assaults. It had been the lack of such spellcasters during Xeal's assault on the fort between Habia and Paidhia that had even allowed him to succeed in faking an assault on them at all. Thankfully, both kingdoms had sent their forces with said ability to aid in the assault of the dwarven lands at the time, a mistake that Xeal wasn't going to allow Nium to make.

Xeal was just grateful that King Victor had agreed to the opening strategy of naval containment, mixed with raids on the countryside where forces were thinnest and border defense were the softest. This strategy truly played to Nium's strengths as the elven, orc and beast-men lands that bordered it also bordered level 200 to level 250 lands. This meant that even if Nium did nothing to shore up its defenses there, it would be costly and slow for any NPC army to use those routes to launch an invasion through. Had the war not started until tier-7 players were available in significant numbers, it would have changed this and forced Nium to worry about those avenues of attack far more than they were currently. Especially as a human wave tactic would only be met with a monster wave tactic if attempted in monster-controlled lands.

However, the flaw to this strategy at the current moment was that if Habia and Paidhia knew that it was what Nium was doing, which Xeal had no doubt they did, it would allow them to focus on attacking. The result of which Xeal saw as he looked down at the millions of tier-4 to 6 players attacking the barriers as he reached the top of the wall. While most might have as well have been using bouncy balls to attack, hundreds of millions of bouncy balls would add up quickly. It was this thought that was on Xeal's mind as he stepped onto a platform that had been prepared, such that everyone in eyesight could easily see him as the first round of electrical spells entered him. Xeal felt the surge of power that was fueled by over 1,000 tier-6 and up spellcasters' spells enter him and almost found it too much for him to contain. Never before had Xeal felt like there might be a limit to the how much electricity he could manage without exploding since he had gained mastery of the element. However, now Xeal found himself believing that there was as he struggled to contain the power that he had just been infused with. The strain had been so much that rather than wait for the medium and short chant spells to be added in like he normally would, Xeal unleashed the first wave immediately and just sent it in a straight line.

The result of this was that he missed those in the front of the mass of players that he had intended to be his main targets. However, the spot that Xeal had hit was now littered with over 100 gruesomely charred and smoking corpses, that were likely past any basic revival skill's, or item's, ability to revive. Xeal didn't have long to ponder this as the medium chant spells hit him and he once more felt a surge of power. This, however, was much easier to control as he focused on picking his targets as the short chant spells hit him and he once more felt that a limit might exist. Though, he was still able to control it enough this time to use it as he intended. For those attacking the barrier, this meant that they were instantly killed as over 200 such players found themselves taking a death penalty. Still, Xeal knew that was only a drop in the bucket of what was needed. At killing 300 players a minute, it would take Xeal over 55 hours to kill a million of them and that would still not even faze those ordering this assault.

It was with this thought that Xeal felt the next wave of long chant spells hit him and he once more struggled to even hold it in as he was forced to release it prematurely.

This time, however, he was at least able to control it on release as it hit the frontlines once more and over 500 players were instantly killed. Xeal just smiled as he felt the medium and short chants enter him and he unleashed the power on the front lines, killing another two to three hundred players. At this rate it would only take 24 hours for him to kill a million players, but he knew he could do better as he shouted out.

"Aila! Switch the order of short and medium chants!"

This time when the long chant entered Xeal, he held on to it with all he could as sweat started to form all over his body from the effort. However, it was just a few seconds later that the short chant spells hit him and he instantly sent the electricity into the players below. Xeal smiled as this time he managed to kill over 1,000 players, though when he sent the medium chant spells out by itself it only killed around 100 players. Still, that was a 15-hour pace to kill a million and Xeal knew that like any other ability, his control of electricity could be trained. Which was how Xeal treated the next 20 minutes he was up there before his stamina dipped below five percent. At which point he called for a break for him to recover. While he used his calm mind skill to aid the speed of his recovery, the spellcasters who were fueling him focused on restoring their MP pools.

As Xeal pondered the situation before him during this break, he couldn't help but feel the futility in his efforts as his side was completely outnumbered. Furthermore, he could tell that this attack was simply meant to probe how Nium would react to such a tactic. The fact that Habia and Paidhia had coordinated their assaults meant that there was some form of cooperation occurring, be that between the kingdoms, or the players. As Xeal thought about this, he wondered if Habia, or Paidhia, even knew of the assaults before today. If Abysses End or some other major power was behind this attack, it would make a certain amount of sense and it would mean that the situation could get far darker in the near future. All while Xeal was still struggling to control a long and short chant spell combo of electricity. He knew that with the multiplicative effects of stacking the spells, it would allow him to have far more of an impact on the situation if he could control all 3,000 spells' power.

Xeal was about ten minutes into his recovery when the word of the first force shield failing could be heard, and he sighed as every single defending player followed the command to descend and attack. This was the moment that the meat grinder started to really get going as one tier-6 player after another charged in with reckless abandon. Clerics and spellcasters began to replace every other player attacking on the wall, as those skilled with the bow made up the rest as they supported those who were built for hand-to-hand combat. The clear level advantage that the defending players had made it easy to push the attacking players back at first, while lower-level shields of all kinds were erected to guard against range attacks from above. There were holes in this that were constantly being breached, but they were only minor annoyances for the players hit, for the most part. The real issue was all the spells that were focused on the walls, since when the first shield had failed and the first line of players had descended, the rest of the shields cast by the tier-7 NPCs had been dropped as well. Like Xeal, they were all focused on recovering in hopes that they could restore the defense before the walls fell.

This remained the state of the battle for another 20 minutes, when the defending players on the ground started to falter as damage started to overwhelm them and their stamina started to run out. Xeal frowned as it seemed that everything was happening faster than he had expected and it was clear that the fort would fall at this rate. For the first time since waking up 20 years in his past, Xeal felt that things were beyond his capability. As much as he wanted to charge in and turn the tide with his efforts alone, he knew that it would only end in his death. As things were, it was only about five minutes from the need to restore the barriers and that would only buy them 30 minutes at best and then it would be time to make a final stand.

"Xeal-san, shall we help them along as they throw away their lives?" asked Takeshi as he walked to Xeal.

"Do you have a plan in mind, or is sitting here watching this just as unbearable for you as it is for me?"

"I have told you that I will never throw my life away. I have already called forward those who are under me that could be considered elites and have been focused on reaching tier-7 like you and I."

"Takeshi-san, just how many do you expect to lose in this charge?"

"It is the retreat that we will take losses in."

Xeal frowned as he considered things before sighing and replying.

"Hold them back for now. It is the next wave that we will need them for. Just make sure they conserve their strength as there will be no retreat when we charge."

"I understand," replied Takeshi while wearing a smile as Xeal contacted Kate.

Xeal frowned as he got the update that the southern forts were in even worse shape as despite the reinforcements, the larger area had led to it being harder to defend. As such, they were already preparing to sabotage the fort that had once been Paidhia's, before the mist that had been created by the dark elves had encompassed the area. After that, they would fall back to the second fort while laying traps between the two that would hopefully inflict damage and slow the attackers down. Either way, things there were looking worse than at the Habia and Nium border. Still, Xeal went forward with his request for all of FAE's main force that was available to assemble. As he finished sending out this order, Xeal watch as the battlelines collapsed as the defenders that had gone over the wall were finally overwhelmed and the advanced force shields were put back in place.

At the same time, Xeal returned to his role of sending one concentrated blast of lightning after another, into the mass of players that truly seemed endless. As he did so, he focused on maintaining his calm mind skill, as he attempted to do everything he could to improve his control over the electricity, only to see modest improvements. This also saw his stamina reduce even faster as he needed to take a break after only 15 minutes into it and roughly 17,000 more attackers killed. Xeal knew that he had killed over 40,000 players and yet it was insignificant in the grand scheme of things. Millions of players were still attacking, despite the likely over 2 million players who had taken a death penalty on just the attacking side, compared to the roughly 100,000 on the defending side. As Xeal was about to begin his recovery once more, he turned to Takeshi and spoke.

"Takeshi-san, I am trusting you to organize things to the right and left of me. Just make sure that no one is within 50 feet of me."

"You're not intending to die now are you, Xeal-san?"

"No more than you are, Takeshi-san. Just let me lead the charge and make sure Gale and Kate make their way to me before the charge, and let Aila know that I need to talk to her."

"Very well, I will ensure that it is done."

With that Takeshi left and five minutes later Queen Aila Lorafir arrived as Xeal let her in on his plan before she went to relay it to the others. With that taken care of, Xeal sat quietly as he ignored the world around him as he both visualized what he was about to do and recovered as much as he could. That was until the call finally came that the shields were about to fail once more and he opened his eyes to see Gale and Kate looking at him expectantly.

"I would love to take the time to explain my intent to both of you, but right now time is too short. Kate, I need you to help make sure Aila's group's spells hit me. Gale, I love you and I am sorry, but I need to soul bond with you again."

"What are you going to do once we begin our period of separation as I officially send you off to war?" asked Gale with a frown.

"Know that I can't use any plan that would normally kill me like this," quipped Xeal.

"Hope that our enemies don't realize that you are vulnerable in a way you weren't before," corrected Kate. "Xeal, you have used this tactic before. Yes, it has been a long time since you made a fool out of Abysses End and Atius, but you have to know that they are well aware of the tactic. They are going to have a plan to counter it and your electrical abilities at any cost."

"I am counting on it."

As Xeal said that, he pulled Kate into a kiss before turning to Gale as she placed her blindfold over her eyes and Xeal gave her a deep kiss as the soul bond was activated. With that he just smiled as he leapt down the wall and into the space between the force shields and the fort, as he felt the 1,000 long chant spells enter his body. The look of resignation on the players directly in front of him told Xeal that they knew that they were dead and didn't care. Xeal was also sure that they had turned their pain settings down to the lowest possible level. As he drew his blades and held them out to his side and began running right at the attacking players, Xeal smiled as he felt 16 short chant spells enter him. At that moment he focused on extending the electricity out from his body such that it went 50 feet in each direction in a steady output, as every second 16 or 17 more short chant spells came in. Ten seconds after the first 16 short chant spells came in, 17 medium chant spells came in and every second another batch of these would arrive. Ten seconds later 17 long chant spells came in and Xeal was receiving 16, or 17, of each spell level every single second as he maintained the output to his sides while running forward.

The result of this was absolute mayhem as while it was enough power to kill the players closest to Xeal, the others found themselves convulsing as they dealt with the attack. Many of them even found themselves attacking and attacked by the players nearest them due to how they were convulsing. Then if they survived that, the wave of players that followed 50 feet behind Xeal took care of the rest. All of this had the effect of allowing Xeal to push through the attacking players like a hot knife through butter. That was until eight tier-6 players came charging at him as the players in front of him did their best to open a path to him for them. Each of these players had gear that Xeal knew was designed to ground them and insulate them from electrical attacks. Still, Xeal didn't even slow down as he closed the distance between them and him, until he let out a dragon's breath attack when they were five feet apart. That sent one of them backwards as Xeal wielded his swords while still sending out electricity from his hands. The result of this was that the 50 feet around him became a completely forbidden zone, that other than Xeal and those equipped like the players that he was fighting, entering was a fool's endeavor.

As Xeal clashed blades in what should have been a one-sided fight as his stats were leagues beyond theirs, Xeal could tell that each of them were not taking damage. No, each of them were clearly soul bonded just like he was right now and there were likely clerics working right now to ensure that the other halves of each of these pairs stayed alive. While Xeal knew he could overcome them still, it would take time and stamina that he didn't have. So instead he overpowered them enough to create an opening before charging forward once more. At this point his stamina was below ten percent once more and Xeal knew that he needed to start looking at his exit strategy. He had also taken more than his fair share of hits and was expecting one more hard counter to him to happen, as he focused on completing the single most vital role he could play.

As if on cue, a few dozen iron rods landed all around Xeal, as he held in a laugh at the surprise on the faces of the few hundred players with long spears that were charging at him as he ignored them. Neither his electricity, nor the electricity that was constantly being sent into him, reacted to the lightning rods as any normal electrical spell would. Simply put, Xeal had let the players who were wearing gear to counter his electricity think it had worked, and just then a massive bolt of electricity came down on Xeal. This had been directed down at him from Kate, who was strapped to Queen Aila Lorafir in the sky above and who had been invisible up until that moment. The bolt of electricity that hit Xeal was essentially three full charges of Queen Aila Lorafir's strongest spell, as Kate's ability didn't have the same dispersing effect after 30 seconds that Xeal's did. Though, Xeal's didn't either if focused on simply holding it outside of his body like Kate had to.

With this sudden boost in power, Xeal just smiled as he sent it all at the players charging at him and the group he had bypassed that were attempting to catch up to him. Instantly all of them died and Xeal just stood still as for the first time since he had charged in, no electricity was entering or leaving his body. The looks on the players' faces as they debated on charging in or not told Xeal that he had just made them all question what was going on and if he should even be considered a player any longer. Lost on them was just how much support Xeal had been getting to use his broken abilities. If he were the monster that they all saw him as currently he would be able to perform feats like he had just done freely. Still, time passed slowly for a few seconds until the first player, and then a second, came charging at Xeal, only for him to grasp hold of the rope that Kate had dropped for him. The moment he did so, Queen Aila Lorafir began to rise higher as Xeal rose above the mass of players that he could now see the rear line on and had to smile at what he saw there as Atius looked up at him.

That simple fact told Xeal all he needed to know. Without a doubt Abysses End had slipped a few key figures in to wage a war on Xeal. Knowing that, it became clear that the players who were participating in today's assault were likely doing so for one of the many empty benefits that Abysses End loved to give out. These could be things like meet and greets with top players, or the spokespersons like Natalina, or the other models that Nantan had brought with him during his final visit. Either way, it would be something that cost Abysses End next to nothing, but the casual players that dreamed of being a part of Abysses End would happily suffer a death penalty for. It was while having this thought that Xeal felt the 1,000 medium chant spells enter him, then ten seconds later the short chant ones arrived. Finally, 28 seconds after the short chants had arrived, Xeal let go of the rope that had him around 200 feet in the air and felt the 1,000 long chants enter him as he lost control.

The next thing Xeal knew, he was face down on the ground on top of the blackened remains of an adventurer. As he stood on shaky legs and saw that his stamina was completely depleted, all Xeal could see was death as far as the eye could see. The players who had been led by Takeshi stood looking at the scene before them with looks of utter shock, as the area a full 300 feet in front of and to the sides of Xeal were cleared. Xeal had just felt relief that Kate had been able to ensure that all of the electricity had gone forward and to the sides of him as intended. As Xeal stood, he let out a roar as he let out a dragon's breath aimed at the stunned players just outside the area that was covered by charred bodies as he took a step forward. In the same moment, another wave of medium chant spells entered his body and the sight of every tier-5 player that had been held in reserve descending the wall caused the will of the attacking players to finally break. It was then that Xeal received a system notification.

(Quest, Defend Nium's border from the assault from Habia complete. Calculating completion rate... 105% completion, rank SS. Rewards: 100,000,000,000 XP, 7,000 guild renown points and an increase in the morale of all allies when you are present.)

In a manner that could only be called a stampede, every player near Xeal turned to run and this caused a chain reaction that spread through the entire army. The only pursuit that occurred, however, was done by the players that were not considered a part of FAE's main force and 20 minutes later the whole battle was over. The final estimates had over 3,000,000 players on the attacking side dying and 150,000 on the defending side. Thankfully no NPCs had been included in these numbers and Kate figured it would be at least a few weeks before they tried to attack again. Still, the other battle had not gone as well and while it ended shortly after Xeal instigated the rout on his end, the costs were much higher. One of the two forts had fallen and 300,000 members of FAE, plus 100,000 players from other guilds had been killed, to the 2,000,000 deaths on the attacking side. This was not the worst scenario and was much better than losing the few dozen tier-7 NPCs that it would have cost to hold the lost fort.

Still, Xeal was frustrated at the results as he saw most of the death penalties that FAE players had just suffered as unnecessary. Especially the ones of those who could be considered part of FAE's main force. It was with this thought that after handling the consequences of using the soul link skill, Xeal found himself accompanying Kate to visit Levina on day 101. As they arrived, Xeal could see the look of pure joy that spread across the electrical phoenix's face at seeing Xeal as she spoke.

"Xeal, you have finally come to pay me a visit!"

"Yes, I am in need of your assistance as it seems that I need to master my ability to control electricity. I had never thought about having issues handling too much power and I need to correct that mistake as fast as possible."

"There shouldn't be such an issue. I mean, you handled controlling me with no issue and that is essentially unlimited power if you ask me."

"He was trying to have over 1,000 tier-6 and up spellcasters hit him with a short, medium and long chant spells while holding it all in," interjected Kate. "While it didn't cause him any damage, he had major stamina and control issues while manipulating it against an invading army that numbered in the millions."

"Oh, interesting I think I know what the issue is. Very well, I know just what to do, though I need you to let me do so," replied Levina.

"I am not sleeping with you," retorted Xeal.

"While I will always say yes should you ever change your mind, that was not my intent, though you will probably want to be practically naked as I am sure your gear didn't appreciate what you put it through either."

"Yah, Darefret looked at me like I was insane when I handed it over to him for repairs and told him how it had gotten so damaged," admitted Xeal. "So, what's your plan? Just load me full of electricity and have me try to control it?"

"No, I am going to convert myself to my rawest of forms and work to enter your body which will force more electricity through you than you could possibly handle. I am expecting you to not last long before your stamina and other stats hit zero and you actually start dying due to the strain on your body. At which point I will stop and allow you to recover before doing it again and again, until you can take me into your body without any issues."

"Wait, you can enter my body?"

"I should be able to, though that is mainly based on my deductions on what you are and the fact that I know I can enter Kate's if and when she reaches tier-8."

"Is that what breaking that seal will cause?" asked Kate.

"No, it will enable it, but I will still be stuck here and so you could only do so while here. Not very useful if you ask me," replied Levina with a smug smile.

"Still more useful than needing to track you down whenever I wished to do so," retorted Kate. "I was not born yesterday. I am well aware that you entering me is not the same as me forcing you into me. Also, you will never get to enjoy using it as a way to satisfy your desires to embrace Xeal, even in such a roundabout way."

"I am aware. My only hope of ever having that is to

convince him that he loves me, a concept that is foreign to me as raw desire and power are what such things have always been predicated on for me."

"That is a discussion for another day," interrupted Xeal. "I need to use the time I have to train, so let's get started."

Xeal switched to the set of trash clothes that were indestructible and bound to each player in case of all of their gear being destroyed, as he entered the barrier that kept Levina contained. At the same time, Levina removed all of her clothing before tossing them outside of the barrier where they wouldn't be destroyed. Xeal only had a moment to take in her form before it shifted into one of pure electricity as a chirping sound could be heard. Once she had finished this transformation, she spoke to Xeal in a voice that sounded like it came from all around rather than from her mouth.

"Right now you need to focus on simply releasing the power the moment it enters you, as my intent is to simply increase the amount of it until you can't keep up."

"Alright, do your worst!"

At those words Levina flashed as she appeared right in front of Xeal with her hand inside of his chest. Suddenly a surge of power entered Xeal that was easily more powerful than the 1,000 long chant spells had been, but not quite as powerful as it had been once the 1,000 short chant spells had been added. That changed in the next moment as he failed to release the power right away, as he passed the state that he had been in when all three set of chants had been stored up. This caused Xeal to lose control as the electricity poured out of his body from every cell before being reabsorbed by Levina, as she held nothing back. With each second the amount of power she was sending into Xeal increased as he simply gave up even trying to hold it in and release it in a controlled manner. All he could do was watch as his stamina disappeared at an alarming rate, as five minutes later he was panting on the ground and Levina who was still in her pure electricity form spoke once more.

"If you have a limit, it is only based on how long your stamina lasts. I expect you here every day if you want to continue to reduce the strain that controlling my element seems to place on you. Now, Kate, if you would return my clothes to me, I will play nice and give Xeal here as little of a show as possible."

"Give him as much as a show as you like. After all, it will only work against you," quipped Kate as she tossed the dress that she had been wearing back in.

Xeal just closed his eyes until Levina spoke once more.

"It's safe to look now, though I would rather that you at least allowed me to give you glimpses of what you are denying yourself."

"And that is a large part of why you and I will not work," commented Xeal. "Attraction only goes so far."

"Whatever. Now, are you going to leave, or do I get to have some time where we can actually talk?"

"Oh, what, are you not satisfied with the sounds I made while you sent enough power to power a city in my reality into me?"

"You see, there is something that I would love to hear about as I have next to no knowledge about it. With Kate it is always about giving me food and idle chitchat that has no substance to it, despite me knowing anything that I would like through our bond already."

"Still not happy about that one," retorted Kate. "Xeal, please stay quiet about our reality as it is the only place that she has no ability to see, or know about."

"I have four daughters and two sons there," replied Xeal. "I will talk about them and only them if you wish to know about my reality."

"Are any of them Kate's?"

"Not yet, but we will get there…"

Xeal just smiled as the next 20 minutes passed as he talked about his children both in and out of ED, as Kate just sighed helplessly. For her part, Levina seemed to really enjoy the topic as she talked about the memories that she had from becoming a mother and how she had always taken pride in the experience. This also included a few comments about how it had been so long and how her current incarnation had never experienced the process of creating a life within oneself. Xeal just let these comments sail over his head as he focused on keeping the topic away from anything that he saw as potentially troublesome. As they left, Xeal could tell that Kate wasn't in the best of moods as his time shifted to admin work that he needed to go over. This included the payouts that FAE would be giving to players who had experienced a death penalty on their side.

"Kate, are you alright?" asked Xeal when they arrived in his office.

"Yeah, I just wish the war had come after our wedding night."

"Ah, your intent is to be pregnant as soon as possible at that point. You don't think I am going to make you wait, do you?"

"Can you really say that we can afford to dedicate the time that it will cost? I am not like the others, I am a crucial part of what keeps FAE running."

"Kate, we will manage. Besides, the war will be nearing its one-year anniversary when it comes time for our wedding. In fact, the war is a good thing for it, as now we don't need to explain to Victor why we won't be at the royal party that night. After that, I will have over two years to handle the issues with the war before it's time for you to deliver and if the war is looking bad at that point, well, we will have likely already failed."

"I am more worried about it being a situation where we are making slow progress that gets turned around when I am only available 27 out of 72 hours, like Luna and Selene are right now."

"Kate, life happens and I know you are smart enough to know that I am not going to stop you from having a child because it's inconvenient at the time you want it. Just like how I will never force you to have one if you don't want one, even if I would be saddened by such a choice. So, what is going on?"

"Huh, fine, I worry that I will never live up to the others. Each of them have basically gone full mom mode since giving birth and I can't see me doing that. I don't even want to breast feed like the others, though I am going to give it a try as I can see the looks they all get while they do, but once more I don't think I will have the patience for it."

"Not hearing any real issue there. Sorry, Kate, but I already knew all of that and I love you for it, not in spite of it. You are all different and I am grateful for it. It's why you all are all my kids' moms. Just because you are more of a working mom and the others are more of the nurturing mom types doesn't mean that you are any less than the others. Instead of worrying about how you're going to live up to their examples, just let them help you be the best version of a mom that you can be."

Xeal could tell that Kate wasn't satisfied with his response from the way she was frowning at him, so with a sigh he continued.

"If you want to yell at me for whatever I misread, or pissed you off about with that statement, feel free to, but it is how I see the situation. I am willing to be told why I am missing the key point to whatever you are going through."

"No, you aren't wrong as I have told myself the same things. My biggest worry is that I will always be the mom who gets the shortest hugs and is none of their favorites as they grow up."

"Kate, who do Ahsa and Moyra always make hold them when all five of you are around and they aren't hungry?"

"Me."

"Exactly. So stop worrying even if Ahsa and Moyra love you more than Sam and Nicole, and yours loves Sam and Nicole more than you. It will be fine as you are all their moms. The key is for you to love them all the same regardless and just let things play out, as the last thing I want to deal with is the five of you having a best mom competition. In fact, I think that best mom mugs will be banned in our house!"

As Alex finished his half-serious joke, Kate couldn't help but smile a little as she held in a short laugh and Alex pulled her into a hug as he continued speaking.

"Kate, I love you. I will keep reminding you of that as often as needed. So, just promise to love me back and work with the others to make sure things work."

"I can do that. After all, I love you too. Now, we need to talk about the costs from the last battle before the players revive and expect to be paid."

"You mean the over 250,000,000 credits worth of gold that the two battles will cost us in just death penalty compensations?"

"Yes, we can't pay that out every three days as that is about what we are taking in every month right now and even if it becomes a monthly bill, that will still cause us to stagnate."

"Have we figured out what Abysses End did to gather that many players so quickly and without us hearing about it ahead of time?"

"We did, we just didn't realize it," replied Kate, sounding annoyed. "Put simply, they traded access to a teleportation network for the cooperation of every major guild in both Habia and Paidhia. From what I can tell, each network has 20 destinations and they offered a month in reality of access to each guild that agreed to the terms and held up their side of the deal."

"Large upfront cost and no additional cost, as I am sure that they aren't covering the cost of each use either."

"That would be correct, though it will be harder for them to sell access in another month as each gate will be overburdened and they are going to need to do scheduled location transfers to make it work. After all, the second it takes to pick a location adds up and will make it so that rather than being able to transfer over 5,000,000 players in an hour, it will be less than 72,000 an hour if they go in singles."

"It is still better than having to walk and if they do three-minute windows every hour it will work out well for them still."

"Fair. Inconvenient, as they will only have around ten seconds between the groups and will need to staff each location, but you are right, it would be doable."

"Let me guess, you already are making preparations to attack these."

"No need to. Abysses End is claiming that as all the forts didn't fall and the players retreated without their order, that the guilds didn't hold up their end of the deal. They are trying to force the guilds to repeat the assault, only this time the deal is that if over 60% of the players present die, that Abysses End won't argue that a retreat broke the deal."

"Are they just trying to bankrupt us?" pondered Xeal out loud as he thought over the matter for a long second. "No, they are likely trying to get us to expose where our external networks are to make their plans outside of this continent. They definitely already know about the Muthia and Huáng empires, but they are watching our moves to figure out the rest as they have to know that we know that another wave is coming. In fact, by now anyone with half a brain knows and their next attack is doomed to fail because of my abilities. So, they are either trying to get us to look at them while they do something else off to the side, or they are just gathering intel."

"The question is, what do we want to show them?"

"Pay every player who took a death penalty according to the rates we put out and start prepping to do a raffle. We want to do two things. First, make it clear that we are hurting financially after paying the players, to the point where we are offering items that normally would not be offered to the public as prizes. Second, we need to have our players based outside of Nium seem to be prepping to transfer here at a moment's notice."

"You are going to make our actions seem erratic with that as they are contradictory actions. Is your goal to get Abysses End to think we are shifting to a conservative model to avoid taking a major hit to our finances?"

"They will think that we can't react to any moves they make outside of Nium, or they will think we want them to think that. Either way we win as if they attack it will play into the trap and if they don't, we will only take a moderate loss while we act defensively. Though the key needs to be the spreading of a rumor that the first wave of our main force is about to attempt to reach tier-7 in the next few weeks in ED time."

"Xeal, that is going to require way more work than just spreading rumors. They are going to need to disappear to somewhere after heading to the locations where they can start their tribulations."

"We are only going to have 3,000 of our members playing into this ruse. Other guilds don't know just how few players are going to pass right now and we are going to play into that. Coordinate the ruse and make sure they are all ready to spend a full two weeks in a dungeon between now and then, as they will need to stay there until it's time to spring the trap. Also, have another 7,000 set up that look like they will be part of the second wave."

"So, who is going to be running the guild during this as I am expecting you, Takeshi, Amser and I all to be included in this ruse and Taya is good, but not that good."

"Taya will get by with Aalin's, Gale's and Clara's help. Besides, they can reach out to us with any questions they have and it will be a good dry run for when they need to step in for a few weeks."

"Fine. I think you are leaving us a bit too vulnerable, both now and when we actually attempt to reach tier-7."

"Kate, two weeks after we disappear, the 7,000 other players will as well and about two weeks after that we all should actually start our tier-7 trials at the current pace we are going. Between now and then is just to muddy the waters and catch Abysses End and the rest of ED by surprise when we actually reach tier-7."

"I know. There is just the issue of our meeting with Eternal Dominion Inc. on May 4th and I am sure Abysses End knows about it."

"What about it? My goal is to start my tribulation directly after it."

"Wouldn't Abysses End expect-" started Kate before pausing a second before continuing. "You are really going to bet that they know we know that they would expect that and hope they are faked out by it?"

"Kate, that will depend on if we are able to make them

hesitate after they make their next move due to how much we make them pay for it."

Kate frowned as she thought over what Xeal was saying. She knew that with his knowledge from his last life, he at least had a frame of reference of the different outcomes. However, she just couldn't see this plan working out well, but at the same time, she couldn't see any that would yield a decent result for FAE in the short term. It was with this realization that she responded.

"The war starting this early really has put us into a bind, hasn't it?"

"Yes. There are no good options as no matter what we do, most of our top leaders need to be unavailable for about two weeks in game. While my plan creates more issues between now and then, it should at least give us a chance to avoid the worst of it."

"You know that they are going to attack the moment the system notification goes out that one of our members hits tier-7, right?"

"I do. We just need to hope that our members can hold the line and make sure Taya and the others are ready to weather the storm."

"Alright, let's get into the details..."

Kate and Xeal spent another hour going over the various scenarios that could play out. These were based on both what Xeal knew from his last life and Kate's current read on the situation. However, everything was uncharted waters for both of them, due to no major wars starting before players reached tier-7 in Xeal's last life and this being the first such conflict that Kate had been a part of in ED. Though she did have past experience from other VR games that was applicable due to Abysses End's involvement in them to fall back on.

When they finally finished, Xeal returned to grinding for

a few hours until it was time to return home to spend the night with his family in ED. As he sat on his balcony overlooking the lodging that had originally been set up for only the three-day marriage interviews between beast-men and the nobles of Nium, he couldn't help but smile at its current state. While there had been more than a few nobles who had left of their own accord, most had stayed and were working hard with the beast-men. The crafters that Xeal had supplied to train them had been an excellent idea, as while none of them were close to being masters, they were decent novices already. While this meant that making cheap arrows, processing materials to save other crafters time, or basic sewing tasks were all they could reliably handle, it was still more useful than what they would be up to if they left. Even if it was pissing off most nobles in one way or another as they called for Xeal to accept more young nobles, or return them all to their houses. Xeal had rejected both as he commented that as far as he was concerned, those that remained had already accepted him as their patron. Even if there were still more than a few formalities to take care of before they were officially sponsored.

When day 102 arrived, Xeal once more found himself with Kate and Levina as he got ready to log out for one of his short breaks. He also once again found himself being overwhelmed by the amount of electricity that she was pushing through him like it was nothing, as like last time he only lasted around five minutes. As he worked to recover enough to move, Levina got dressed before speaking in a tone of mild annoyance.

"I would have thought that you would have at least shown some improvement since yesterday, but it seems that you just don't have the motivation to make this happen on a short timetable. Perhaps you will reach where you need to be in another decade or so, but not before the next major battle."

"So I will return from my break and spend the next week here as you repeat this over and over again whenever my stamina recovers."

"Won't do any good. You gained all of 2 seconds. That isn't even a one percent increase. If you keep that pace, you won't even reach ten minutes after 100 of these sessions. As much as I love seeing you and you letting me touch you like this, if you are going to improve you need more motivation."

"Are you saying that ensuring Nium wins the war and my family is safe isn't enough motivation?!"

"Xeal, your family will be safe regardless and while your guild collapsing would devastate you, it is not enough to truly push you to your limit any more. No, you need something far more immediate and undesirable to you for motivation. Any ideas, Kate?"

"Having to show you affection would certainly do the trick," quipped Kate. "But you would simply increase the difficulty and ensure that he failed to get your prize then. So, let's go with you have to spend your recovery time letting either Ekaitza, Lumikkei, Malgroth, or Lughrai hold you as you do so."

"You are so mean to me." Levina pouted. "Though I was going to suggest him having to give a kiss to either me, or one of my sisters selected randomly."

"Not all of them would say yes to that," retorted Xeal. "Also, Kate, are you really saying that I dread showing any of them affection more than the fall of Nium?"

"Yes, you are utterly terrified of letting one of them in as you believe it will allow all four in. Of those who are actively expressing interest in you, you only fear letting the phoenixes in more right now. Yes, you would rather let

Princess Bianca, or Princess Lorena in at this point!"

Xeal wanted to deny Kate's words, but a part of him worried that she was right as he responded to her.

"Fine, I will leave this to you to explain to the others, but you aren't to even let Ekaitza, Lumikkei, Malgroth, or Lughrai know about this until I fail to reach whatever goal we have for our next session."

"Very well," replied Kate, "Five minutes and 30 seconds, as you made it to five minutes and 18 seconds this time."

"Great, so I only need to show six times more improvement. Kate, are you still in favor of letting one of them in?"

"Yes, but not to the same extent that I once was as I think you are pretty much at 16 already, assuming that Daisy, Violet, Bula and Dafasli all reach tier-7 with you. They are more likely than not at this point."

"How did things get to this point?" asked Xeal rhetorically.

"You fell in love with two women that couldn't refuse to share you and they let a princess in who sees the number of brides you have as something to be proud of and well, you were love starved in your last life," replied Kate half sarcastically.

"Last life?" asked Levina in a tone of genuine curiosity. "What does she mean by that, Xeal?"

Kate blinked a few times as she mentally cursed herself for slipping up, as Xeal sighed before replying.

"The concept of reincarnation exists in my reality and it is said that part of who we are is influenced by who we were in a past life at times. In this case, the joke is that I must have been a sad and lonely man who lacked the care and affection of others in my last life, despite having a deep desire for it. So, now I can't help but find something to love about any woman I allow to get close to me."

Xeal could tell from the slight frown on Levina's face that she wasn't buying his story. However, a second later she smiled as she responded to him.

"I see, so there is hope for me to find a way into your heart, I just need to get close to you. Is this close enough?"

As Levina said that, she lay down on the ground right next to Xeal as she let her body brush up against him and smiled. Xeal just shook his head at the playfully taunting look she was giving him, as he stood up and left for the day before logging out. He knew that just like Kate would have, she had calculated the pros and cons of pushing for the truth at that moment and had made the right call for the greatest long-term benefit.

(*****)

Morning April 20 to Evening April 28, 2268 & ED Year 6 Days 103-129.

Time in reality might as well have not existed for all the productivity that Alex got done during the two one-hour breaks he was taking each day. He didn't even see any part of the house but the VR pod room, his bathroom, the hallway and stairs to the upstairs dining room, the inside of the elevator and the nursery. Most breaks it was roughly in that order as well, as Gido brought him something to eat while Alex focused on his kids and the few moments he got with Sam, Nicole, Ava, Mia and Kate. All of whom were being great about dealing with the current state of things, though time would tell if they could deal with it long term. Especially once they were barely seeing him in ED once things really started to get going.

While Alex remained in his 22 hours a day in ED schedule, the rest of the house continued life as usual for the most part. Ava and Mia were still keeping to a feeding schedule for their kids, Kate was pulling a few 22-hour days as well and Tara was beyond overworked as she took on even more responsibility, both in and out of ED. Thankfully, Sam, Nicole, Clara and Fred were able to help Tara out with most of it, but it was clear to all that once this phase was over, Tara would need a vacation from work for a good bit. Still, everything was running as smoothly as could be expected in reality with everything considered.

Days 103 to 121 in ED were a blur to Xeal, as he remained focused on simply leveling and improving his and his party's abilities. This of course included trips to Levina every time he was about to do admin work, to exhaust his stamina while trying to improve his control over electricity. Surprisingly to Xeal, Kate's threat of being held by one of the four dragonoid women actually was effective, at least in part. Xeal had only made it four days before he missed a target. At this they had learned of the deal and one of them was making themselves available each day on a rotational basis. Xeal found that he was also failing to reach his goal one out of every three daily visits after they had arrived. A fact that Kate was quick to point out after he had repeated this pattern three times. As she put it, he was slowly giving into them and if he wasn't careful they would find a way in, after which Xeal started to succeed nine out of ten times.

Though each time he failed, Kate was quick to ask him if he was just looking for an excuse to be held to relieve some mental exhaustion. Xeal had just smiled at this idea as he suggested that she let him rest on her whenever he succeeded then. So it was that that Xeal found himself enjoying ten minutes of laying his head in Kate's lap most of the time after that, as she used it as an opportunity to get a head start on their meeting that would follow. The pouting faces of the dragonoid women during this made Xeal decide to keep his eyes closed to avoid seeing them as he focused on relaxation. He felt slightly guilty about the system Kate had set up where Ekaitza, Lumikkei, Malgroth and Lughrai were only allowed to respond to Xeal's words and weren't allowed to initiate a conversation. He knew that they had agreed to it simply to have any chance of gaining ground, but he was also just staying quiet in an effort to keep the interaction as awkward as possible. Still, they had taken to doing things like stroking his hair, or humming softly as they tried to mimic the same things that they had watched Xeal do with his wives in similar situations.

It was also this situation that Xeal had found himself discussing with Austru when he had visited her. For the most part she had been satisfied with Kate's explanation that had been included in a letter. Though she had several questions for Xeal. These revolved mainly around his feelings on the situation and if he thought it was working. After which they had enjoyed a good night of snuggling as Xeal focused on just enjoying the break for what it was. When the time had come for him to leave in the morning, he reluctantly did so after a few more hugs and kisses. That was until the ruse in ED started on the 26th, though all that changed was that he was offline for four hours a day as he mimicked what he would be doing during his tier-7 tribulation.

When day 122 came around, Xeal found himself at level 197 and quickly approaching level 198 as the next arena league started. Once more, few if any members of FAE's main arena team were participating as they were instead joining Xeal and others in the main force that had been selected in vanishing from the public eye. Kate had been sure to only select the members that she was absolutely positive wouldn't leak the details of the ruse as they all entered clearable dungeons like the kobold mines, or the Vault of Ucnuc had been. For Xeal and his party this was the dungeon at the center of the Mist Woods, where they used safe zones to get rest and recover regularly. Xeal realized that this was also the first time that he would be spending downtime with both Lucy and Sylvi, as he still assessed if the cleric of Freya that Gale had found for his party was a fit.

"Is this really how the next month plus here is going to go?" asked Lucy, sounding bored.

"You should really learn how to be grateful for times like these," replied Sylvi. "They are important as when we are out in the field like this, they will be how we recharge between each struggle that is before us."

"I get it. I just have so many other things that I could be taking care of right now if I was allowed to!"

"Lucy, we can't," replied Xeal. "If our work is getting done like normal it will ruin the ruse."

"I know that, though I just think you wanted to get out of doing any of the work that the arena leagues create for you."

"What are you talking about, I have you for that now," quipped Xeal. "Or did Kate fail to let you know that your job includes that?"

"You still need to look over it, or have you been approving it without looking at it?"

"No, he has been having Aalin handle it," interjected Eira. "Gale, Luna and Selene do a fair bit of work behind the scenes as well now."

"Oh, what are they trading admin work for time with you?" questioned Lucy. "Xeal, that is not how things should be run!"

"Lucy, I know what all of them are capable of and trust them to handle things how I want them to be done. If I didn't delegate everything that I possibly can, I would never get anything done. You need to be building a team that you can do the same with. Speaking of which, how has yours and Gale's recruitment been going?"

"How any of the women you are in a relationship with can stand you shoving work off on them is beyond me. As for the special players, well, let's just say that they are currently gathering in Muthia until you can find a way to get them here."

"Good, that will work for now. As for me shoving work off on those I see as my wives, well, they are just as much owners of FAE as I am in my mind. Are you saying that if you were married and your partner owned a business that was bringing in enough income that it covered all the bills, that you wouldn't be willing to lend a hand?"

"He has you there," interjected Sylvi. "A marriage is a true partnership when done right. While each member of it may have different roles, they still need to work together and support the other where they can. For me that was ensuring that my late husband could count on me to heal him in battle and I could trust him to keep me safe from attack at the same time. You're a cleric as well, you should know what I am talking about."

"No," replied Lucy. "I don't expect that I will have the same relationship with my partner if and when I find one. I don't want them doing my work and I have enough work of my own to handle to take on any of theirs. Also, I don't see myself being attracted to someone who just wants me to stay back and heal them."

"That just sounds sad," commented Daisy. "We hope that if he lets us in, that Xeal will be happy to let us have that kind of relationship with him."

"Yes, else we will feel like a burden to him," added Violet.

"Lucy, you are free to handle your relationships however you like," cut in Xeal as he took control of the conversation. "However, for me, those I am with, it is nothing short of a full partnership. That said, I am also lucky enough to not need to withhold information from them as you might find yourself being forced to do. Unless you plan to only date other vice guild leaders of FAE."

"Oh god, no! I want to be able to leave work at work," retorted Lucy. "I will leave the sharing the work to cooking, cleaning and raising the kids if we have any."

"The ways of your kind are weird to me," commented Sylvi. "To me there is no difference between being at home and work. Life is work. Yes, there are moments of relaxation between the work. Killing monsters, raising kids, cleaning, cooking, even practicing one's faith is work. To separate them by where they are performed just ignores reality as a whole."

"You are not wrong," agreed Xeal. "It's part of why I believe in paying others to handle any work that I don't need to do when I can afford to do so. Work that others can do, but I need full confidence in it being done correctly and discreetly, is where my wives come in when possible."

"Sure, now can we change topics?" asked Lucy. "Like how long until you see Abysses End taking the bait...."

Xeal just smiled as he obliged Lucy as they shifted topics for a bit, before setting up guard shifts and getting some sleep in. Xeal was just thankful that the dungeon's safe zones were closed rooms in this one that had enough room to set up a proper camp, as he snuggled with Eira in their private tent. The look of contentment on her face at knowing that she likely had over four weeks that would be spent like this was obvious. At the same time, seeing the others in the morning was rather awkward for Xeal, especially Bula who was still doing her best to ignore her desires towards him. Desires that Xeal was intimately familiar with thanks to Freya and he couldn't help but wish that he wasn't.

Days 123 to 127 continued like this as Xeal reached level 198 while the rest of his party, save Lucy, had already reached the tier-6 level cap of 199 and started to focus on leveling up their experience items. Xeal had to hold in a laugh as he thought about how he would only have a few days at best to focus on his own experience items. This was one of the real costs of Xeal's need for one and a half times experience, as his whole party had weeks to focus on leveling such gear up and he didn't. The fact that having such equipment could be almost necessary to reach tier-7 for any but the top players, depending on their tribulation, made Xeal feel like he was going in at a disadvantage. He just hoped that his elevated stats didn't increase the difficulty of his tribulation too much. Though after comparing his tier-6 ordeal to what he knew was normal, he didn't hold much hope of that being the case.

Day 128 started out normal enough and Xeal thought that it would be an uneventful day just like the ones before. Only just before they would have normally been calling it a night, he received a message from Taya. Abysses End was launching simultaneous attacks targeting FAE members in every single country outside of Nium and another human wave attack was headed for the border forts. Xeal just wanted to sigh as he pondered how to respond to the threat as his reemergence would likely have multiple effects. The first of these would be the nature of his reemergence as if he reappeared at level 198 like he was, the instant rumor would be that he failed his tier-7 tribulation. The result of this would depend on a few different scenarios and how the story got spread as if he willingly failed it to counter Abysses End's assault, it could elevate his image significantly. However, it would also encourage Abysses End to continue their assaults in hopes to keep Xeal from being able to reach tier-7 at all. On the other hand, if he failed due to not being up for the task, his image as the top expert in all of ED would be shattered and it could have worse effects than not showing up at all. Though it would also likely cause the assaults to pause for a longer time as Abysses End would think that Xeal was going to undergo extensive training to attempt to reach tier-7.

It was for these reasons that Xeal decided to make a spectacle out of his and the 3,000 players who were supposed to be attempting their tier-7 tribulation. They would all also be wearing their items that disguised their levels as it would allow the rumors to really get going and confuse the situation between the three main possibilities. Those being the two failure scenarios and the reality that FAE had lured Abysses End in to attacking them. The beauty in this plan is with just a bit of effort, most people would believe the version that they agreed with and waste theirs and Abysses End's time as they pushed their narrative. Thereby increasing the noise and obscuring information in the short term and possibly lasting long enough for Xeal to actually reach tier-7.

So it was that with a few messages everything was set in motion, as Amser led the operations to counter Abysses End abroad. Meanwhile, 80% of the available forces went to hold the line on the Paidhia and Nium border, and Xeal and the 2,999 others arrived at the Habia and Nium border. As they did so, there was once more over 5,000,000 players assaulting it as the defenders used everything at their disposal to attack them while Xeal received the same quest as last time. Along with the 3,000 players, Queen Aila Lorafir arrived with 1,000 tier-7 spellcasters that could wield high-powered electrical spells. This was about every single one of such spellcasters in all of Nium and it had taken quite a lot of convincing to get them all to be available for this stunt. King Victor was expecting a spectacle that would convince the populace of all three kingdoms that just having Xeal already meant that Nium was destined to win.

Xeal, however, was just hoping that all the training that he had done with Levina had paid off, especially as it had been a hassle and a half to continue it while carrying out this ruse. Still, it was time to see if he could handle the insane levels of power that were about to be channeled through him. Especially as he wasn't holding anything back as he descended the wall the moment he arrived, as all 1,000 spellcasters prepped their first long chant spell. As Xeal started to slowly walk the ten feet between the wall and the force shields, he just smiled as he drew his swords and let out a dragon's breath at the nearest players. With that, there was no doubt on who Xeal was and looks of dread spread across the nearest players as they forgot to even attack the barrier. As Xeal paused just before crossing into the enemy ranks, he spoke in a low and even tone.

"This isn't personal, but you all are about to die in a rather gruesome display."

As he finished saying those words, Xeal felt the surge of power from all 1,000 spells entering him as he realized that Kate and Levina had been pulling one over on him. These 1,000 spells felt like only a third of what he endured at Levina's hand, as he held on to the power while waiting for the other two rounds of spells to hit him. At seeing him not attacking, the players across from the barrier were confused for a second before a few realized what that meant. Judging by how quickly they tried to escape, Xeal could tell they had at least been present at the last assault and once the medium chant spells arrived, the whole area near where Xeal was standing was empty. Xeal just smiled as he stepped through the barrier a moment before the short chant spells were due to arrive. Instantly Xeal saw thousands of arrows, rocks, spells, javelins and whatever else that attackers had on hand that could be launched at him. However, before any of them could reach Xeal, he had already received the 1,000 short chant spells inside of his body.

The next instant slowed down to a crawl by Xeal's perception. All around him were desperate players that just wanted to have access to a teleportation network. Most probably didn't even care if Nium, Habia, or Paidhia won the war, or the state of the continent after it was over. All they were worried about was the ability to play ED while enjoying their time, but instead they found themselves as pawns on a chessboard. As this moment ended, Xeal unleashed a massive bolt of electricity that shot right through the mass of players before him as if they didn't exist. One after another, each of these players didn't just die. No, they were turned to dust and in all likelihood their gear would be ruined as well. As it traveled through the players, Xeal received a system notification.

(Congratulations, you have killed 20,000 humanoids with a single attack. Rewarding title: Annihilator and 15,000 renown.)

Xeal found himself surprised by this notification and was curious about what this new title did, but he didn't have the time to worry about that as he observed the results of his attack. The bolt had been around 20 feet wide and he had aimed it towards the area that he knew the main command unit was. To say that it was like looking at the first row of wheat after harvest would be an apt comparison, if the rest of the wheat wasn't running in fear. As for the command unit, it had survived, but Xeal could see the look on Atius's face as he looked at the destruction that had cleared a path directly to him in an instant. He looked frantic, if not slightly insane, as he shouted and tried to regain control of the millions of remaining players. Meanwhile, Xeal gripped his blades while activating elemental blades and getting a bit of electricity back in his system, that he used to create an effect of his still having more electricity to release. This took the shape of bits of electricity jumping in and out of his body as he slowly walked forward as the players surrounding him simply worked to create distance between them and him.

None of the invading players even tried attacking like

they should have and Xeal just smiled as the real issue with human wave tactics reared its head. None of those present were anything special, with the vast majority of them not knowing how to react to the sudden devastation that Xeal had inflicted on their ranks. No, they were not the type to fight a boss monster that could kill them with a single attack, as they lacked the ability to exist on that knife's edge. It was only players like Takeshi and Amser who would be willing to take on such challenges with a smile, as they came out on the other end unscathed. This was a category that Xeal didn't even place himself in as while he liked his odds against any player in ED, it was only due to how broken his stats and abilities were. Even now Xeal knew that all it would take was the players nearest him rushing him and he would die and waste the drop of phoenix blood that he had protecting him. However, he smiled as the first 17 short chant spells entered him and he began releasing it all around him such that anything that came within 20 feet of him would be engulfed by it as he started running at Atius.

Ten seconds in and the first wave of medium chant spells entered Xeal and he increased the field around him to 35 feet. Finally, when the long chant spells entered him, the field around him increased to a full 45 feet in every direction from him as he charged forward. As Xeal ran, any player who was unlucky enough to find themselves in contact with this field didn't even last a second before dying. This surprised Xeal slightly as even with it basically being the combination of around 50 tier-7 spells, it still shouldn't have been that effective against the stronger players in his way. Though Xeal just assumed that it was a side effect of his new title and kept running forward. However, Atius wasn't just going to sit there and wait for his doom to arrive as Xeal closed the distance.

No, he knew that there was nothing to gain from allowing Xeal to kill him as the rout had already begun and the 200,000 players that had just descended the walls behind Xeal only added to the chaos. For a brief moment Atius thought of having the millions of players pay the price for not holding their ground until the 60% casualty mark had been met, but he couldn't blame them. Xeal's single attack had exceeded anything that should have been possible by his own understanding. They had been ready for Xeal's tactics from the last battle and even rejoiced at seeing what seemed like a limit to his ability to control electricity, which was still a sore spot for Abysses End. They had sent multiple complaints through every channel they had about just how broken it seemed to be, only to be shut down at every turn. All they were able to learn was that he had gained it through an unlikely sequence of events that were extremely difficult to achieve and unrealistic to be done by anyone again.

Atius and the rest of Abysses End had their own theories, knowing everything that they did at this point. This included the generous supply of phoenix feathers that Xeal had been using and his inclusion in the godhood quest that was absolutely top secret. Luckily, Frozen Sky wasn't loyal to the shell of the workshop that Jingong had once been. Instead, he had reached out quietly and made deals to counter Xeal. It had been him who warned of Xeal already being far more than any player could hope to face one on one right now, even when he wasn't in top form. Abysses End had told him that he was exaggerating things at first. That changed after he easily beat several of their top players and then told them that Xeal had defeated him even more easily. It was this that had convinced Abysses End that they had to go all in to remove Xeal and FAE as a threat now and join the war effort in both Habia and

Paidhia. Yet it seemed that even their most unrealistic estimates had been short of Xeal's true power and it was with this thought that Atius ordered the full retreat.

As the orders spread, it was only a matter of minutes before every player had used their return scrolls, or found themselves being attacked by one of the players that followed behind Xeal. As this happened, Xeal just smiled as a message came in that the assault at the other border had suddenly ended as well. Still, he looked at his stamina and frowned as the five minutes of activity that he had just done had him down to 66%. At that rate, 15 minutes was all he could handle while using the method he had just executed. Xeal also took a moment to investigate the details of his new title.

Title: Annihilator: when using any attack with an area of effect, or more than 100 targets, all damage is increased by one plus the difference in levels divided by ten. With a minimum multiplier of one and maximum multiplier of three. Killing 1,000, or more, humanoids with a single attack induces a fear effect on all enemies and an inspiration bonus to all allies.

Xeal looked at this title and couldn't help but frown as he typically didn't walk around with the needed support to pull off what he just did. Even his dragon's breath was technically a single-target attack, unlike most other breath weapons that he had seen. Xeal knew that it had to do with the beam nature of whatever Watcher's element was, though if Xeal had to guess it was plasma. Still, if he could vary it and use it in a cone, even if it would become less powerful on its own, with this new title it could be far more effective. Xeal was still thinking about this and if he had any ways to easily pick up a skill that would allow him to gain an easy AOE attack when Queen Aila Lorafir landed and started to speak.

"It seems that your training was effective."

"Yes and no. I still need to fix my stamina issue, but my ability to control large amounts of electricity has certainly improved."

"Yes, well, I am not sure I could have survived that attack you unleashed to start this battle and it was definitely the most destructive attack I have ever witnessed."

"I doubt any but Levina could take that attack and not come out significantly worse for it. It killed over 20,000 of the attackers and I got a title out of it..."

Xeal shared his new title and his thoughts on it to Aila who stayed quiet as she took on a thoughtful expression before responding.

"You are quite possibly more valuable as a siege weapon than anything else at this point. Even the best magic cannons that have been recovered from lost ages would be nothing compared to what you are. Though you are right that you need to find a way to use it outside of a full-scale battle. It is just a question of how and do you do it now, or later."

"I need to find the time to really see what my options are as I have never thought about picking up any such skills. My goal is to only take on large groups when I have the support of others who can supply me with the electricity I need."

"Xeal, you never know when you will need to deal with a large group and anything that relies on others is at best situationally useful rather than another trump card."

Xeal paused to think as other members of FAE started to make their way over to him as he thought over his options before he responded to Queen Aila Lorafir.

"It is something that I will need to consider in another month, or so. For now, I need to make sure that FAE's holdings are doing well."

"Alright, shall we get you back to the fort then?"

"In a second. I need to send a quick message."

As Xeal input his message that was set to go to every member of FAE, he smiled. All it said was "counterattack." With that single word, it gave all of FAE notice that Xeal was personally taking command over the current operation. A second later, a message from Taya came in instructing every level 190 to level 197 member of FAE to report to guild headquarters for assignments. At the same time, all level 198 and level 199 members were to stand by in case any other actions were taken in Nium. With that taken care of, Xeal found himself being transported back to the fort before he teleported back to Nium's capital and headed straight for the royal palace with Queen Aila Lorafir in tow. When they arrived, they were greeted by a pair of nervous royal guards as they looked at Queen Aila Lorafir with concern as one of them spoke.

"I am sorry, my lady, but–"

"But nothing," interjected Xeal. "She is with me and is an ally of Nium. If you fear that King Victor will hold it against you for letting her through, then feel free to go check as we waste time here."

"Duke Bluefire, you know that–"

"Anyone more powerful than the king's guards are not to be allowed to meet with him without prior arrangements. Is that going to include me now?"

"Excuse me?"

"Xeal, word of your exploits at the border have yet to reach here," commented Queen Aila Lorafir. "Though once they do, I wonder if it will gain you friends, or simply make them fear you."

Just then a messenger came running, as the man came closer and realized who was standing at the palace gates. It was clear that he didn't know how to react as he came to a halt. Queen Aila Lorafir just smiled as she continued to speak.

"It seems that we arrived a tad early, though it is convenient as we can now just send him to see if King Victor wishes to allow my entrance today."

Xeal could see the messenger tense up as he looked at the other guards, before one of them told the messenger to get a move on and Xeal found himself waiting. So, rather than stand idly, he started checking over the progress of the fight outside of Nium and the transferring of personnel through the temporary teleportation gate that was connecting Muthia and his guild's headquarters. Xeal was grateful that Empress Sakurai Jingū had been more than happy to allow FAE access in such a way, despite the drawbacks. Included in these was the real possibility of war coming to her lands as Abysses End had already positioned itself to attack both the Muthia and Huáng empires when the time was right. Lucy and Gale were also slipping into Muthia to gather and return with the dozen or so divine scions that were currently gathered there.

Once the deployed players were in Muthia, they would be transferring to all over Eternal Dominion and in total some 60,000 members of FAE would be participating in repelling the attacks. Additionally, Kate had activated the clause in all the contracts that she had required the other parties to assist to 'sustain endeavors in times of constraint to ensure continued production post constraint.' This move had been met with a fair bit of complaints and pushback on this notion, especially as it was essentially forcing them to aid in the effort to push Abysses End back. However, when it became clear that both Fire Oath and Salty Dogs had been caught by the same clause, the others had stopped making noise. This was for two reasons. The first was that they didn't want to insult either of the super guilds and the second was that they were enjoying seeing the super guilds fall for the trap as well. Fire Oath was particularly upset as they were in the process of cutting ties, but were roped in until they had paid off the debt in full.

Even so, the one who was most irate was surely Abysses End as they found themselves not just being forced to back off, but losing territory that they had held for years in ED now. In one single motion, Kate had managed to set Abysses End back years and force them to take a defensive stance, as they were forced to abandon their operations in several countries altogether. Especially when others who had a grudge against Abysses End took advantage of the situation to join in. Once FAE's reinforcement arrived, it was going to be time to see just how far Abysses End could be pushed back, but before that they needed to meet with King Victor. Thankfully, the messenger had returned with an irate King Victor, who wasted no time in letting his mind be known.

"If I need to make it known that Duke Bluefire is trusted to pass with, or without, Queen Aila Lorafir accompanying him when they are returning from defending our lands again, I will hold you two personally responsible. So, ensure that that is made known to all who need to know!"

Xeal had to hold in a chuckle with how fast the two guards let Xeal and Queen Aila Lorafir pass, as they found themselves walking with King Victor as they made their way into the palace in relative silence. Once they were in King Victor's private study, he sighed before he spoke to the room as a whole.

"Zylah, please join us for this discussion."

At that, seemingly from nowhere, Zylah appeared with a frown on her face as she spoke.

"I don't see what I have to add to this discussion. Your brother-in-law and my apprentice's husband is a true monster, end of story."

"Please, the amount of prep I need to do to pull off what I did-"

"Doesn't change the fact that you did it," cut in Queen Aila Lorafir. "Xeal, I don't think you fully appreciate your current situation. You displayed an attack past what we would expect for even a deity. All any can do against it is avoid it, or hide behind something made of stone like the palace and hope it holds."

"Honestly tell me that a skilled tier-7 earth mage couldn't counter it," replied Xeal. "All they need to do is cut me off from my source and they will eliminate the threat of it."

"Yes, but that is easier said than done when you have me above you. Xeal, you have put the world on notice and if you think that every nation isn't watching this conflict and adjusting their own invasion plans accordingly, you would be mistaken."

"Aila is correct," commented Zylah. "They even have evidence of the results of you being there and not being there because of the synchronized assaults."

"All it means is that you can scratch off large-scale armies being used," quipped Xeal. "After all, all it will take is me showing up with the support I need and the battle will be over."

"No, if I were them, I would lure you in with such an army and aim for your support," replied King Victor. "Yes, the battle would be costly, but if I could weaken your support I would. Though that will change once you have enough of your kind to offer the same level of support."

"That will take a fair bit of time and there is a fatal flaw to my ability that you are overlooking and was hidden in this battle. Victor, I can't show up and win you a battle with just 1,000 spellcasters and a force designed to defend them. Doing what I did cost so much stamina that I would only last 15 minutes doing it and just the main attack that I used took a full ten percent of it."

"That is still enough to easily kill 100,000 fodder troops and tilt the battle in our favor," replied King Victor.

"Only if it is an army made up of solely my kind. I will not murder the populace of this world in such a manner."

"Xeal, you will likely have to at least once," replied Queen Aila Lorafir solemnly. "If such an army is brought forward and you participate and don't do so, it will send a clear message that simply mixing in the people of this world in will counter you. They wouldn't even need to fight, they would just need to be mixed in enough to tie your hands."

"Aila's right," agreed King Victor. "You may permanently kill many that day, but it would also lessen the likelihood of them using such a tactic in the future."

"Have I mentioned that I hate war?" grumbled Xeal. "Even if I know that it is inevitable in this world."

"Only every time the topic comes up between us," commented Queen Aila Lorafir. "If I didn't know you as I do, I would think that you were trying to get on my good side about it. After all, no sane person wishes for war. At the same time, you recognize that without the ability and will to do just that, none can sleep in peace. Even when this continent is unified under a single nation as you dream, there will still be need of those who recognize that truth, else rebellions and foreign forces may still bring about its ruin."

Xeal sighed at her words as he shook his head before responding.

"Reality is cruel, even in a world designed to be an escape from it for many of my kind. Now, let's move on to the meat of the issue that we are here to deal with. Victor, are you really fine with declaring war on Abysses End and declaring that any nation that deals with them are subject to an extra tariff on all goods that they export to Nium?"

"It will result in a similar tariff being placed on us, but it will not have a significant impact on things and other nations will actually be happy to pay it. After all, most will simply pass the bill on to Abysses End with interest while publicly denouncing us. The main exceptions will be the nations where Abysses End is a major power, but even there they won't go to war over an entity that seems to be a mercenary force at best."

"Excellent. Then if you would please prepare your message and I will ensure my guild members that will be acting as the messengers are ready to depart within the hour."

"Hey, Xeal, I'd like you to give me the same thing you have given your wives to ensure that I live and escape what is about to come."

As Zylah's words registered, Xeal looked at the tier-8 woman who was looking at him with a look of cold resignation on her face as she awaited an answer. It took Xeal a long moment to connect all of the implications of what she was saying and how it would affect his own plans as he weighed his options before responding.

"You won't like the price of it."

"You can collect it if I make it to the other side of this war with it still in place."

"No, I can't trust any contract that I would make with you. I need payment up front."

"Fine, what did you have in mind?"

"Kill Saul Drerzen five times."

"Who is that?"

"One of my kind."

"You just want me to give one of your kind a death penalty five times?"

Xeal could tell that Zylah was confused as it sounded simple, but Xeal just smiled as he responded.

"Yes, I want you to kill the largest stakeholder in Abysses End five times and make sure they know I am the one that paid for it to happen. I'll even let you borrow one of the talismans that I have that will guard your life, but not allow an escape until you have completed your task. Oh, and make sure it's done in a very public setting."

"Are you sure that you don't want me to just kill five different key figures in Abysses End? It would let me get it done much quicker."

"No, I want them to increase security, know it's coming and still not be able to stop it. Now if he starts refusing to come out in public you can go ahead and hang his body from a wall, or something, where it can't be missed by my kind. Just not near anywhere that kids play."

"And what about when he just stops coming to this world?"

"He won't and if he does, Kate will look into it and I may pick a different target from Abysses End."

Zylah looked like she was weighing her options as she thought over Xeal's words before she responded.

"Fine, but none of the targets can be above tier-6."

"Alright, here is the talisman. I look forward to seeing the results of your efforts."

With that Xeal handed over one of the copper talismans that he had made for the young noblemen that he had focused on training and the dwarven VIPs that had been transported to Nium by ship. He knew that the reason that she had required that her targets remain below tier-7, was simply due to her desire to never need to use anything that would identify her actual power when killing them. If she wanted to make it seem like it was only a tier-7 assassin carrying out the act, Xeal wasn't about to stop her from doing so.

"Alright, now let's get into the minutia of what we each need to do before we all get completely derailed," commented King Victor, as he returned the conversation to its main purpose.

The following hour saw them address several possibilities and scenarios, that were all highly likely outcomes of all the moves that were being made. Still, they all knew that these scenarios were just a fraction of the possible outcomes from the way things were currently going and that the actual results were impossible to fully predict. Once more Xeal couldn't help but sigh at the state of things, as it was likely that with the dominos that were about to fall, that half of all of ED's nations would be at war by the year's end. This was a full year in ED before such a state had been reached in his last life and it just added to the strain that FAE would need to manage to ensure it came out on top.

Once Xeal was finally free of the impromptu war council, he kissed Queen Aila Lorafir goodbye and made his way to his office at his guild headquarters where Kate, Taya and Lucy awaited him. From there they got to work as they focused on getting through the backlog of paperwork that was waiting for them, while also monitoring the ongoing operations. Xeal knew that he would be sent in if any area seemed about to get out of hand, but it was clear that with the other guilds' aid, Abysses End was stuck on the defense. It had become such a one-sided struggle that many countries happily accepted denouncing and expelling Abysses End from their territory. Many of these had cited reasons that boiled down to that their insertion into a struggle between countries on multiple sides of a conflict posed a danger to their own security if ignored. This also served as a warning to all other guilds with major presences in multiple countries on the drawbacks of doing so. Especially for the ones with major presences in neighboring nations as they weighed their options and looked at the implications of how they would handle a war between said nations.

By the time day 129 had come to an end, Kate had been ecstatic by the state of things as she shared the early results of their efforts in real time. Rather than being upset about the fact that FAE had called in so many guilds to force back Abysses End, most guilds and players were seeing it as a brilliant idea. After all, no partners in the agreement had lost anything significant as Kate and Taya had included outs that allowed for fines to simply be paid if abiding by the contract would violate another contract. These fees would be determined by the number of losses sustained by FAE and those who did respond to that call for aid and divided among all parties equally. Suddenly small and large guilds with a significant portion of their funds tied up in trade were copying this model and working to implement it.

Xeal wondered just what the result of this would be as it was almost guaranteed that it would simply be turned into a giant mess. He expected it to reach a point where everyone was unable to make any aggressive moves for fear of the coalition that would be created to oppose them through such deals. In turn, this would create a situation where conflict arose behind the scenes and eventually, like a house of cards, it would fall when the first true conflict of interests arose from within. Xeal had seen similar results come from such deals in his last life and knew that the clock had started on even the one FAE had established falling apart due to such issues. Still, he had no issues taking advantage of being the first guild to establish such an organization while it lasted.

When it was finally time for Xeal to log out for his break, he just smiled at the constant requests that he had received from Abysses End for a meeting after Zylah carried out the first assassination. Poor Saul had been killed while on his way to meet with an important noble of Vefreora. Apparently only his head and a note arrived, stating that by Duke Xeal Bluefire's order, Saul had been killed and that he must die at least four more times in the next 20 days, else said noble would bear the responsibility instead. It left it vague just how said noble would pay, but the context was such that it could be anything from his own life to the lives of those he held dear. Additionally, it had included instructions that if they wished to allow him to take his own life, that it needed to be as public and humiliating as possible. This had been followed by four different scenarios for him to act out and how the body was to be treated once the deed was done and forbade any revival techniques.

Unfortunately, Xeal knew that refusing to even meet with them would result in issues that he would rather avoid dealing with. So, he had agreed to hear their complaints during his next logout, assuming that they would agree to have their guild leader handle it directly. With that not so fun experience to look forward to, Xeal smiled as he logged off for the night after enjoying a few moments of just being with his family in ED.

(*****)

Morning April 29 to Evening May 3, 2268 & ED Year 6 Days 130-144.

As Alex made his way to the conference room with Kate and Tara in tow while everyone else made their way to the morning kendo lesson, he couldn't help but sigh. Once more Jacob had handled all of the setup to ensure that the call was a single button away and would be secure on their end at the very least. As much as Alex was dreading this meeting, he could tell that Kate was actually looking forward to it from the look of smug satisfaction that had been on her face since she stepped out of her VR pod. When he had asked her what she was looking forward to, she just smiled and told him not to worry as they left the others and met Tara at the elevator.

Once they were all seated, it didn't take long for Jacob to establish the call as the hologram of Dommik Aimes, or Leo Dangrareth in ED, appeared in front of them. The guild leader of Abysses End wore a frown as he looked at what must have been the three of them sitting together on his own holo display. Alex just waited for the middle-aged man to open the discussion as he wasn't in the mood to waste any courtesies on the likes of him. After what was a long awkward pause, Dommik spoke in what was clearly an annoyed tone.

"You could at least act like you had even the slightest intent on being civil during this discussion."

"Sorry, but I think we are long past such a stage," retorted Alex. "How's Nantan by the way? Things just haven't been the same since all of that went down, though I must thank him and you for introducing me to Ava and

Mia."

"See, not everything that we have done to you has been unwelcome. Congratulations on the four new little ones by the way. I must say that you certainly have been busy and from what I know, you are just getting started on the whole family front of things. I am also glad that it seems that you don't simply hate Abysses End, but any that would seek to control you from how you have dealt with Fire Oath and the Astor family. Now, let's see if we can't figure something out before things reach a point such that mutually assured destruction is the only option."

At that Kate stifled a laugh before she responded to Dommik's words in a light-hearted tone.

"It seems that Abysses End still believes it has the capacity to force us into such a situation. Dommik, you and I both know that you are annoyed at having to be here after FAE paid to send your guild a message by killing Gabriel Trevils's character, Saul. The fact that he targeted a member of Abysses End whose only true value to your guild is his wallet and not you is already us showing restraint. Does it look bad for your organization? Yes, but trust me when I say that if you would like we could shift that target to you, or any other members of Abysses End rather easily."

"I am aware. It is why I am only getting you to drop the humiliation factor in the note they left-"

"We had nothing to do with that," interrupted Alex. "It can be tricky when dealing with those who hold more power than oneself and I am sorry, but that is just part of the personality of the assassin that we were able to hire. All we told them was to ensure that your guild couldn't hide the fact that Saul died all five times. The rest was left up to their discretion and if I were you, well, I will refrain from giving you advice that I wouldn't follow myself."

"So, there is really nothing to discuss here is there," grumbled Dommik. "Our relationship has reached the point where there is nothing to lose by targeting individuals for assassination that serve no purpose but to humiliate the other."

"Please, there is still much to lose on both of our sides," commented Kate. "Saul is nothing but a warning. We are at war and it is likely that both of us will find ourselves over extended before it ends and collateral damage is inevitable, but certain lines should not be crossed. One of those you have already done, by directly aiding both Habia and Paidhia, despite them being at war with each other. It is why Nium declaring war on you was so effective and it's why you are going to find Abysses End is seen as nothing but mercenaries. Whether or not you can fix that perception is your own issue."

"How is this still at the level of a warning?" retorted Dommik. "You are working to remove us from over 30 countries!"

"All we are doing is what you attempted to do to us," countered Alex. "Though you're right that isn't a warning, it's war. Us targeting Saul is the warning that FAE can easily play the assassination game and I invite you to do everything you can to avoid the next four strikes on Saul, outside of him not logging in."

"So, shall I start targeting your wives and children then?"

"Dommik Aimes, you are free to do whatever you think Abysses End can handle and thinks is in its best interest," replied Alex in a voice filled with malice. "Just know that there are certain actions that will result in results far worse than Abysses End's dissolvement for those involved. I mean, my grudge will mostly end once Abysses End is no more."

"Dangerous things, grudges, they can take us to places

that we should never venture. You may even say that yours is the whole reason that we are attacking you now," responded Dommik. "I mean, you could have easily avoided much of this by simply including us in the deal that you made with the other super guilds regarding the dragonoid slots."

"Perhaps," commented Tara breaking her silence. "But then it would have looked like FAE was just another doormat to the super guilds. Sorry, but I doubt any of our members want us to follow in the footsteps of Eternal Valhalla and become nothing but the super guilds' new piggy bank."

Alex could tell that Dommik wasn't pleased that Tara was even present as he responded to her in a condescending tone.

"And who do I have the pleasure of addressing as your guild leader failed to allow for introductions and I simply assumed that you were a secretary who was here to take notes."

"Tara, though you most likely know me as Taya and I assure you, the only one who needs to be taking notes is you. After all, I am sure that you will soon forget the lessons that we try to teach you every time you attack us and you wind up on the losing side of the exchange."

"Interesting. You say that, but why has FAE not come and finished us off if that is the case? I would think that if you keep having to teach us lessons that you would have just taken care of the problem once and for all."

"It's not worth the cost," retorted Alex. "Sorry, Dommik, but on my list of problems, you and Abysses End don't even make my top ten. No, while I could see your guild reduced to a state that makes Jingong seem intact, it would cost more than it's worth. So be grateful and stop trying to volunteer to be the guild we destroy before another guild destroys us."

"At least you admit that FAE wouldn't survive a conflict with us!"

"No, I simply stated that if FAE tried to actually eradicate you, we could, but it would leave us vulnerable. Now if there is nothing else, I believe we have verbally sparred enough for you to tell poor Gabriel that he needs to just accept that his character is going to die four more times."

"I think I want to see just what your assassin plans to do if he stays offline."

"Suit yourself," interjected Kate. "I wonder what the reaction would be from seeing your body turn up on that noble's front gate?"

"Ha, you will just make that noble hate you more!"

"Oh, I mean that it will be done on his orders. I mean that would be a way for him to bear responsibility. While you are respected in Vefreora, you are not as important to them as the half dozen major guilds that are tied to the fate of the nation much more than you are. If I were them, I would see it as a reasonable price to pay to avoid the alternative. Though I suppose that is just my thoughts on the matter."

With that Kate cut the call as she smiled at Alex and continued to speak.

"Zylah has already discussed things with me and that is the exact plan should Gabriel not log back in, only it will be him and three others."

"Is that why you were smiling smugly?"

"Yes. Sorry, but you needed to be able to claim ignorance for a bit longer and now we get to see what will happen."

"It's fine. Tara, do you have anything to add before we move off this subject?"

"Yes, when are we going to actually ruin Abysses End?"

"It will likely be right after I attempt to reach tier-8. Either I will succeed and see if I can't do it single handedly, or lead a full assault before any of their members can reach tier-8."

"No," replied Tara. "You are going to wait until I have had a chance to try to reach tier-8 as well. I want in on ruining them."

"I think that goes double for Amser and a few others," added Kate. "That said, I expect you to allow any who reach tier-8 with you to join your assault. Many hands make light work after all."

"Kate, this is personal."

"Alex, it is and not just to you. After all, if it's personal to you it is for me, Sam, Nicole and especially Ava and Mia, not to mention the rest of your loves in ED. That is unless we really are just pretty jewels that you wish to show off and not partners in everything."

As Alex gave Kate a look that was clearly saying that she was being unfair, Tara just looked between them before she spoke.

"I am just going to leave and let Kate convince you. After all, I know she will and I don't want to watch this."

Alex held in a laugh as Tara left and Kate pulled him in to a kiss the moment the door was closed. When the kiss ended, she looked Alex in the eye as she spoke.

"I love you, but you have a revenge issue. I thought that you would be better at controlling it, but from what you have shared and what I have been able to gather about your encounter with Frozen Sky, you have almost no control when it is just you. So, tell me, if it had been just you when you woke up and none of your friends had been around, what would be different right now?"

"Nothing-"

"Everything. Talking with Sam and Nicole and getting the story about you when ED first launched, I can tell that you put aside your revenge for them. Just like how you have shifted your plan when Ava, Mia and I came into your life. No, had it been just you, you would have long since reached tier-7. You would have never gone the route of the knight as building up your guild would have never been a focus as you would have never started in Nium. Though I am unsure which super guild you would have chosen to attempt to take over."

Alex paused for a second before sighing as he replied.

"Salty Dogs. I would have convinced them to increase their presence on land with the first guild boost and aimed to become a co-guild leader with Mittie. It is the only path that I can see having more than a 50% chance of actually working out for me."

"Hmm, I would have thought that you would go Dragon Legion. Either way you would have done nothing but amassed power and sought revenge, if not for your friends. That is not the man any of us love. It is your personal demon and when you finally satisfy it by destroying Abysses End and forcing Frozen Sky to quit, you need at least one of us at your side. Else I fear that you will be consumed by it and take things beyond what is necessary!"

Alex frowned as he thought over Kate's words, while she looked at him in a mix between care and frustration. He couldn't deny that he had tossed aside any long-term considerations beyond ruining Frozen Sky's resolve once and for all when he faced him in a one-on-one battle. Alex could also tell that this wasn't just Kate's normal calculating move from the look of worry in her eye that he rarely saw. No, this was the Kate that only he and the other ladies in his life ever saw as she never let her emotions speak when anyone else was present. It had also been these same emotions that had pushed her to come up with the plan to overload him with affection and attention seeking. It was with that thought that Alex finally responded.

"Kate, we are still likely a few years away from the day that any of this matters, but I fear allowing any of you to come because I know the monster that I will become. With the sole exception of the moves I made with you and the rest of my family in mind, every move I have made has been about getting to the point where I can actually carry out my revenge."

"I am aware, especially with the contracts that you have given Night Oath to handle some of your less personal targets. However, what point is there if you are consumed by your own revenge? And don't you dare say that I don't know what I am talking about!"

"I would never dream to do that. I am well aware that you want nothing more than to ruin the Astor family. You have wanted that since before you came to me. While I didn't see it when you first arrived, it is clear that you want nothing more than for them to beg you for help."

"Alex, I only want them to realize that my skills are every bit as valuable as my father's and to not judge me based on being a woman and who my mother is. Though you should thank them for all the conditioning they put me through, as it is what prepared me to be fine with our current arrangement."

"Kate, you're not fine with it. It's why you are focused on the legislation that would allow Sam, Nicole, Ava and Mia all to become wives to me as well."

"No, I am focused on that because as much as I hate to admit it, you've won. I could never walk away from Ahsa and Moyra and I am sure it will be the same with the other four soon enough. I don't want them growing up as your mistresses' children, as while I know you will never see them as any less for it, the world is not so kind!"

"Huhhh, fine, you win. I will stop planning to shoulder the whole responsibility for driving the knife in, but I will not ask anyone else to help me do so either. You have volunteered and you better reach tier-8 with me, else I will likely have to still drive the knife in on my own."

"No, it is Ava and Mia that will be next to you when you drive that knife in. The rest of us who come with you that day will be busy handling the minor players. Though, you may need to let Amser have a few of the bigger targets as well. Now, let's put that aside and just focus on our own prosperity rather than schadenfreude, as doing so is never anything but self-destructive."

Alex just smiled as he took a deep breath and gave Kate a kiss as they left to join the others for breakfast. With this, Alex found himself pondering on his own motives rather often that week, as he enjoyed having the normal two-hour logouts again and with it, time to spend with all the others. This included Ava and Mia who were finally getting a bit more free time with Aidan, Nadia, Evan, and Nova being fed every third hour instead of every other hour. It also didn't hurt that they had been cleared for other activities as well and had been quick to seek out Alex's affection. Still, a fair bit of their time was focused on the prep for the upcoming meeting with Eternal Dominion Inc. that was rapidly approaching.

When Xeal returned to ED on day 130, he quickly made sure that nothing had changed on the overall situation before he got ready to depart for the next pressing issue. As he did so, he found Mari waiting with Maki in her arms and Lillemor standing behind her ready to leave. At 32 months old, Maki was already over three feet tall and liked nothing better than playing with her siblings. As Xeal went to join them, Maki was inquiring about where the other three were by simply saying "Where And, Where Een, Where El." Mari was reassuring her that they were off to visit Grandma Gū and Xeal had to hold in a laugh at the nickname Empress Jingū had ended up with from his children. Though Xander being And, Xin being Een and Ellis being El were also works in progress as all his kids were speaking, but in what he would call a limited and altered vocabulary. They each seemed to have a particular issue with no as they seemed to think it was a word that only they should use, or that they could use it to get out of having to do things like go to bed. Still, Xeal couldn't help but smile at the adorable nature of all of them and even more so as Maki noticed him coming over and was the first to greet him.

"Dada! Play!?"

"Not right now, Maki, though I am sure that Grandma Gū will be happy to play with you and I am sure at least one of your aunts will be around."

"No, play now! Pleeeease?"

"Okay, we will play in the carriage. Just you, me and Mommy," replied Xeal as Maki smiled happily while reaching out for him.

"The others have already left to spend the day at the palace," commented Mari as she handed Maki over to Xeal. "They said to have us join them once we return."

Xeal just smiled as he gave Mari a kiss and they made their way through the teleportation network that Xeal had connected to the Muthia Empire and his guild headquarters. As they arrived, they were greeted by a dozen tier-7 guards, all of whom looked a bit on edge as they ensured that no unauthorized players used the gate. The fact that the gate had been set up in a building next to the capital's teleportation hall made it a convenient location for quick travel to the rest of ED once any player arrived.

However, at the same time, it also made it a prime target for an attack by Abysses End, or any other group that would like to attack FAE, or Nium.

Upon seeing Xeal, Mari, Maki and Lillemor, the guards all bowed slightly after a slight delay as they processed that they were not a threat. After the moment passed, a pair of the guards separated themselves from the rest to accompany them to the imperial palace. So, after a quick exchange of courtesies and waiting for the carriage to be brought around, the four of them found themselves on their way. With the two guards sitting atop the carriage, Xeal was able to enjoy his time as he played with Maki for the 20-minute ride until they arrived. Upon disembarking from the carriage, they were met by Empress Jingū's consort, Arai Sadanobu, who like always looked at Xeal with mild disdain. Though he softened his expression when looking at Maki as he greeted them.

"Thank you for responding to our request for a meeting on such short notice. Lady Sakurai is awaiting you in her private garden."

"It's good to see you too, Dad," quipped Xeal. "I take it my other dads were busy today. Either way, feel free to tell them I say hi."

Mari gave Xeal a look as Arai attempted to resist responding rudely as Maki just giggled in Xeal's arms. In the end the exchange simply ended there as Arai motioned them to follow him as he turned and led them to Empress Jingū's private gardens. Once there he excused himself as Xeal, Mari, Maki and Lillemor entered to find tea and a late evening meal awaiting them, alongside Empress Jingū who smiled widely as she greeted them.

"Xeal, Mari and of course little Maki, it's wonderful to see you all. I am sorry, but Kuni and Momo are both busy with possible suitors. Honestly, those two have become even more annoying since they started to accept offers to explore possible courtships. Especially Momo. She has really been finding every possible issue with those who are seeking her hand and I blame you for that, Mari."

"No aunty?" asked Maki as Empress Jingū took her from Xeal and replied.

"No, but you have Grandma. Isn't that better?"

"I want Aunty Uni and Momo. Please, Grandma Gū."

Xeal just smiled at the look of helplessness that Empress Jingū had on her face as he spoke.

"Maki, I am sure both will return by the time Grandma Gū and Daddy are done talking. For now, do you want to try the food that Grandma Gū has for us?"

"Not hungry, play!"

"Lillemor, would you mind walking with her in the gardens while Xeal and I eat and discuss things with my mother?"

"Not at all, Lady Mari. I will ensure that we stay in view."

With that Empress Jingū reluctantly handed Maki over to Lillemor and joined Xeal and Mari in sitting at the table. Before Xeal could even begin enjoying his meal that looked to be some type of fish with rice, Mari spoke.

"Now, Mother, what is it that you so urgently needed not only Xeal, but Maki and I here for?"

"Straight to the point. You really don't wish to take time to enjoy a meal before talking politics."

"Mother, I want to enjoy my meal, not be distracted by my worries."

"Very well, I would like to recognize Maki as having inheritance rights to my throne. Now can we enjoy our meal?"

"Mother! You know just what doing so would cause, so why would you do that to her!?"

"Yes, it is a move that will essentially say that I find all my own children as lacking and that I wish to place my hopes on the next generation. Opportunists will be quick to seek permission to have members of their house with young sons immigrate to Hardt Burgh and it will not be an easy situation for her to grow up in. However-"

"No," interrupted Xeal. "If you wish to use my daughter as a distraction, or political tool, I will not hear of it."

"Xeal," responded Empress Jingū calmly. "It is not meant to be a distraction and anything I do can be seen as political. Your very marriage to Mari was arranged for political reasons. Like it or not, you and all your children are part of this world and are destined to be seen as political tools!"

"Mother, you know what Xeal means. By naming Maki as having inheritance rights you would draw her away from Nium and towards Muthia in the eyes of many. Considering that she is already seen as a potential bride for Prince Vicenc and her family governs territory in another nation, it is a highly inappropriate action for you to take. So, just why are you wanting to pursue it?"

"Fear," responded Empress Jingū. "Just because I am in Muthia and war has yet to break out here, doesn't mean that I don't see what is coming. Right now, Kuri is the one most likely to survive among my heirs, simply because she is under Xeal's protection. Momo is the second most likely, though that is because she is the most likely to be used by a ruler who wishes to legitimize their rule. Should all but Kuri and you die as Muthia somehow survives, neither of you would be fit to rule. You are tied to a husband that kneels to a king already and Kuri will have hidden from the plight of the empire. Maki, on the other hand, would be seen as acceptable, but only if I name her as having the right to be considered beforehand. So-"

"So, Kuri can return to fight," replied Xeal. "If she falls in battle, she will escape to Nium with how her life is guarded."

"Just how many times can you allow her to do that?"

"Not nearly as many as I would like, but once is enough for now as it can be readdressed at that point."

"I would still prefer to have Maki as a safety net."

"Mother is your true fear from within?" asked Mari seeming to realize something.

"I said no such thing, but one cannot be too cautious of such possibilities. After all, my own siblings' families would love to trace the rights back one generation and then apply them."

Xeal wanted to yell at the top of his lungs as he once more was reminded that many times it was the enemy from within that posed the greatest threat. Mari and her sisters getting along was the anomaly, not the rule. If anything, the relations between Emperor Huáng Jin and his father, or Princess Syretia and Prince Arnost of the Ivurith empire, were more aligned with the norm for relationships within royal families of this world. Xeal wondered just how many rulers in ED had only accomplished their rise based on treachery as he responded to Empress Jingū.

"You will not name Maki to have inheritance rights. You will name me as the final heir should no other of your line survive besides Mari."

"My ministers would never-"

"Your ministers can swallow it. Just tell them that they better pray that it doesn't come to that as no amount of treachery will see me die and leave a throne to rule intact."

"Xeal, you won't even risk sitting upon Nium's throne, or sharing Aila's," commented Mari, sounding confused. "Why would you do this?"

"Because I will never need to sit upon this throne this

way. Were Maki to become empress in the next few years, who would act as regent?"

"Mari, Xeal is right," answered Empress Jingū. "Though I am going to need to officially ally our nation with Nium for this to be accepted by the populace. You will need to declare that should you become emperor, you will relinquish your holdings, titles and any fidelity to Nium."

"Better get ready to have FAE move in and prepare for war from all sides," retorted Xeal. "That isn't going to happen. I will not act like allowing my son Xander to inherit my house with Enye acting as his regent will not create the same conflict that doing that would create. No, if anything, the fact that your empire would instantly find itself as a subordinate kingdom, will only motivate your ministers to ensure that your line survives."

"Very well…"

With that the topic shifted to lighter topics as they started to enjoy their now slightly warm meal. After which, Empress Jingū enjoyed time with Maki and Xeal could tell that she was still wishing that her plan to use Maki and not Xeal had worked. For his own part, Xeal did his best to just ignore the reality that was right in front of him should he somehow end up actually becoming emperor. He also was asking himself why he had even suggested such an idea when he just needed to stonewall Empress Jingū and keep Kuri alive to avoid it even being an issue. Still, he knew that by doing this it was almost certain that Empress Jingū and her children would be safe from their relatives at the very least.

As they left a few hours later, it was with a message for King Victor to look over before Xeal would be named as the emergency heir. Thus, as Mari took Maki to the royal gardens where Enye and the others were, Xeal made his way to meet with King Victor. As he read the contents of the letter, Xeal could see the frown on his face deepen further and further, until he looked at Xeal and spoke in a voice of pure frustration.

"Xeal, you are aware of all the issues this will create right here in Nium, correct?"

"You mean besides the calls for me to be branded a traitor, opportunist, power hungry, unreliable, and unfit to be a noble. I can go on, but that is where it is vital to address it through the treaty that will be signed between both nations. So long as you use my house as a bridge between both nations, it should lead to a result where my loyalty is seen as what ensures that the alliance is preserved."

"Should I expect a similar treaty to be sought out by the Huáng empire?"

"It is likely that it will come, though unless they are willing to make more changes than I believe they would, no such alliance would make sense."

"Oh, and just what would they need to do?"

"Declare themselves as a new nation, with every minister and local ruler agreeing to go into exile while Lingxin becomes empress and my house would end up ruling there. As things currently are, my goal is to save the capital and claim it as a guild city-state which will remain neutral to all powers, save for those who would attack it."

"You believe you will have the power to back that up?"

"Victor, I believe that I have laid the foundations such that if they are allowed time to mature, that it is a realistic possibility. Though now it would require Nium's own war to drag out until they do, if a war was to start in the Huáng empire right now."

"The sheer chaos that all of this is going to create-"

"Is something that my guild is in a position to handle, Nium not so much. Victor, if you allow any of this to occur, it will be tying the fate of all those who are party to the agreement together. It is a deal that will likely cause wars to instantly break out and create the first ever true world war in this world, at least since the gods fought the primordials."

"13. 13 nations. That is what this alliance requires to be solvent and you can only provide three."

"Five. I can deliver five nations if you care not for the details of the arrangement, or who the others are."

"Oh, and what nations do you believe you could deliver and what would it cost me?"

"The Ivurith Empire and Zapladal Theocracy, but you would likely need to marry two or three women. Princess Syretia Eudoxia who is currently going by Alyson and either Lois Auger or Sciencia Auger, who are both participating in the beast-men marriage interview process, but haven't had any luck yet. Honestly, they were more likely to find husbands after the first wave of you awarding titles of nobility to soldiers for meritorious deeds."

"Xeal, just what have you been up to? I knew about Lois and Sciencia, but Princess Syretia is said to be dead!"

"I may have helped her fake her death and hid her in Aila's care."

"Did I say chaos earlier, this is sounding like true pandemonium. You could not pick a more absurd set of countries to form this alliance around."

"Which is why I need to reach tier-7 before we make any moves. Oh, and I will need to borrow Zylah if possible."

"Xeal, just what are you planning?"

"Nothing much, just walking in to negotiate the deal with seven tier-8 entities as I would rather not involve Cielo city if possible."

"Are you planning to negotiate with them, or coerce them into your deal?"

"I simply want to impress upon them why this alliance makes sense. Oh, and depending on how things play out, your first-born child with Princess Syretia may become the heir to the Ivurith Empire."

"Ha, hahaha, oh, you are really going to make me want to kill you. Fine, let's go ahead and play this game, but I will only accept either Lois or Sciencia, and Nora will pick, while the other marries either you, or one of your vice guild leaders. Xeal, you do realize you are basically saying that this plan will see me gain ten brides by the end of it, right?"

"And you would still have less than I! I am sorry, Victor, but I don't care if you end up with 18 extra brides if it means that I can avoid adding any more to my plate."

King Victor took a deep breath at Xeal's response as he brought his emotions under control before replying.

"Xeal, I need to visit Nora to discuss this. If you would please arrange everything for that to happen I would greatly appreciate it."

"I will have Enye bring Ekaitza around and coordinate it. Also, you should bring Enye with you."

"Hoping that she can keep Nora from wishing to ruin your life by helping Princesses Bianca and Lorena find their way into your bed?"

"No, I have no fear of that. Nora may wish to discuss it with someone who is not her husband before she agrees to allow you to take a bride."

"Fine."

"Great. Now I just need to convince Princess Syretia that sharing you with all the others is in her interest, else things might get rather complicated."

King Victor just looked at Xeal like he wanted to yell at him as Xeal held in a laugh as the meeting drew to a close. Xeal just smiled as he finally was able to join the rest of his family as they relaxed in the gardens as his children played.

This included Kate, Luna and Selene, as well as Daisy and Violet, who continued to integrate into his family in any way they could. Xeal had to laugh as if they didn't catch him, they would very likely catch one of his sons one day, just as the five-tailed fox-woman Chiharu had said. Still, for the moment, Xeal just enjoyed the peace that came from this scene for him as Mari had already taken care of sharing the details of the visit to the Muthia empire with them. So, after a brief summary of his meeting with King Victor and letting Enye know about his request to visit Queen Nora, Xeal was able to enjoy one last day off before it would be time to return to the grind.

Days 131 to 145 saw him do just that as other than handling some more paperwork, he found himself and 9,999 members of FAE act as if they were starting their tier-7 tribulation on day 133. During this time, Xeal and his party focused on technique over experience, though Xeal still managed to reach level 199 on day 142, as he shifted his focus to his experience gear necklace accessory as he saw it reach level 170 before the end of day 144. With that it was now providing a 17% boost to all seven items that it currently held. This caused it to essentially be worth 1.19 items in its current form and Xeal wished he had been able to add more levels to it as he logged out one last time before he attempted to reach tier-7.

(*****)

Morning May 4 to Evening May 8, 2268 & ED Year 6 Days 145-157.

As Alex sat down in the conference room after enjoying a light breakfast, he couldn't help but smile at seeing Kate and Tara as they went over the presentation that they were about to give one last time. The pair of them had really revamped it since the last meeting with Ellayina Walsh as they made sure that it met her requests. That said, nothing in the content had been changed. They had simply trimmed the fluff and reduced the avenues of approach as to why they should allow FAE to secure a quantum-entangled server for their city. Kate had profiled each and every member of Eternal Dominion Inc. who was on the docket to participate. This had been far easier then profiling Ellayina Walsh for their first meeting as she was an enigma in many of her tendencies and as Kate had put it, she was likely playing the same games Jasper enjoyed.

Finally, the time came for the meeting to begin as first Gaute joined and then the members of Eternal Dominion Inc. Altogether ten individuals, that Kate and Tara had been working with their assistants to ensure all relevant information was already in each of their hands before this meeting, were present. This made them relatively sure that Eternal Dominion Inc. would be in favor of the deal. However, there were two other key figures that would need to be swayed. One was Ellayina Walsh, who Alex felt relatively confident about and the other was the current president of Eternal Dominion Inc., Kevin Hansen.

Kevin Hansen was one of, if not the most, influential man in the world in Alex's last life, as Eternal Dominion

Inc. expanded to insane proportions. While the only revenue that was ever earned by Eternal Dominion was through the five percent processing fee that all in-game credit transactions required, that was still in the trillions of credits each year. With 20% of the world's economy based around his game in one way or another, he had more power than any single government, as without a replacement ED's end would wreck the world's economy. Yet right now Alex knew that he was just beginning his rise as there were still a few competitors who were holding on with player bases in the hundreds of millions. Still, if Alex were to rank him at this current time, he would be about on par with the leader of a medium-size country. So his presence alone made this meeting something that Alex could only dream of in his last life as Kate began speaking to open it.

"Welcome. I hope everyone is doing well and we are grateful to you all for taking the time out of your extremely busy schedules to meet with us today to discuss the possibility of a limited partnership. Are there any questions, or comments, that you would like to address before we start our presentation?"

"Yes," replied Kevin Hansen. "Alex, this is slightly off topic, but is there any way that you would be willing to trade your first guild bonus and electricity control for my agreement to allow the server to be housed in your city?"

Alex blinked a few times as what he was being asked registered in his mind and the fact that they were being brought up here confirmed just how much pressure his actions had put on Eternal Dominion Inc. After the implications of what he was being asked to do sunk in, Alex smiled as he responded.

"Mr. Hansen, if you are just trying to ascertain the value that I place on securing this server I am sorry, but that trade would leave me at a major loss. Though if you are simply seeking to find a way to convince me to willingly surrender the two things that give me the greatest confidence in my guild's survival, you are wasting your time."

"Interesting. You know we could simply strip them from you if we so chose to, right?"

"And you could strip every player who has converted their race to half-dragonoid of that benefit. Mr. Hansen, forgive me for saying so, but right now, even if I gave up both willingly it would cause irreparable harm to your position. You need to stand by your system and say that it rewards players for true excellence and while some rewards can seem excessive, changing them will only cause more issues. After all, if Abysses End, or other guilds think that they can pressure you into solving their issues, then when will they stop making demands? What happens after you remove my ability to control electricity? They demand that you compensate them for the two assaults that failed because of it?"

"So you would have me ignore one of the industry's backbones after another one has already all but collapsed? Do you really see yourself as more important than them?"

"None of us are truly important to you," interrupted Kate. "At least not as individual people, or companies. What is important is the confidence that average players have in Eternal Dominion being seen as the most enjoyable way for them to spend their time. It is why we are working to set up a true link between Muthia and Nium that will allow for players to access Nium and the rest of Eternal Dominion during the war. There are still some issues with this, but once FAE has a few thousand tier-7 players, it should be a feasible enough operation to maintain. On the note of player enjoyment, I would think that the human wave tactic that we have been repelling would be seen as the bigger threat to that."

Kevin Hansen looked annoyed at Kate for pointing out the obvious as he responded to her.

"Thank you, Ms. Peirce, but all of those players chose to partake in those assaults."

"To gain access to a way to at least move around their country and enjoy the time they do have to play," countered Alex. "Yes, I have used a similar tactic when recruiting guilds to defend Nium's borders, but I am not forcing them to charge at a fortified position that they have no business being involved with. The point is that most players simply wish to ignore the wars and simply opening up a way for them to transfer to another continent easily would be enough to solve that issue."

"I thought that you just told me to not listen to any complaints from guilds?"

"I said demands. Feedback is always important, especially from those who disagree with our own view. After all, while neither may change their mind, if both can understand the other's reasons, we can start to find a way to establish common ground and a way forward. For instance, if you created an absolute member cap of around 120,000,000 members in any guild right now, you would essentially only allow me to reach that number first. I keep an advantage, but Abysses End, Fire Oath and the other super guilds would have a path to catch up eventually."

"You believe that you will have 120,000,000 members one day?" interjected Ellayina, sounding surprised.

"Ms. Walsh, I am projecting to reach 111,111,111 members and stop there in 11 to 15 years, as that is where how I am designing my guild to be structured will break down. I am sure guilds like Abysses End will happily pass me by and try to control more than any one guild should, at least in my opinion."

"And just what is too much? A whole second world?" questioned Mr. Hansen. "I mean, you seem fine accepting the possibility of gaining that from one of your current quests."

"Yes, the reward that the system is offering to whoever is left standing at the end of my special quest is too much for any one guild, let alone player. It is why my goal is to be the one that does win it. After all, I have already begun to restrict my actual control there."

Alex could tell that the meeting was already heading towards a poor conclusion from the look on Mr. Hansen's face when Ellayina cut in once more.

"Kevin, drop it. You and I have already had our back and forth on this! Unless you want me to follow through on what I already threatened."

"Ellayina, now is not the time for us to be discussing such things!"

"Right, so drop it before it can't be!"

Alex could tell that there was a fracture inside of Eternal Dominion Inc. and it seemed like he was at its center. He knew that Ellayina was the brains and technical side of the equation and Mr. Hansen was the business side of things, including a large part of the seed money needed to create ED. Between the pair of them they held 55% of the company, with Ellayina holding 25% and Mr. Hansen at 30%, while the other 45% was being held by other major investors. It was these other figures that currently were simply silent partners that were unknown in number and influence to the public, that were the biggest unknown in the current situation. Especially if Ellayina and Mr. Hansen were split on a decision that would need to be voted on and if Alex had to bet, they had an alliance to ensure that such an issue never arose. Before Alex could think too deeply on this, Mr. Hansen cleared his throat before speaking as if the exchange that had just transpired had never happened.

"I believe Ms. Peirce and Ms. Moira have a presentation for us. If you would begin."

Kate and Tara both seemed a bit put off by the fact that they were being referred to by their last names, but they recovered quickly as they launched into their 30-minute presentation. Highlighted were all the benefits that the arrangement would have for Eternal Dominion Inc. and the negatives were countered. By the time it was over, Alex wondered if it had been enough to overcome what had clearly been a rocky start to the meeting, as the floor was opened up to questions. These ranged from things like confidence that the current timeline would be met and if Eternal Dominion Inc. could pull out of the city if they decided that it wasn't in their interest at a later date. All of this was, of course, covered in the extended files that Tara had sent all the participants as she directed them to the appropriate sections as she answered them. As for the deal regarding the quantum-entangled server, they could remove it if they wished to, but they would be responsible for covering the estimated losses caused by doing so as it would be a key feature of the city.

Finally, every question seemed to be taken care of and it seemed that the meeting was coming to a close. Afterwards, Eternal Dominion Inc. would have their own meeting as they discussed things amongst themselves and decided what direction they wanted to go. However, it seemed that Mr. Hansen wasn't quite done with Alex as he spoke once more.

"Alex, I must say that you have quite the vision for the future. Now tell me why Eternal Dominion Inc. shouldn't build this and more cities like it?"

"Very well. Mr. Hansen, I am sure that thanks to the success of Eternal Dominion that you could very easily do just that and do so in a way that would align with your plans quite well. However, doing so would be a mistake as it will take decades to see any returns and it will tie up resources that could be used for Eternal Dominion. Especially once others start mapping out your plans and buying up land to try and block you, or sell it to you at a much higher rate than you want to pay just to secure locations. No, the financial benefit is heavily weighted towards guilds to build their own cities over any one entity making such decisions."

"And you would have us provide a server to each of these cities?"

"No, I would expect you to make a benefit analysis for each one and decide if doing so makes sense, or not."

"So if I turn you down and decide to build a city in Montana to act as a testbed for these ideas, what would you do?"

"What can I do, other than obviously scale down the plans for my own city and invest elsewhere. Mr. Hansen, we each should do what is in our own best interests and I believe we have made the case for why FAE's plan accomplishes that. If you disagree, then I see no reason that you should even entertain our proposal, though I hope you will agree with our assessment."

"I think that you have given us much to consider. Now if there is nothing else, I believe that we should bring this meeting to a close."

"Only that I believe that you need to be confident about the future of any organization that you pursue this kind of deal with."

"Oh, and you are saying that you are sure of yours?"

"Once more, wrong word. Few things in life are assured,

and I am not death, or taxes. I am, however, confident that FAE will be around a lot longer than Abysses End."

"So, you do intend to destroy them if possible."

"One of us has to go, as they won't mind their own business and seem happy to dig their hole deeper every day. As such I will be sure to fill it in for them. If they are still at the bottom when I do, well that's their own fault."

"You-"

"Kevin!" interrupted Ellayina.

Alex watched as Mr. Hansen seemed to need to calm down once more as he confirmed that, for whatever reason, there was a connection between him and Abysses End. In a way this made sense with what had played out in Alex's last life as many complaints had been levied against Abysses End, but nothing seemed to happen. It was this that had brought about the public policy of non-interference with anything that wasn't seen as an exploit, like the making of armor from coins and adamantium. Even then, those who discovered such exploits were often seen as helping the game and were rewarded for it in one way or another, as the exploit was patched. Something that Alex had only gotten a modest amount of for everything that he had shared with Daryu. As Alex dwelled on this, Mr. Hansen spoke once more.

"I would appreciate it if you didn't threaten the future of Eternal Dominion by targeting one of our main generators of revenue."

"Who generates more revenue, them, or FAE?"

As Alex asked this question, he saw Mr. Hansen pause for a second as if he realized something as Ellayina answered.

"They are barely beating you currently, but that is looking to shift in your favor when the next report comes in. Honestly, if the initial numbers hold, FAE generated more revenue for us last month than any other guild has ever done in a single month."

"Ellayina! That is confidential information."

"Kevin, if owning 25% of a company doesn't entitle me to let our top customer know that they are just that, then what is the point?

Now let's go so I can force you to accept the deal as it is and avoid a dozen more of these meetings!"

"Ellayina!"

At that, Eternal Dominion Inc. dropped the call and only Gaute remained on the line as he spoke.

"Alex, that was a rather revealing meeting. It seems that you have friends and foes at the top of Eternal Dominion Inc."

"No kidding. Kate, we need to figure out how deep the connection between Kevin and Abysses End goes."

"Agreed. That wasn't just worry about his bottom line that I was picking up, though I don't feel like his own future is on the line if Abysses End is dismantled. It could be that one of his good drinking buddies is a major shareholder in Abysses End, or they have some minor dirt on him, like a hidden mistress, or sex tape."

"Either way, we need to make sure that we don't suddenly find Abysses End has received a benefit beyond what the system would normally allow."

"Gaute, with what Alex has gotten, that is a rather hard thing to characterize," commented Tara. "It makes me wonder about a few things as they have recovered from every setback that we have dealt them."

"We may have just solved that," replied Kate. "What if Kevin was loaning them gold in ED? He could easily do it as he is sure to have a backdoor installed for him and it would help generate revenue in the short term for both parties."

"Speculation will do us no good," stated Alex. "For now we should just be happy that Ellayina seems ready to go to bat for us and see what we can learn."

"Don't expect much," answered Kate. "If it has all been contained to inside of ED, then there might not be any real traces to find, but it would make sense that Abysses End wasn't the only one benefiting. In fact, I suspect that Kenneth might know, but if he didn't even share it with me-"

"It would need to be a 'tell anyone and you will be permanently banned from ED' type deal," finished Alex. "It makes a certain amount of sense, as even with how advanced ED is, to get all five major workshops to abandon all other VR games for it couldn't have been easy."

"So are we going with that they all got some sort of advantage?" commented Gaute. "It would also make sense that after what happened to Jingong, they likely all put more pressure on Kevin to guard their interests."

"More than just the guild leader would need to know then," added Kate. "Though not many and while my father might know, I would have been left out at this point. It could be simply information akin to knowing to talk to a certain NPC, or use a certain map for grinding. The possibilities are endless if it is just at the level of favoring the super workshops."

"We are getting back to speculating," interrupted Alex. "Kate, if you can get a message to your father and you think he would be unable to resist the temptation of responding, ask him if Abysses End might have dirt on Kevin for supplying them with an advantage. Make sure to word it such that he can answer without answering."

"That will be tricky, but I will try to reach him quietly."

"You all are insane," interjected Tara. "Just stop. Don't

look into a thing. We can move forward assuming that the super guilds are being given a major advantage and just plan accordingly. All that digging will do is piss Kevin off and possibly hurt ED, and I for one don't want that."

"Tara, my goal is to oust Kevin as the president of Eternal Dominion Inc. and have Ellayina replace him," stated Alex. "At least if he really is the one behind it and she is relatively clean. If not, well, not much that can be done then."

"No matter what we do, he isn't going to sell his 30% stake and even if he did, who could afford it?" countered Tara. "I would rather work with the devil we know than risk the chaos of what could follow his fall."

"Tara is right," agreed Kate. "If we find anything it could only be used as leverage, just like Abysses End is likely doing right now. Besides that, it would be mostly an empty threat as it would be bad for Ellayina to replace him. She is not suited for the role of being the president of Eternal Dominion Inc., no matter how much she wants to be. Surviving a mind-numbing presentation about financial data is a key skill for anyone in charge of a major organization. That is unless they have someone like I am to Alex, that they are willing to foolishly trust that they are not secretly maneuvering them to be at their complete mercy."

Alex just smiled as he gave Kate a kiss before speaking.

"Alright, none of this leaves this group. Kate, don't dig too deep, but keep your eyes open for any possibilities. That goes for you two as well. Even if we don't intend to pursue it, knowing what the arrangement is can be useful for making our plans."

With that the meeting finally came to an end as they returned to making sure everything was in order for what was about to be a dangerous period for Nium and FAE. For Alex, the only thing of note in reality through Friday the 8th was a tentative agreement for the quantum-entangled server to be supplied. This was based on the facility to house it being done within six months of the current projection and passing an inspection from the engineers who maintained the whole system. There were other details, such as office space and general purpose areas that would be made available for Eternal Dominion Inc.'s use as well. However, these were far simpler to handle as Harrison and the team at the Colorado HQ got to work making sure they were acceptable.

Upon returning to ED in the early afternoon of day 145, Xeal found himself still in the safe room that his party had been using when he last logged off. Eira was still snuggled up to him as she smiled at seeing him return to their world after over 12 hours away from it. She had a warm smile on as she pulled him into a kiss before speaking.

"Are you ready to deal with not having me next to you for around two weeks?"

"Are you?"

"No, but I will deal with it as if I fail, then I will be unable to stay by your side and the last thing I want is for Daisy and Violet to find their way next to you instead. At least not until I am ready to let them that is."

"Oh, do I have you to thank for them not getting to be more forward still?"

"In part, but the moment they reach tier-7, they will have my tacit support."

Xeal just held in a groan as he shook his head to get the thought of the pair becoming bolder with their actions out of his head. Still, as he stood, the rest of the room grew silent. They all knew that it was time for them all to make their final preparations before attempting to reach tier-7. For NPCs this was typically a significant moment that would be handled differently according to the culture of the individuals. For some a celebration of life would be held as they ensured that they entered the tribulation without any unresolved business if possible. Some would see all those near them pray and fast for them as they hoped to not need to mourn them. There were even a few cultures that would hold a wake for the individual before they began, bringing a whole new meaning to attending your own funeral. However, regardless of the specifics, skipping all of that, like those who were present were going to do, was almost unheard of. Had they each not been equipping a phoenix feather talisman on top of most being marked by him to ensure that they wouldn't die, Xeal knew that he would be asking the impossible of them. Even so, he could tell that there were still nerves as he pulled out several large bottles of various drinks and enough food for a feast as he spoke to the room as a whole.

"Well, this time tomorrow we will all be beyond the reach of all others as we rise to what many see as the peak of their ambitions. I do hope that most, if not all of you, don't feel the same as for us this is just another step on our journey to rise above all else. As you can see, there is enough here for each of us to choose two bottles. One is for now and the other is for when we return victorious. So, pick your poison, grab some food and let us spend the rest of the day toasting to our future!"

Xeal smiled as they all came and grabbed two bottles and some food, as Eira was the first to stand up and offer a toast.

"To never giving up and chasing what you know you want!"

A round of acknowledgments and clinking bottles later and it was Lucy who stood up.

"To standing up to the challenges of the world and

becoming stronger for it!"

Xeal just smiled as one after another everyone started to offer similar toasts as they started to drink more and more. While there was definitely enough alcohol to get any normal human drunk present, one of the side effects for having as high of constitution scores as this group did, was that you really had to try to get drunk. Still, that didn't mean that it had no effect at all, as after around 40 minutes of toasts and talking, Daisy and Violet both stood as they giggled while they offered another toast.

""To getting Xeal to look at us!""

As they finished shouting, they turned such that Xeal could see their three tails raise in the air as they shook their hips and kept giggling. It was clear that they were embracing the moment a bit more than Xeal had intended, but he just figured that it was to be expected as they had likely been building up to have the courage to do that. What he had not expected was for Eira to tell him to give them each a kiss on their cheeks. However, instead he just stood up and when they turned around, he pulled them into a hug as he simply let them know that they were seen. The way they nuzzled into him, that included their bushy tails caressing his arms, was enough to tell him that they were relieved as he felt the tension in them release. Though he could have done without them talking about how they looked forward to when he would do much more with them.

Once Xeal had helped the tipsy fox-women down, the party returned to a general state of chatting and laughing. Though Xeal now found himself in between Daisy and Violet as Eira came and claimed his lap as she teased him about being scared of a couple kisses on their cheeks. Xeal just chuckled and agreed as he exaggerated his fear, as it had already started to shift to a complex feeling of inevitability. Especially with the thought of his children being the other option, as seeing Daisy and Violet take that path would be rather awkward to Xeal at this point. Once more this state of general merriment was interrupted as Alea stood to make a toast. Unlike Daisy and Violet, the high elf that looked far too much like her mother for Xeal to be completely comfortable with it, stood steadily and put on a stoic face.

"To putting the past behind us and moving on in more constructive ways as we navigate the paths that destiny has laid out for us."

As everyone raised their bottles, Xeal took note of how Alea was looking at Bula and how Bula was looking slightly surprised. Clearly Freya hadn't deemed it too pertinent to allow the sight to give Bula a heads up, though recently her visions had just been of the chaos of war. As Alea sat, it was Bula who stood and spoke the next toast.

"To humility and acceptance of reality while hoping and working for a brighter tomorrow."

Another round of raising bottles followed as Alea and Rina smiled and a tension that had permeated the party since Bula's declaration that she would stand next to Xeal, seemed to release. Though Xeal felt like all that had changed was the rules of the game, not the end goal as he frowned as the happy chatter returned. Finally, it was time for them all to sleep one last time before departing as Xeal stood, noticing that there seemed to be a sudden resignation that was interrupted as Dafasli stood and spoke before Xeal could.

"Before we call it a day, I'd be forever regretful if I didn't take this moment tur give one last toast. Tur Xeal, our leader, our hope, our friend and hopefully one day much more, at least for me!"

Once more the bottles were raised as Daisy and Violet

added an "us too" to the mix. As they finished, Xeal could see the blush on Dafasli's face as she held the strongest of the spirits that Xeal had brought in her hand. Once more he was reminded just how much of this world was shaped to fit the expectations of the players as despite that, Dafasli was no more drunk than a monk who had taken an oath of sobriety. It was with this thought that Xeal started to speak as he prepared to call the miniature party to a close.

"I, for one, feel ready to face whatever my tribulation has to throw at me! Now, I know that none of us truly face death with what is in front of us, but know that any who fail to return victorious will find themselves stepping away from this party! So, look around you at your companions as this may be the last time that someone here is amongst us, though I believe that all of us have the ability to take this step! Oh, and yes, Eira, if you dare fail, I will simply ensure that you are rarely not either carrying, or nursing another kitten as your mother wishes for! Now one last toast. To taking on the world and standing victorious at the end of it all!"

As Xeal raised his bottle and drained the last bit, the rest of the room did the same and he smiled at seeing the look on Eira's face. He could tell that he had provided her with enough motivation to run into hell to avoid the fate that becoming a house cat would be for her. While he was well aware that she wanted several children, he was also well aware that she was determined to stand next to him as much as she possibly could and intended to wait to become a mother.

That night, Xeal found himself next to Eira as she held him tightly as he found his dreams spinning around the possibilities in his life. These ranged from the absolute collapse of FAE and ruination of his personal wealth both in ED and reality, to the meteoric rise that he was currently on continuing as he and his family prospered beyond belief. The one constant that was always there as these images played through his mind was the smile on his face as the women he loved stood next to him. In all the uncertainty that he had of the future, the one constant was that he would be surrounded by them. For him that made even the worst-case scenario his mind could create better than his last life. This allowed him to sleep peacefully despite the worries that he held surrounding being absent for over a week, if not two in ED, depending on what the system decided to put him through.

The following morning saw them all quietly wait for the now routine movements that Taya had FAE's members making, that always created a flurry of movement to track. It was these movements that would allow for Xeal and the other 9,999 players that were about to attempt to reach tier-7, start their tribulations quietly. There were several options at this point on how to initiate the tribulation, as you simply needed to head somewhere that held significance to you and a void bead. The other option was to bring something of significance to the same point you entered your tier-6 ordeal. The stronger the significance the better and the darker the moment the better, as only a truly trying memory could unlock the hidden difficulty, Demonic mode. In Xeal's last life it had also been known as suicide mode, as the few accounts of players who had challenged it were such that it didn't seem possible. Yet Xeal knew it was, if only for knowing that it was the path that Takeshi had walked, even if he was the only one that Xeal knew had succeeded. Xeal didn't know what demons that Takeshi had in his past, but he was sure that they were significant enough to trigger the mode as Xeal made his way to the Stisea kingdom.

It was there that he had sold everything that he owned in

his last life before sending all his gold to his friends and logging out for the last time in that life. Xeal could think of no point in his life that he had been at a lower point, as he just hoped the system would allow him to use it. As Xeal pulled out the void bead on the very spot that he had stood as he logged out to end his original life, he smiled as he looked at the menu that had the option to select Demonic mode available. There he stood as he took one last look at his stats before he selected the option. At level 199, he had 170 points in constitution, 325 points in strength, 400 points in dexterity, 330 points in MP, 200 points in SP and 265 points in charisma. Once all bonuses were added, all but MP and charisma rose by at least 134 points as his strength reached 566 and his dexterity was 625, both of which were numbers a tier-6 player had no business having unless they focused on a single stat at the cost of all others. A normal player would only have around 1,180 total ability points to work with and Xeal had 1,690 total, or what was normal for a level 263 player or NPC. While Xeal knew that it wasn't uncommon for a player to get a random boost of ten to 50 base ability points by this point, 510 was insane. It was also a fair bit more than anyone else as he had started to get them at level 40, while Aalin and Gale were next at level 80. That gave him a 40-point advantage over even them and the rest of the phoenixes' marked were even farther behind.

As Xeal considered this, he also considered that his hit points were at 160,891, his SP pool had 72,635 points and his MP pool was at 75,272 points. This meant that he could execute 1,452 double upward and downward slashes, all charged with elemental blades before he emptied either his SP or MP pools. He could also forgo using elemental blades and just fire off 376 level 3 dragon's breath attacks instead. The fact that his dragon's breath was the only skill that Xeal had to wait to reach tier-7 to unlock the fourth level of it, made him wonder if he would have to be tier-8 to access any advanced skills related to it as well. While to many the inflated stats that Xeal was looking at would be a source of confidence on reaching the next tier, Xeal was just dreading what the system was about to throw at him as he selected to start his tribulation.

(Requirements met to attempt tier-7 Demonic mode tribulation. Do you wish to begin? Yes, or no? Warning, you will be forced to log out every ten hours in reality for at least two, but not more than three, hours during your ordeal. Time will be stopped in your tribulation while logged out and any failure to return will result in your failure. Warning, all details of your tribulation must remain secret until you complete it and revealing them in reality during your logouts will result in your failure. Repeat WARNING, ALL DETAILS of your tribulation must remain secret until you complete it. EVEN SAYING IT IS HARD WHILE OFFLINE can cause this clause to trigger! IF TRIGGERED, it will result in your FAILURE!)

Xeal smiled at the emphasis that the system put on shutting up about what was occurring in any tribulation. These were deeply personal experiences and Xeal was just happy that he had warned all of his members beforehand of this restriction. Still, he expected 10% of those attempting to complete their tribulation to fail for this very reason, as not being allowed to talk about something made many want to do just that. Resisting that urge was a whole other skill in itself, one which some would have it easier than others. With this thought, Xeal selected yes as the world around him dissolved and he found himself standing in a tent that was set up to act as a command center as he received the tribulation details.

(You must lead your forces to assault and capture the

enemy keep. The percentage of your troops that arrive at the keep will directly influence your results.)

Xeal frowned as this setup was extremely weird for a tribulation and felt more at home as a tier-6 ordeal setup. That was until the tent flap opened and three individuals entered and Xeal's blood ran cold. At the front of them was the spitting image of Frozen Sky, on his left was Atius and Lodovico Michelangelo stood to his right. Xeal could not think of three people that he wanted to see less than these three and was about to attack when Frozen Sky spoke.

"Commander, everything is ready for our trek across The Salt Deadlands. Are you sure that this plan is the best?"

(Notice: all individuals in this tribulation are taken from your memories and you must follow the plan to cross The Salt Deadlands.)

Xeal wanted to scream at what he realized would be an absolute nightmare for him, as he had to work with all those he hated to assault a keep. Still, he worked to hold it in as Atius spoke.

"Sir, we are just waiting for your word to break camp."

"Yes, Lodovico, see that it is done. Frozen Sky, Atius, I wish to review the dangers that we will face and check that we are prepared for them one last time."

"Of course," replied Atius as Lodovico turned and left. "Missing a single detail could cost us greatly and it never hurts to take the time to be sure."

Over the following hour, while the rest of the camp packed up, Xeal learned that The Salt Deadlands was a desert that was as white as snow as it really was all salt. Not a single drop of drinkable water existed within it and it would take ten days to cross if everything went right. Then there were the undead that rose at night. While weak, they were an unending horde that was made from the very salt that they would walk on. The legend that surrounded the region was that there was once a prosperous civilization that angered the gods with their ways and were destroyed for it. According to this, the salt was actually the bodies, buildings, roads, carts and everything else that existed within that civilization when the gods leveled it. Now, however, it served as a source of salt for the surrounding regions and was slowly shrinking.

The keep that they were setting out to capture was just the first step in what was a generational aspiration to create an empire. The force Xeal was working with contained 1,000 able-bodied tier-6 combatants and another 1,000 made up of their families. Once they captured the keep, this would be enough to establish their dominion over the area and prepare to expand from there. The more that Xeal looked over the details the less he liked them, as they would have to travel across the blinding white desert during the day and deal with the undead as they tried to sleep. Xeal's kneejerk reaction was to flip things and have them sleep during the day and travel at night, but that would lead to major losses among the non-combatants. Luckily the system gave him the times for the current day and night cycle, and they currently had fourteen-hour days and ten-hour nights. Setting up camp took about four hours and tearing it down took one hour. With the need to add an eight-hour rest in, that left eleven hours to work with to fight the undead and travel.

The current plan had them stopping two hours before sunset to erect the camp fortifications, while the next two hours the force divided between setup and defense. After that, those who were defending would rotate out and sleep in shifts until morning, when they would pack everything away and continue the march. The fortifications that they were using was just a rope and metal pole fence that a single swing of a sword could destroy, which necessitated blunt weapons. Even then, Xeal was well aware of the fact that repairs would be needed regularly as they traveled. Though Xeal also got an idea around how they could try to travel at night and only needed to do a few tests on the first night to confirm things.

With that idea in his head, Xeal ordered everyone to move out and what followed was one of the more miserable days Xeal had experienced. As they moved, they were constantly dealing with the reflected light off the salt, as any gust of wind would send dust clouds made of salt at them. It didn't help that behind the masks that everyone was wearing were the faces and caricatures of the personalities of those he despised. The one bright side to the current situation is that none of them had the ability to bug Xeal as they marched, beyond the occasional exchanges when they stopped for water. Each of these stops was very controlled as they had strictly rationed their water to last 11 days and if they ran short, they would be doomed.

When it was about two hours from sunset, the wagons with the poles and ropes were brought forward and Xeal got his first good look at them. The poles were simply iron bars with two-inch rings at their tips, that were about five feet in total length and when placed in the ground, would stick out about three feet above the ground. The rope was just rope, nothing special about it, other than there was a lot of it. After the 500 poles had been pounded into the ground and the rope strung through, Xeal just waited to see what happened as he had everyone hold off on setting up the rest of the camp.

As the final ray of light vanished, one skeleton after another seemingly formed from the salt at their feet. This included inside of the camp as more than one scream could be heard as the combat forces quickly dispatched the level 20 monsters that were only a threat due to their numbers. Thankfully, none of the non-combatants were below level 39 and even they were able to handle these monsters. As Xeal looked at the area in front of the camp, there were around 2,000 visible skeletons within a distance that he could see. Some of these were headed towards them while others just stood still as if they were a statue as Xeal gave his next order.

"Atius, Frozen Sky, get the 500 most able-bodied of the extras and have them each hold a pole. We are continuing for at least another few hours. Keep the pace slow and assign a guard to each pole bearer."

"Xeal, the men are tired," replied Atius. "Should we not spend an hour or so continuing to recuperate if we are to push on?"

"No, we are only going to continue for another four hours tonight, but ensure that everyone is paying attention to their condition. The last thing we need is someone collapsing and creating a hole in our defense line."

As Atius and Frozen Sky left, Xeal kept telling himself that they were all not the real ones over and over. However, it was easier said than done, especially as he wasn't entirely sure who the full 2,000 present were yet. Xeal worried just what he was going to be confronted with before the week was over, with what he thought about many of those he hated.

Ten minutes after Xeal had given his orders they were moving once more. It was only at half the speed that they had been able to manage during the day, but it was a much more pleasant experience, even with dealing with the undead as they moved. As such, Xeal instantly adjusted his plans and by the time they stopped a few hours later, everyone was happy when he announced a 12-hour rest past when they finished setting camp up.

Xeal had just finished giving Frozen Sky, Atius and Lodovico, who seemed to be his main lieutenants in this tribulation, orders when the next headache arrived. Looking tired but wearing the same sweet smile and pink bob cut that Xeal remembered from when Nantan had brought her to visit, was Tao Saki. Xeal wanted to yell for her to leave as she opened her mouth and started to speak.

"Commander, I came to see if you needed anything before turning in for the night."

"I am fine, thank you. Now if you would leave so I can get some sleep in."

"I hear it gets very cold at night here. I wonder if you need someone to share your body heat with?"

"I will be just fine."

"You always seem to like to play hard to get, commander. Tell me, are you ever planning on accepting any of our offers to be yours?"

"No, I am quite content in my solitude."

"Ah, you fear creating divisions between the camp if you accept any of us. I understand, you are such a special existence, I don't believe that there will ever be a man that can measure up to you again. So worry not, I will allow you to embrace all of those who would share you, so long as you didn't shut me out."

It was taking every ounce of Xeal's self-control to not behead her and place her head on a pike as a warning to whomever else was making such plans among the women of the camp. However, after a deep breath, Xeal looked at Saki's smug face that seemed to think that she had put forward an irresistible offer and responded in a cold voice.

"Saki, we are marching to battle. Death in one form or another lies before us! I will not be accepting any women into my bed until the battle is behind us at the very least!"

"Ah, I can see that tonight is not the right time, but you will need to find a way to relax before the battle. Else you may find yourself too wound up and not able to give your best when the time comes. Perhaps you would prefer Elin, Irene, Polina or Natalina instead."

"No, and if anything is going to wind me up, it is you and the others seeking affection from where there is none to be found!"

Xeal gave Saki a hard stare as she gave him a pouting look that told him that this wouldn't be the last such move that she made on him. The fact that she confirmed all four spokeswomen that had accompanied Nantan on his final visit were here as well just added to his annoyance. That night, Xeal frowned as he lay down to sleep. He found it a herculean task, as he felt as if the moment he passed out he would be pounced upon. Either by one of his lieutenants that thought they would do better as the commander, or a woman that was after his attention. So when he woke alone and unmolested around eight hours later as the morning sun graced the sky, he sighed in relief.

Ten minutes later and Xeal was walking the perimeter and seeing how the night had gone, as he found that other than a few cut ropes that had been hastily repaired, nothing had been damaged. During this walk, Xeal found himself recognizing more and more of those present from both this life and his last life, as it seemed that the system had really reached deep to recreate all those he would happily kill. Even Hugo Mercer was there. It also seemed that every woman that he was attracted to physically, but would never touch under any circumstances, were present as well. This went past just Saki and the four spokeswomen, as Xeal found Lina Chun's, Mittie Alabaster's and Vanessa Mercer's doppelgangers as well.

By the time the rest had ended it was late morning and Xeal only had a few hours before he would have to log out and take his first break from this madness. So, with a sigh, he put out the order for camp to be broken down as he held a meeting with Frozen Sky, Atius and Lodovico. During this, Xeal was quick to explain that they would be shifting to starting to walk in the night and setting up camp in the late morning and not breaking it until after sunset. To prep for this, they were going to practice moving quicker during the day and he instructed that the 500 who would be manning the poles be given an extra quarter of a day's water ration. Both Atius and Frozen Sky opposed this, but Xeal ordered it as necessary for morale and to ensure that they didn't collapse during the march. With that handled, Xeal found himself going offline right before they were set to move out.

When Xeal returned it was another hard day of walking, though he took note that it seemed that Saki had taken to walking in front of him. Thankfully the atmosphere of the march was such that casual conversation was hard to maintain due to the dryness of the air and the need to conserve the moisture in one's mouth. Xeal could tell that by the end of this trek most, if not all, of his force would have nagging status conditions from crossing The Salt Deadlands. Still, they continued walking until it was well into the early morning hours before they set up camp and Xeal held his daily meeting. This was followed by Saki making another pass at him without making any blatant notion of actually joining him in bed. After Xeal had successfully sent her away, he retired once more and fell asleep, being tormented by visions of giving in and ruining everything he had with the women he loved. Instead of those he loved, he saw visions of him with hundreds of women serving him with and without swollen bellies, as he became a true harem king.

Like this, one day after another passed as Xeal fought to continue his resistance to what the tribulation was doing to him. He didn't think that it would cause him to fail if he gave in and accepted Saki, or one of the others that had made a pass at him, into his bed. However, even if it wouldn't cause him to fail, he doubted that he would be the same afterwards, or be able to forgive himself and that was far more important to him. Slowly they reached the point where they were setting up camp in the late morning and sleeping through the day and making good progress as they did so. Still, Xeal could see several status conditions that affected him and the others start to build up, to include poor hydration and hypertension. Thankfully, after ten days, they arrived at the end of The Salt Deadlands and found themselves back on normal dirt once more. From this point it was only a half-day's march to the keep, which guarded the only reliable fresh water supply in the form of a lake, for days. This lake was fed from underground springs and was like an oasis in the arid desert that surrounded The Salt Deadlands, from what Xeal could understand. The fact that they only had just enough water to arrive before being in real trouble was another issue that Xeal was contending with. Especially as they would have another half day's worth, had he not given the pole bearers the extra water each day along the way.

Even so, Xeal set their course and after one last logout, they arrived at the keep to find it guarded by around 500 individuals. This was in line with the information that Xeal had expected, but what he had not expected was the final cruel knife that the system was playing on him. On top of the walls, as clear as could be with Xeal's senses, were only those who he cared for. This included Kate, Gale, Aalin, Enye, Dyllis, Eira, Lingxin, Mari, Luna, Selene, Aila,

Austru, Takeshi, Taya, Casmir, Amser, the rest of his party, his and all his wives' parents and many more. There were even faces that he had yet to find any way to approach in this life that he had shared a true comradery with in his previous life. To make matters worse, it was clear that many of them were all not as strong as they were outside this fake world and his force would easily overwhelm them. As Xeal thought on this, Frozen Sky, Atius and Lodovico approached Xeal with wide smiles on their faces as Lodovico spoke first.

"Just look at all those women. I wonder what they will sound like under me? Hey, commander, are those two redheads twins? If so, can you please let me have them?"

Xeal gripped his sword tightly as Frozen Sky spoke next.

"Lodovico, let's not ruin their value now. Besides, there is a battle to be fought before we can claim them as ours and they may not survive that."

"Hey, we need to make sure that as many women survive as possible," complained Lodovico. "How else are we going to triple, or more, our population in the next 20 years."

"As much as I hate to say it, Lodovico is right," conceded Atius. "Though I think that we should wait until after we win to start claiming prizes and decide based off merit."

"So, commander is going to end up with half of them to himself," quipped Frozen Sky. "Commander, if that one with blue hair survives, can you let me at least break her in?"

Something finally broke in Xeal's head as he stood there looking at his wives while these pigs discussed doing unspeakable acts to them. Rather than fly into a rage though, Xeal just remembered the wording of his task. All it mentioned was capturing the keep and getting his force to it and he had arrived with his full force intact. They were definitely in a weakened state, but they would still easily win in this fight and it made Xeal sick to his stomach. However, he pushed that down as he spoke in a tone that dripped with menace as he gave out his order.

"Lodovico, you are to go forward and seek a parley. Tell them that I wish to attempt to negotiate terms of their surrender and that they can send as many as they like, but I will go alone to a point just out of range of those in the keep."

"Why me!? Shouldn't that be the kind of thing you send Saki or Natalina to handle?"

"No, you wish to earn the right to touch any of the women that will be captured, so you can start earning achievements."

"Xeal-"

Atius's attempt to talk ended with a single look from Xeal, who looked ready to kill the next person who challenged his orders. Ten days and eight logoffs of frustrations of not being able to even share the burden of this tribulation with those he loved was already too much, but this latest twist took the cake as he spoke.

"You all may be able to still succeed without my help with taking the keep, but it will come at the cost of being able to hold it from the next group to arrive. So, let me be clear, the next person to question my orders will find themselves a head shorter!"

All three of them looked like they were terrified as Lodovico almost tripped over himself as he hurried to follow Xeal's order. At the same time, Frozen Sky and Atius stepped away as they went to spread word through the rest of the force. Xeal just focused on his breathing as he thought over the insanity of what he was planning to do and just hoped that the system would allow it. Otherwise, he would have just wasted the entire time that he had spent on this tribulation.

Thankfully, it seemed that Lodovico succeeded in arranging a parley as Xeal walked until he was about a quarter mile away from the front of the wall as he stood there alone. Lodovico looked like he was going to head to Xeal to update him, only to rethink it after taking a single look at Xeal as he made his way back to the rest of the force. At the same time, five individuals emerged from the front gates of the keep and Xeal recognized each of them. At the lead was Kate with Luna and Selene flanking her, and Takeshi and Eira another step back from them. Xeal could see Aalin, Gale, Aila, Dyllis, Daisy, Violet and Bula atop the wall standing at the ready and he was sure Enye, Austru, Lingxin, Mari and Dafasli were behind the gates ready to charge in to aid in a retreat if necessary.

When Kate's doppelganger stood ten feet from Xeal, he felt like he was being looked at the same way he would look at those who had betrayed him in his last life. It didn't help that no matter what action he took at this point, Xeal would feel as if he was betraying someone. It would either be those who looked and acted like those he despised, but had suffered through the trek across The Salt Deadlands with him, or those who looked like those he cared for, but had no connection with within this fabricated world. Xeal knew that all of this might as well be in his head, but that still didn't make it any easier to make the decision that was before him as he started to speak.

"I will be the lord of these lands one way or another before the day ends. Now how that occurs is still partially based on your decision."

"You fear us dealing enough of a blow to you that your ambitions stall here," replied Kate's doppelganger. "So, the question is why would we allow ourselves to be placed beneath you when it is clear that we would be signing up for more bloodshed in the future?"

"So long as men desire power, bloodshed is inevitable. It is just a matter of how much blood needs to be spilled to transform the desire for power into one for peace."

"Unless the one in pursuit becomes addicted to the bloodshed along the way, or is disconnected enough to never feel its effects."

"I do not see you as one who would happily allow their own blood to be spilt to avoid that of another's from being spilt."

"Nor am I one who will open my legs and bear the child of my enemy to save myself."

"So, I ask once more, what route do you wish to walk today?"

"The one where I give you water and you return to where you came from."

"I can do no such thing as no matter the cost, I need to capture your keep."

"Then a battle is the only option before you as I am not going to simply allow you to have it."

How Xeal wished he could use the logic of all of this was fake and that if she simply agreed to allow him to capture the keep he would vanish. It would be as simple as him entering the keep alone and them declaring him as its owner. Once they did so, if he didn't vanish they could just recapture it from him as they killed him in the process. However, the not sharing of any information about the tribulation applied to within the tribulation as well and even saying that he had to capture the keep regardless of the price was pushing things. Still, Xeal was determined to avoid becoming what he refused to be as he responded.

"Single combat. I will face all five of you in single combat and if I win you surrender to me."

"And just what happens when we kill you? All we will gain from this is a more ferocious enemy and don't suggest a hostage exchange, as I don't believe for a second that you care for a single life beyond your own!"

That single line delivered in the voice and from a body that looked like a woman that Xeal loved was more wounding than he had been prepared for. At the same time, it lit a fire inside of him that he had not known was there as he responded.

"Fine, I will capture the keep single handedly, so let's just agree that if I manage to reach the top of that tower, you will bow to me!"

"You intend to fight your way through all of us?!"

"Yes. Now make your preparations as when I am done doing so, I expect your people to become mine. Accept this deal, else I have no other way to avoid watching as you all are subjugated in every way possible."

"You have to reach and remain at the top of the tower for a full minute to claim victory and if we push you off of it, you will bow to me!"

"Fine, you have a deal. I will begin my assault the moment the gates open to allow you to enter the keep once more."

"Very well, at the very least we will kill you before your force attacks, regardless of this deal. I will at least take pleasure in that as I take my own life over the alternative."

With that, all but Takeshi's doppelganger began their retreat as Xeal motioned for Frozen Sky, Atius and Lodovico to approach. They arrived just before the gates of the keep opened and Xeal spoke while drawing his blades.

"No assistance is to come. I am doing this by myself and any who interfere will die by my own hand!"

At that he charged right at Takeshi's doppelganger, activating the active state of his fighting spirit skill and opening with a dragon's breath aimed at the area inside of the gate. As Xeal did this, he slipped into the same headspace that he did when sparring with the other members of FAE, only he added a new level of intensity to it as he held none of his strength back. With this he had expected Takeshi's doppelganger to be overwhelmed, but instead Xeal found his charge halted as he locked blades with him. Xeal just smiled as he realized that he was facing off against what was likely the final boss of this tribulation for him. After all, there was no player who Xeal built up their abilities in his own mind more than Takeshi and now he had to overcome that very embodiment of his beliefs.

This had led to the scrapping of the plan that Xeal had at first, as he instead simply focused on defeating Takeshi's doppelganger. With each exchange of attacks, Xeal just smiled as he pushed himself farther and farther towards perfection. He had even lost sight of caring about winning, losing, or the consequences of either. Instead, all that existed was the opportunity to grow to a whole new level as he slowly gained the advantage in the fight. Still, slow was the operative word as it was taking everything he had to gain any advantage and a single mistake would spell defeat. Even the 30 seconds of electrical charging with elemental blades that Xeal was doing was easily countered, as Takeshi's doppelganger resisted reacting to it in the slightest. This meant that while it was dealing damage, it didn't create the opening that Xeal needed to gain an absolute advantage like he would have liked.

Meanwhile, Xeal was constantly needing to readjust his stance as Takeshi's doppelganger used one skill after another to maneuver into advantageous positioning. Xeal knew this strategy all too well as it was what Takeshi used himself to always avoid being surrounded, or cornered, when vastly outnumbered. However, while Xeal only had his first level piercing thrust skill to serve a similar function, he did have the dexterity to at least react in time to parry each attack that came. This led to a near stalemate that Xeal knew would end when one of them ran out of SP, stamina, or got effective outside help. While most would fear the possibility of someone stepping in to interfere on either side, both Takeshi's doppelganger and Xeal had no worries of that. Takeshi's doppelganger, because if aid came to Xeal he would have forfeited his right to demand the keep's surrender. Xeal, because he knew that the way Takeshi's doppelganger was fighting would only be weakened by the aid of others due to how hard it was to coordinate with others while using such a style.

Like this the fight continued and continued, with neither side backing down as Xeal began to worry that his stamina running out would be the deciding factor. Had the pattern that Xeal had identified in Takeshi's doppelganger's movements not felt like a trap, Xeal could have used a dragon's breath attack to create an opening, but now it felt like it would be him that was left exposed. Xeal knew that there was a split second where he was open with each release of the attack and that it would be more than enough to get himself killed in this fight. However, Xeal saw no other way to break the stalemate, so he went through the motions to activate the skill, only when he would have normally fired off the breath attack he didn't. This caught Takeshi's doppelganger by surprise as he had gone in for the kill and was now presenting an opening as well.

Xeal didn't let this opportunity pass as he activated his piercing thrust skill and followed through with his combo lock of double upward and downward slashes. Takeshi's doppelganger did his best to break free, but even when he finally did the damage was done, as he found himself dealing with enough minor injuries that Xeal was able to overwhelm him. Finally, after a full hour of struggling, Xeal came out victorious as he breathed heavily with less than five percent of his stamina left and the mortally wounded Takeshi's doppelganger standing across from him. Both of them were as an arrow at the end of its flight as Takeshi's doppelganger spoke.

"At least my death comes at the hand of one whose skill has surpassed my own."

"Ha, you think you're allowed to die," retorted Xeal. "No, you are far more valuable than my own lieutenants. I will have you live and fight for me no matter what method that I must use."

"You seek your own death. How do you know that I won't kill you the moment you show me your back?"

"Because you never once attempted to maneuver such that your attack would have landed on my back. If you ever seek to kill me, it will be from the front as your honor demands such be the case when facing a foe who has your respect. Now sheathe your sword and accept your loss as I figure out how to survive getting over that wall now that you thwarted my plans to catch you just before the gates closed."

"Ha, you would have lost had this battle taken place inside those walls."

"Just as you would have been unable to move in such a manner with others interfering with our fight. The real question would have been if you had what would have been needed to push me off the tower."

"No, but there are others more suited for such a task than I as well."

With that Takeshi's doppelganger knelt as he sheathed his sword and Xeal cautiously approached him before binding him with ropes and calling for a few clerics to tend to his wounds. At some point during all this, Saki and several others had arrived next to Frozen Sky, Atius and Lodovico. All of them were heaping praise on Xeal while telling Takeshi's doppelganger that he was going to love serving Xeal. For his part, Xeal did his best to ignore this while using his calm mind skill to recover from the battle as thankfully none of them interfered with him. During this time, Xeal was also reflecting on the battle as he thought of every time Takeshi's doppelganger had slipped attacks past his defenses. While none of them had been decisive enough to cause Xeal to expose a major opening, they still had taken over a quarter of his health. Even if that was insignificant in the grand scheme of things, it and every other move from that fight was worth examining.

When Xeal finally stood, he was met with the sight of Takeshi's doppelganger giving him a look of disgust over what Xeal was sure were the words of the others. Xeal simply frowned as he looked at the celebratory group that surrounded Takeshi's doppelganger, as he received more than one smoldering look from the women that made him want to vomit. Xeal once more reminded himself that none of this world was real and that he needed to complete the task before him as he spoke.

"All of you are to stay here and watch the show while leaving our guest alone! I will believe his word over any one of yours when I return and I will need three new lieutenants if he is dead."

With a quick look at Frozen Sky, Atius and Lodovico, who all looked like they actually feared for their lives, Xeal began to slowly walk towards the keep. As he closed the distance, arrows, spells and all sorts of ranged attacks started to rain down upon him, but Xeal simply kept his calm mind and fighting spirit skills in their active modes. This, plus his dexterity, was enough to deflect, or dodge, almost all of these and the ones that did connect were only minor inconveniences to Xeal. Still, he started to run at full speed as he closed the last 100 feet to the 30-foot walls, and as he closed the last few feet Xeal pulled a pair of daggers out and leapt at the wall. Hitting the wall at around the 15-foot mark, Xeal wasted no time in pushing himself to the ground, leaving both daggers imbedded in the wall. One was as high as his arm could reach and the other at where his waist had been. This was followed by him running parallel to the wall as he did a full circuit as the defenders tried to keep attacking him.

However, they were at a considerable disadvantage from atop the wall and it became clear why taking this keep would be easy. It was too big for 500 people to properly man it. This created multiple points that Xeal could use to climb the wall while only taking minimal attacks and he took note at which points offered the least resistance as he saw the two daggers once more and pulled out two more. With a leap and pulling up his leg, Xeal managed to use them like stepping stones as he dug the first of the other daggers in at around the 25-foot mark. Immediately following this, he pulled himself up with his arm as he drove the last dagger in at the 28-foot mark and pulled himself over the wall.

As Xeal got to his feet, he found himself looking at the startled faces of dozens of familiar figures as he executed a piercing thrust to break through them. With that, he headed straight for the tower which he needed to stand atop of to win. Xeal almost felt as if his path there was too easy, as he only suffered from moderate resistance, but when he looked, he could see that most of the defenders looked shaken from feeling Xeal's fighting spirit. So it was that he was able to almost run straight to the tower and reach its top with little issue.

However, waiting for him there were the doppelgangers

of Eira, Enye, Luna, Selene, Mari, Lingxin, Austru, Dafasli and seemingly for good measure, Amser. None of them wasted a second as they charged at him and Xeal found himself being overwhelmed by their coordination. While Amser was a bit out of sync with the rest, she was excellent at adjusting her moves to not harm the harmony of the others. Around 15 seconds into this struggle, the doppelgangers of Kate, Aila, Gale, Aalin and Dyllis arrived. Instantly Dyllis's doppelganger started to sing and Xeal could feel his abilities weakening while the others became stronger. Aalin's doppelganger focused on placing force shields where Xeal would try to dodge to and Gale's doppelganger was casting debuffs at him as well. Meanwhile, it was clear that Kate's and Aila's doppelgangers were prepping the attack that would send him flying off the side of the tower.

45 seconds into the minute that Xeal had to hold the tower and he was already in worse shape than he had been at the end of his fight with Takeshi's doppelganger. It was at this moment that Kate's and Aila's doppelgangers unleashed their attack and Xeal almost had to laugh as two bolts of lightning entered his body. When Xeal seemed unaffected by two attacks from peak tier-6 spellcasters, there was a single moment of hesitation as Xeal unleashed the electricity in a burst, hitting all of them on the top of the tower. Normally Xeal would have wanted to celebrate a plan well executed, but Kate's doppelganger fought to control the electricity as Aalin's doppelganger charged at Xeal with a force shield in front of her. He had gone to brace himself only to realize that the floor had become ice as she slammed into him and he saw the wall of the tower quickly approaching. If he did nothing he would be headed over it with about ten seconds left before the full minute ended and so he stabbed both his swords into the stone

beneath the ice and held on for his life as he managed to stop himself. Only the next thing he knew, all 14 of them came charging at him as they slid on the ice and with five seconds left, they all collided with Aalin's force shield as Xeal released his swords and dropped to the floor.

As Xeal found himself against the wall and at the feet and mercy of the doppelganger women surrounding him, the minute mark passed as he smiled. There was a look of confusion on most of their faces as several blades were being held at his throat. Still, he looked at Kate's doppelganger and saw the complex expression that she was making and decided to speak.

"I believe that a full minute has passed and I won our wager."

"How can you be so calm and trust that I will honor it?" retorted Kate's doppelganger.

"That is simple. It is the only path forward that doesn't end with all of our deaths."

"There are worse things than death," interjected Amser's doppelganger. "Much worse things. Would you have us join you and fight those we have been friends with before, or force us all to carry the children of the one who raped us among your men?"

Xeal was once more slapped with the cruel reality of the situation as he knew that they weren't lying and he knew just what his force would expect after capturing the keep. He also knew that he was a single wrong word off from being killed as they all awaited his response.

"Ha, this is the worst. Just kill me, or honor our bargain. I have no logical answer to your quandary and I would rather not help the idiots out there win by killing a few of you in my final struggle."

"You think that you could kill us?" scoffed Luna's doppelganger.

"In the position you're in we could kill you in seconds," added Selene's doppelganger.

"Perhaps we should put you through what you would do to us first."

"We could make a real show of it up here."

"I am sure that all of your followers would be able to see it."

"I wonder if you would be loud enough for them to hear you from here as well."

"That's enough," interjected Kate's doppelganger. "Why are you so ready to just give up?"

"Ha, it's simple. Either you accept my deal, or no matter the path I take, I will become what I refuse to be. Yet if you accept my deal you would become the same, so just kill me and be done with it."

As Xeal just lay there, he thought about how easy his tribulation had been in his last life compared to this and at the same time this one felt easier. That was if he had no qualms about betrayal and was willing to treat this as just a game with no real consequences and move on. Last time he had just had to deal with crossing a wilderness as he lost one friend after another, as he cleared the way for a caravan. The worst part of that one had been the fact that he had realized after the third death that nothing he did could save them, as the system was automatically killing them one at a time. This time Xeal had to betray one group, or the other, at least in his mind and he just couldn't do it and just closed his eyes as he waited to feel a blade come down on him, or hear that they would honor the deal.

Only neither of those happened. Instead, he found himself in an open space where a single old man sat at a table with an empty chair across from him as he looked at Xeal expectantly. Xeal stood with a frown and made his way over to the empty chair, before sitting across from the old man. There was a long moment of Xeal studying this man as the man studied Xeal, before the old man finally spoke.

"Fascinating. I can see why the system forced me to meet you here, rather than where others could see the record of it."

"And where is here and who are you?"

"Who I am is not important. This is simply the space that your tribulation occurs in. As they tread on personal matters, the system locks out all admins, AI or otherwise, save for me."

"And what makes you special?"

"Ah, I monitor the psychological wellness of all players. It is my main job to kill you before you become traumatized to the point of not being able to function."

"Is that what was about to happen to me?"

"No, you are a bit of a special case. You are, hmmm how to put this, an anomaly."

"So, what am I doing here?"

"Talking of course. All I ever do is talk and if you let me, I will talk to you about it all, this life and your last. Though I must say that we should address your current situation first."

"I can't talk about it, or I will fail, remember?"

"Interesting, you still think there is a path to victory?"

"Until it says I have failed it, I will believe that there is."

"You certainly are resilient to be able to say that and believe it. Here, how about now?"

At that Xeal received a system notification.

(Notice: your tribulation has been paused until further notice and you are free to discuss it until you log off, or receive notice that you aren't.)

"Fine. What the hell would you expect me to do? The

system literally pushed me into a no-win situation. I can either betray those I lead, or I can feel like I am betraying those I love!"

"It is too late now, but simply sending your forces in and having them deal with most of it would have left you needing to only keep a few enemies busy to succeed."

"Right, as I would be left to imagine what happened after as I completed it. Sorry, but no thanks. I would rather have ended up in a cell as they keep me prisoner and have to choose to fail than that."

"Which is why we are here. The system is debating on whether or not to accept the path you took as completing the tribulation successfully. You checked every box that it was looking at, up until you reached the keep, which was where it created a true conflict for you that went beyond what should be allowed without realizing it."

"Great, so what I get a pity pass. Sorry, but no thanks. If the system did that, it would go against how things are meant to work. Either they give in to my offer, or I fail."

"Why is it that you feel the need to deal in absolutes? What do you have to lose from passing your tribulation on a technicality?"

"Nothing, but I have full confidence in what will happen next."

"Oh, please share."

"If they are truly accurate representatives of the women I love, they will not kill, or imprison me. If they are only pale imitations of them and go for the kill, or try to imprison me, well, I will have resolved the conflict in my head at the very least."

"I see. Then let's put that aside for now and speak on the other matter that fascinates me. Your memories that should not be there."

"Sorry, but unless you know how they got there, I think

that I have said all I need to about them."

"Yes, well humor me for a moment as this is my first time being granted access to your mind and the main system thinks that I may have played a role, though I would obviously not know, now would I."

"What, do you have to do a psychological check when players restart?"

"I do, actually. You would be surprised how often your kind just wants to run away from the messes they make. Often times simple conversations are all that is needed to help them process things in a way to avoid things, like if for instance a player like Frozen Sky thought restarting would get you to leave them alone. That said, I will only sit down with them if it is deemed that they are unstable and highly prone to do something that they and others would truly regret."

"Ha, Cui Zhi can make as many characters as he wants. I will never allow him to reach tier-8 in this life."

"But you will allow him to exist, which is better than what one Lodovico Michelangelo, or David Roberts has experienced at your hands. Tell me, is it really fine to punish them for what they did in a timeline that no longer exists to you?"

"Lodovico made the mistake of targeting two women that I love. It didn't hurt that he was an easy target and release for my need to feel like I am righting the wrongs from my past life. And as I say that, it makes me feel like some petty villain who can't let anything go."

"Your words, not mine, but as someone who has needed to have extensive conversations with poor David, I can honestly say that he was in danger of a complete breakdown. He hasn't actually quit, but is only logging on to chat with me once a week at this point. Thankfully the system gave me enough information to point out the root cause and no true damage has been done to him."

"Oh, and just what does he know?"

"Only that he treated the wrong woman in a manner that was unacceptable."

Xeal just smiled at that as he could see it actually doing some good if the sleazeball learned not to mistreat women as the NPC continued.

"Don't justify your actions from the results. The ends do not justify the means."

"Is this where you tell me to stop seeking revenge on those who wronged me and others in my last life?"

"Not exactly, as I know part of your revenge is really just you trying to shape events to avoid a scenario that is untenable. That said, I believe the term an eye for an eye makes the whole world blind fits your situation well."

Xeal resisted rolling his eyes at the overused phrase that was commonly inserted in any argument about retaliatory actions. Still, it was fitting for the situation and he couldn't argue the universality of the sentiment as he responded.

"Was this the whole point of this tribulation? To get me to see that I am out of control and need to resist my urge to seek vengeance?"

"Yes, your ability to pass any tribulation was never in doubt. It is why we had you experience being that which you hated. It is also why there is no need for you to return to that world, as you successfully resisted betraying anyone and simply accepted your own fate. That is unless you wish to spend another month there as your wedding to Kate's doppelganger is arranged, as that was what was about to happen."

"Why would that take a month?"

"You tell me. She is based off your thoughts about her."

Xeal just laughed as he realized that she would set things up to facilitate the other nearby lands surrendering before

Xeal's forces raided them, to avoid backstabbing them. At the same time, it would give them an opportunity to attack first and clear her own conscience. Knowing what he did, he expected that she would have a plan designed to cause either and she would tilt things based on what she saw as the best option for her. As he thought on this, the elderly NPC continued to speak.

"Amazing how both good and bad can come from the same source. Xeal, our time here is coming to an end, so I will leave you with this. Give those you wish to see laid low a chance to earn such a fate in this life before you carry out the sentence you have condemned them to."

Before Xeal could respond, he received a series of system notifications as the NPC faded from existence.

(Tier-7 demonic mode tribulation complete. Calculating completion rate... 107% completion, rank SS. Rewards: 75 class skill points, level will automatically be raised to 200, 20,000 renown, 1,500 gold.)

(Congratulations, you are one of the first 100 tier-7 players. Rewarding a bonus 2,000 renown and 10 class skill points.)

(Congratulations, you are the first player to complete a tier-7 demonic mode tribulation. Rewarding title: Master of oneself, 20,000 renown and 100 class skill points.)

(Caution, the elder dragon mark is ready to break its fourth seal. Please find a secluded location within an hour of returning to the main Eternal Dominion world, or the seal will break on its own.)

As this last notification came in, Xeal found himself back in the Stisea kingdom, not far from where he had initiated the tribulation. Xeal just smiled as he started to make his way to the teleportation hall to return to Nium, through a quick stop in the Muthia empire. As he did so, he quickly looked at the details of his new title.

Title: Master of oneself. The height of a man's success is gauged by his self-mastery. Immune from being negatively affected by the charisma of others who have less than double your own score, no max tier.

Xeal almost did a double take as he realized the implications of this skill. While most would think it was useless as players already had a high resistance to NPCs tricking them with honeyed words, this would likely go much farther as it could mean a bard's debuffs could be ineffective as well. While he would need to spend considerable time with Dyllis to test this out, it could put him into another category of unstoppable if it did. Especially when facing monsters who relied on charisma-based skills to lure in and kill unsuspecting victims, like succubi.

It was with this thought that Xeal made it to the teleportation hall, only to discover that the Muthia empire had closed its gates down and so had the Huáng empire. When Xeal looked into the reasons why, it was clear that Abysses End had launched attacks on both that very morning. Having instructed the others to not bother him for anything until his tribulation was over, Xeal figured he better get up to speed as quickly as possible. So, he sent a message to Taya letting her know that he had finished and was heading to an inn to rest before working on finding a route back to Nium. The response that Xeal got back was one of relief, as she told him to hurry up as ever since the first player that passed had returned, Abysses End had really ramped up their assaults.

This was annoying as Xeal had hoped that it would take longer for Abysses End to recover from the combined offensive that FAE had executed with all other contracted guilds. The issue this time, however, was that Abysses End wasn't targeting any of FAE's holdings directly and instead acting as a mercenary force for all forces that were assaulting both the Muthia and Huáng empires. As such, FAE couldn't justify activating the clause again without pushing their partners to end the agreements. Especially as it would essentially be asking them to act as ground forces for a war between countries and not a strike directly on another guild. Additionally, Fire Oath had found a way out of being bound by the agreement through accelerating the removal of their crafting members from FAE. With this Fire Oath had become free to join any war on whatever side they wished even if it brought them into conflict with FAE directly. As they could still claim to be neutral towards FAE, but not the country that FAE was supporting to get around the rest of their agreement with FAE while they still owed them credits.

After Xeal was safely inside of an inn, he sent a message that just said he would be there as soon as he finished recovering after breaking the seal. Xeal knew that it would be an experience that took a fair bit out of him as he selected to start the process. Pain wasn't the right word for what Xeal felt next, as he had never felt anything like it before; he felt like his blood was literally boiling. However, unlike last time, he didn't find it coming out of him as steam. No, it seemed that his body was holding it in and the pressure made him feel like he was going to explode as he let out a soundless scream. It felt as if every cell in his body was being destroyed before it was replaced with a new one and it wasn't happening fast, at least not to him. Had he known that he had unknowingly entered the state that was normally reserved for combat, as time slowed down to the point that each second was equivalent to four and two-thirds seconds for him now that he was tier-7, he would have cursed the feature. Especially as it took 45 seconds of hell and made it feel like three and a half minutes of it, which might as well have been forever to Xeal. Had he not activated his calm mind skill on reflex, it would have been unlikely for Xeal to even maintain his consciousness.

When it finally did end, Xeal was hunched over on the ground, with a pool of blood that he had vomited up at some point beneath him, as he struggled to breathe. His eyes were struggling to process the world and his nose was smelling way too much as he pulled up the details of the elder dragon mark. Thankfully, he was able to read it without any issues as he looked over it.

(Elder dragon mark: you have been marked by an elder dragon and your body has almost completely integrated with the mark, increasing its sturdiness even more. Natural armor trait gained: it takes more to wound you now. You ignore the first point of physical damage per level. All debuffs from injury are reduced by 35%. 1.25% boost to all stats and enhanced senses. 2 extra attribute points in MP and 3 extra free attribute points per level. Access to dragonoid skills through class skill points. All levels take 1.5 XP to reach. Lost upon death. Cannot safely log out while marked. As you increase your tiers, you will unlock more benefits. Four seals broken.)

Xeal knew what the issue was right away and was grateful when the system allowed him to take a closer look at what was meant by enhanced senses.

(Enhanced senses: you can perceive some of the unperceivable. You can smell fear, see some active spells and much more with practice. Warning, due to intensity level of new sensory input, it is recommended that you disable this ability until you have time to train it. Ability can be turned on and off at will and will slow MP recovery while active.)

Xeal instantly selected to disable it as he finally returned to the normal level of heightened senses that he was used to. The fact that it had been in a default on position was annoying to Xeal, as he rolled over onto his back and just breathed. It was currently the tail end of day 157 and he knew that he had a lot of important moves to make before he could log off, but first he needed to sleep and recover. The Muthia and Huáng empires could wait eight or so more hours as he would be worthless as he was regardless. Finally, the last thing Xeal did before losing consciousness was sending off a message to Taya saying that his recovery wasn't going to be quick, but he would be heading to Belladonna once he was back on his feet.

(*****)

ED Year 6 Days 158-159.

Upon waking, Xeal wasted no time in checking his messages and seeing the detailed situation report. It showed that Abysses End had moved about four hours after the announcement of the first player reaching tier-7 went out. This had been a full-out assault that leveraged every avenue that they had to use, to attack countries with a strong connection to FAE. The situation was the worst in the Huáng empire as in just the 12 hours since the assault had begun, a city had fallen and it looked like the next dominoes were about to fall in another 12 hours. At the current moment, 86 members of FAE had passed their tribulations with over 5,000 failures and Amser had finally been the first to reach the new tier. Takeshi had also finished his demon mode tribulation an hour after Xeal and was done recovering and was just waiting on orders, as it was a mess everywhere that you could look. Particularly as the second wall fort on Nium's border with Paidhia had fallen and they had pushed into the countryside. This meant that Paidhia was occupying territory in both Nium and Habia, while neither of them had gained any of their own.

The situation at the Nium and Habia border was only stable due to the lack of an assault there, as Abysses End seemed to be planning to wait for the forces there to be sent to reinforce elsewhere before attacking. Kate, who had also completed her demon mode tribulation two hours after Xeal, had put forward that they were waiting for Xeal to be spotted on another battlefield before moving to take that point. Either way, Xeal couldn't sit still as he started to make his moves as he put out the orders for all new tier-7 players to carry out a counterattack in Nium, with the exception of Takeshi and Kate. Xeal needed both of them if he wanted to salvage anything from the situation in the Huáng empire, as Xeal started to make his way to Hura Crepitans's home where Belladonna the poison phoenix was located.

As Xeal started what would be a four-hour trip thanks to his level and his fighting spirit ability that made all monsters run from him at this point, he looked at his class skill menu. Thanks to him saving his points up and the 185 bonus points he had earned from completing his tribulation, Xeal had a total of 406 points to spend. The first thing he did was spend the 75 points needed to upgrade dragon's breath to level 4 and find the advanced skill aura control and pick it up for 50 points. Xeal just smiled as aura control was a passive and active skill like fighting spirit and calm mind, and basically replaced both of them as a better version of both. For two MP and SP a second, Xeal could essentially weaponize his charisma, mixed with his strength and constitution scores, to create an effect similar to what bards' basic inspire courage, or dread, would do. It was potent enough that it could even affect those well above your levels, even if it was much less effective as their own stats increased. Xeal could only maintain this effect for around ten hours at a time currently and only if he didn't use anything else that required SP, or MP.

Next Xeal had been dissatisfied with how the fourth level of dragon's breath just increased the damage and MP cost to 300, until he saw that he had unlocked the ability to take the advanced skill elemental filtered dragon's breath. This skill cost 100 more points, but unlocked every possible element and form of dragon's breath for his use.

While it would cost 400 MP to use and be just as powerful as his level 4 dragon's breath from the sounds of it, it had two advantages that made it extremely worth it to Xeal. First it had its own cooldown, which meant that he could fire off twice as many breath attacks and second it had the ability to use it as an area of effect. This would allow for his title of Annihilator to kick in and increase the damage even further and counter the negatives of using a cone over a line breath attack.

With those skills selected, it left Xeal with 181 points to work with as he looked at what other advanced skills he had unlocked. Unlike normal skills, advanced skills wouldn't even appear unless the prerequisites were fulfilled and they could go beyond what other skills you had. While theories were the best that anyone had on everything that could influence what advanced skills appeared, Xeal knew it included base ability scores, skills, titles and abilities at the very least. That was why when he saw the lightning form advanced skill, he didn't think much about it until he read it and quickly paid the 100 skill points to acquire it. Even though using it would cost him a full 100 MP per second that it was active, Xeal could take on a form that was similar to the one Levina took on during his training. While in this form all of his gear would be stored in his inventory and he would be immune to all physical attacks. He would also gain a movement skill called flash step while in that form, that would allow him to practically teleport to any spot that he could see. Despite the clear dangers inherit to it, such as the vulnerability to magic attacks, inability to pick anything up and the need to reequip all his gear after returning to his physical form, it was a must get for Xeal. Especially when he saw that he would be able to essentially generate as much electricity as he wanted, so long as he had enough MP points left in his MP pool. Xeal was already thinking of using it for one massive attack as he activated it, shot up into the sky and used all of his MP in a single strike.

As Xeal thought on this, he was wishing that he had more MP as while the 332 points that he had in it was a respectable amount, it was nothing compared to the true glass cannons. However, Xeal also knew that very few of such players were ever successful due to the nature of needing to be self-reliant in most tier-up events. The exception was for those who were like Luna and Selene, that had something that caused them to be considered one entity by the system. This was the relation that Alea and Rina shared as well in the path of sorceress and dame. It was these situations that created the most common situation for glass cannons to exist at the higher tiers. Still, it was rare due to the level of dependence such players had on their partners and the weaker of the two always hindered the stronger one's growth if their abilities were unbalanced. Even so, Xeal knew that the over 75,000 points that he could release would be about 12.5% of what he had held when the full 1,000 tier-6 and tier-7 spellcasters had hit him with their long chant spells. That was definitely enough to take care of most tier-7 NPCs, but would likely fall short when dealing with around a half dozen of them. While thinking on this, Xeal decided to leave his final 81 points untouched for the moment as he wanted to consider a few different options. This included a quick equip basic skill option, which would help when he shifted back to a physical form.

With that and other possibilities on his mind, Xeal decided to give his new lightning form a try as he instantly had his whole perception of the world alter. The feeling of being pure electricity was disorienting as he just kind of floated and could only travel through its flash step ability.

While this was great for speed, Xeal quickly realized that it also made it extremely difficult to keep a frame of reference and after two minutes of using it, he needed to take a break. His head was spinning as he had basically activated the ability constantly and covered what would have normally taken him three hours to run in that time. Still, as he focused on his current position while reequipping his gear, he found that he was a good bit off of where he wanted to be due to poor navigation while he was in his lightning form. This was another drawback of that form as it disabled all menus and interfaces that most players relied on. All that Xeal could do was see his MP, hit points and select to end the ability, as all his other non-passive skills were disabled as well.

Even so, Xeal was looking forward to seeing how it did in action as he traveled the remaining hour that he needed to, to reach Hura Crepitans's home. As he did, he sent an updated timetable to Taya, who just replied with "?!" as he sent her simply "new skill." With that a few more questions came in, but he just said he would say more when they saw each other.

When Xeal arrived at the medicine valley that Hura Crepitans called home, he saw that it had definitely grown in popularity since his last visit, that had ended with Lily being marked by Belladonna. There were now tier-7 guards standing at a gate that was the only entry point to the valley, thanks to a wall that had been erected in the last few years. Xeal knew to expect all of this as he approached while wearing a cloak, as FAE had paid for most of it in exchange for a few favors from the orichalcum-level alchemist. This had also been in FAE's own interest as it hardened the target enough that it ensured that it wasn't worth Abysses End trying to attack it. After all, just like Xeal's last life, the Stisea Kingdom was one of the few places that Abysses End's presence was practically nonexistent. Still, as Xeal approached the gate, he could see the guards tense up as he sent a message and a moment later Lily, who was also among those who had just reached tier-7, appeared and spoke to the guards.

"He is expected by master and no, you don't need to know who he is, why he is here, or even remember that he was here."

Xeal had to hold in a chuckle at the terrified looks that each of the guards got, at seeing Lily give them a look that clearly said any argument would result in their own misfortune. The look in her ice blue eyes, that now contained a strong undertone of purple just like her hair, was enough that even Xeal would have taken a few steps back if he was the guards. However, he was not, so he just smiled as they passed through the entrance and continued on towards the modest mansion that Hura Crepitans lived in. The fact that everywhere Xeal looked was full of players focused on learning alchemy wasn't lost on him either. Especially as a quarter of them were FAE members and many of them had looks of concern on their face over the recent situation in ED.

By what the forums were showing, Abysses End had successfully mounted a new offensive without FAE and its partners being able to push them back like the times before. While they hadn't regained any of the lost ground from FAE's last counter-offensive, this assault focused on gaining new ground that they could easily defend in the future. However, Xeal knew that things were much worse than what the forums were saying, as Abysses End was in position to secure the entire continent that the Huáng empire was on as a base of operations. The fact that all five other nations were focused on the elimination of the Huáng empire was likely enough for Abysses End to play all sides, while promising to stay out of any other conflicts on the continent. With a deal like that in place, Xeal would find just holding the Huáng empire's capital to be an impossible task if he didn't take care of a few issues first. Xeal was still going over his plans when he arrived inside of the courtyard that Hura Crepitans spent most of his time and hid the entrance to Belladonna's prison.

"It has been a long time, young Xeal," greeted Hura Crepitans. "I see you have grown much since then, but it displeases me that you are wearing metal in my sanctuary."

"I do apologize. Perhaps you would prefer this."

As Xeal spoke those words, he activated his lightning form skill and waited for Hura Crepitans's response.

"What the hell!" exclaimed Lily. "What kind of insanity is this!"

"Incredible," commented Hura Crepitans with reverence. "To be able to personify one of the absolute forms of nature. I dare say that you have reached a point that few can ever dream of reaching."

"Thanks, I guess," answered Xeal in a distorted voice. "I am still getting the hang of this form. Now if you would be so kind as to open the path, I need to be on my way."

"Very well. Lily, you will be joining him, correct?"

"Yeah, it is time for us to show the world that FAE is here to stay!"

Xeal smiled as he ended his lightning form skill and found himself in the trash clothes that were bound to his account once more before speaking.

"I dare say that the next few years will determine the fates of many nations, including the Stisea Kingdom. Master Crepitans, if you can think of a way to entice the rulers of this land into joining a rather peculiar alliance with FAE at its center, let Lilly know about it on her return."

"I will consider it, but I would rather this land avoided

war for a bit longer."

"As would I," agreed Xeal. "But rarely do we get what we want when we want it."

Hura Crepitans just smiled, as he nodded and opened the pathway as Lily led the way and they made their way through the underground path. As they entered the opening to Belladonna's prison where the teleportation gate that they were about to use was, they found Belladonna smiling at them. In the same moment, she forced her hand out of her prison and pulled one of the stones from the gate, rendering it unusable until she returned it as she spoke.

"Now, before I allow the two of you to hurry away, I need a moment of your time."

"Bella! Now is not the time," retorted Lily.

"No, now is the time, as I am aware of the urgency that you are under and I want something."

"I am not freeing you," stated Xeal plainly as he started to pull out the pieces to another gate that he had on him. "You are right and leaving this gate here will suck, but I am sure it is better than whatever you have in mind."

"You haven't even heard what it is yet!"

"If you think that you need to hold us hostage to get it, then it can't be anything good."

Xeal just smiled at the frown that Belladonna had on her face as she spoke.

"Fair, but at least let me say it and I will return this stone and save you from losing that one to me."

"Just be quick about it."

"I want you to convince Hura to give me a child and have Lily raise it."

Xeal paused for a second as he processed the request, while frowning and looking at Lily who looked beyond shocked at the request, before he responded.

"Sorry, but I am not going to get in the middle of that issue. That is something that is between you and him. As for raising that child, I would leave it to Cielo city as it is much more equipped to handle something like that."

"No, I want to be a part of their life. I just don't want to doom them to being down here, or rarely leaving the valley above. Lily would at least be able to bring them by weekly at the very least once I relinquish them to her."

"Lily, what are your thoughts?"

"Thoughts, me, umm---"

"Belladonna, it is clear that Lily needs time to think about this, so for now can you restore the gate, or I will just finish setting up this one."

"Lily, please."

"What Xeal said, and right now is a really bad time with the war and everything."

"That's the point," replied Belladonna. "Hura is planning to fight. After hiding here all this time while he slowly mastered himself and reached the peak of tier-7, he is considering trying to reach tier-8, or just fighting as he is."

"You believe that he will die?" asked Xeal.

"Everything that is not me and my sisters will die at some point. Even the deities aren't as unkillable as they would like you to think. All I am after is to have a piece of him growing within me before his time is up."

"If his only reason to say no is that he doesn't wish to raise them, then I can promise you that I will ensure that someone will raise them while having at least weekly visits with you. However, that is all I will promise. You need to convince him, not ask me to."

Xeal could tell that Belladonna was conflicted as she silently placed the stone back in place and the gate reactivated. With a quick "thank you," from Xeal, he and Lily stepped through and found themselves in Queen Aila

Lorafir's palace as she greeted them.

"Welcome back, though I wish it was under better circumstances."

"As do I," replied Xeal as he walked over and kissed her. "Are Kate and Takeshi here yet?"

"No, but your party is and I think that I will tag along today as well."

"As will I," commented Zylah as she appeared out of seemingly nowhere and she tossed the talisman that Xeal had given her back at him. "I am just happy that I managed to complete the task you sent me on and return before these assaults started, if only barely."

"Are you sure you wish to no longer have any doubt of just how powerful I am?" stated Xeal as he caught the talisman and activated his enhanced senses and fought through the over stimulation that flooded in.

"You-" started Zylah as she seemingly disappeared and reappeared next to Xeal with a dagger at his throat. Only her wrist was in his hand as she did so and a look of fear crossed her normally smug face as Xeal focused his aura on her. Part of the issues that she had was the need for a lopsided dexterity and SP for her build. This left her constitution, strength and charisma that made up the base of her will weaker than it would be otherwise. Though she was still a tier-8 NPC and was quick to recover as she released her dagger and slipped free, before retreating beyond Xeal's reach as he smiled and spoke.

"You are correct in that I am still no match for you, but I am no longer a defenseless lamb that you can slaughter at will."

"No, you are a true monster," retorted Zylah. "I love it. Your enemies don't know what they are about to face."

"Agreed. I doubt that anyone of your world that is below level 250 would offer me much of a challenge at this point. That said, I am no one-man army just yet."

"Perhaps, but to make me feel danger at your level, is something I wouldn't think possible. It tells me that even those like myself should ignore you at their own peril."

"That is all I can really do to you," retorted Xeal. "Now, where are Kate and Takeshi?"

"They will get here soon enough," responded Queen Aila Lorafir. "I believe they are stuck getting up to date information from Taya as you arrived way too quickly. Which is something that I am curious about as well. Also, why are you not wearing any combat gear?"

"This is why," stated Xeal in a distorted voice as he activated his lightning form and flash stepped directly in front of Zylah, before moving to the far side of the room. "I can only hold this form for about 12 minutes right now, but I can move rather quickly while it's active."

As Xeal returned to his physical form, he smiled at the look that Zylah was giving him as he continued speaking.

"I can also convert all of my MP into a single attack if I so choose to while in that form. My estimate is about…"

The next ten or so minutes were spent as Xeal went over the changes that he had undergone upon reaching tier-7. Though when pressed about what his tribulation had contained by Lily, he avoided the subject and just said that he needed to unpack that when it was just him and those he loved. At that Queen Aila Lorafir suggested that they all join the rest of Xeal's party in waiting. So, after placing a pseudo mark on Zylah, by using one of Eris the chaos phoenix's drops of blood, they made their way to a room designed for entertaining guests. There Xeal got his first look at his party after their tribulation. Only Sylvi was absent and they seemed to grow quiet when Xeal entered. As far as appearances went, none of them looked any different, beyond Daisy and Violet having four tails instead of three now. Still, there was a different aura about them as Bula was the first to stand as she spoke.

"Sylvi will not be returning to us. She sent this with a note back to us."

Xeal took the talisman that Bula held out and looked at the note that had been sent with it.

"This will likely be the last words of mine that are ever shared. I am sorry, but my life will either end, or I will pass my tribulation. I am at peace with my life and I am happy to have been given a reason to face my fate. If I do perish, do not mourn for me. Celebrate me being able to fall facing what so many run from and finally getting to reunite with my love."

Xeal just frowned as he looked at the rest of the room, which included Lucy, who looked like she was waiting to be yelled at. Instead, he just took a deep breath as he addressed the room.

"It is too soon to know that she has perished with certainty, but I expected this to happen. Lucy, I hope you're ready to live in this party for the foreseeable future as until peace comes to Nium, you're stuck. So, as Sylvi asked, we should be happy that she will finally be able to reunite with her husband after being separated for so long. Lily, if you would head off to get orders from Taya, you are going to be rather busy for the next few weeks as you are going to be filling in for her as she attempts to reach tier-7 since Lucy will be unavailable."

"Oh, come on, can't Kate handle that?" complained Lily.

"So, you want to do Kate's job and negotiate with five-plus countries to create an alliance that will see FAE open access to as many continents as possible."

"Taya's job sounds great!"

Xeal just smiled at how quickly Lily shifted tones before hurrying away, as Xeal turned his attention to his party as they shared a long silence before Bula spoke once more.

"Xeal, she is almost certainly gone from what I have been shown. Though I believe that the best thing we can do is just move on. We honored her life and made peace with what lay before us already, and I know that she did the same with her family before joining our party. My vision also shows me that she was happy when she died, as her last hours were spent failing to let go of her husband in her tribulation."

"She literally couldn't bring herself to move on," commented Eira. "Though I can't blame her as he isn't waiting for her here like you were for me, and yes, my tribulation forced me to deal with losing you. Only, I know that is impossible, so it was kind of ineffective."

"Eira, let's not go around sharing what we suffered through," stated Alea. "Else we may make those who wish to not share feel pressured into doing so."

"Alea is right," agreed Xeal. "Each of us likely faced what makes us the most vulnerable and even if we knew it wasn't real, it is still something that should only be shared with those you truly feel that you should. Eira, after we are done with this mission, you and the other women I love will learn about mine, but I doubt I will ever share it again after that."

"Right, I was just trying to let off a bit of the pressure. It's just the first time since I have been with you that someone I got used to seeing isn't going to be around anymore. I mean, she always did seem to separate herself from us slightly, but she was still nice enough to have around."

"Yes, she was," agreed Lucy. "Honestly, I feel like I should have known that she was planning to do this as I was around her the most. Perhaps if I-"

"Lucy, it was her choice tur make," interrupted Dafasli. "We all have tur dur what we see as right for us…"

Xeal just stayed quiet as the room continued to awkwardly work its way through the situation, as it seemed that his arrival caused the discussion that they had all been avoiding to happen. Finally, after over an hour of this, things seemed to come to a close as they took the second bottles that they had taken the night before their tribulations and headed outside. There they made their way to a corner in Queen Aila Lorafir's garden that she guided them to, as they each took a single drink of their bottles before emptying them on the ground. After one last moment of silence, they made their way back into the palace to continue waiting.

When Kate and Takeshi finally arrived, it completed the group that would be headed to the Huáng empire on this trip. Xeal knew that for most of those present that this would be the first time that they met one of the phoenixes, as he had left all NPCs behind when leaving the continent. So, Kate gave a quick briefing, which included crouching when they use the teleportation gate as they made their way back to the room which Xeal had arrived in. Five minutes later and Xeal was looking at Bīng as she spoke to him.

"Xeal, has the time finally come for the rule of the Huáng family to end?"

"That is yet to be determined. If you are focused on only the name then most likely. However, if you are speaking of the bloodline, then possibly not."

"I see. Tell the fool that sits upon the throne to accompany you here then."

"Bīng, what are you planning?"

"I have an offer for him and only him, one that I expect you to facilitate, or I will stop giving you my feathers and blood so freely."

"Is there a reason you and Belladonna have both been so demanding today?"

"Ah, so I am not the first that you have seen since it started. Xeal, it can be said that the ten of us are the mothers of this reality and even imprisoned as we are, we can feel the coming death that will cover the land. I am not talking the death of your kind as you are a foreign entity to us. The inhabitants of this world are fearing for their lives and I am not just talking about humanoids. Even the monsters that seem to repopulate faster than any amount of culling could keep up with feel this fear and so we do as well."

"You're not going to force him to give you a child, are you?"

"Would you rather I ask you, as I am willing if you are?"

"Absolutely not!" interjected Eira. "Xeal isn't a stud horse."

"Eira, you need to calm down," stated Kate as she joined the conversation. "Bīng knows that and she also knows that she would be committing to Xeal for as long as he exists if he were to accept her. That said, she also knows that he isn't even slightly interested in including any of the phoenixes in his list of wives, no matter how hard Levina tries."

"Levina is the one you should have mercy on and embrace," replied Bīng in a somber tone. "I have realized through seeing things through Aalin that accepting any other, to include our old mate, would all but destroy her at this point. Xeal, you have completely dominated her and you wouldn't even need to exercise the power you have over her to get her to do as you wished any longer."

"I didn't ask for that to be the case," replied Xeal. "Besides, even if I did embrace her, or any of you for that matter, I would fear ever giving her, you, or any of your sisters a child."

"Oh, and why is that?" asked Bīng with curiosity.

"I fear that it would be on the same level as a deity in potential."

"Ah, you think that so long as you keep your children on the mortal tier, that mine and my sisters' great-grandchildren will tolerate their existence. Yet, you are aware that that will not be possible."

"It is so long as the gods are divided on the matter. Creating something that could threaten them would unify them rather quickly."

"Against something that they can't kill," retorted Bīng.

"How well did that turn out for you, your children and grandchildren?" countered Xeal.

"The day will come where the bill is due," stated Bīng coldly.

"And that day will also spell the end of the human civilization as they run in fear of you. I get it, you have been wronged and you wish to walk freely and do so with your children while punishing the ones who did this to you, but what would that mean for everyone else?"

Xeal could tell that Bīng wasn't appreciating him pointing out the obvious, as she looked at him with a disappointed look as she spoke.

"Is it your responsibility to worry about how the ant makes its home?"

"It is when I am the ant. Bīng, the moment you and your sisters break free, the only side that I will be on is the one that sees humanoids like myself, my wives and friends prosper. I am well aware that even now the war between you and the gods is raging and that I am a key piece on the board for both sides. Heck, I could free Levina at will right now, had I not tied my hands until more of my kind reaches tier-8."

"You would force Levina to fight against us and submit to imprisonment once again!"

"If that was what it took to ensure this world's survival, why wouldn't I?"

"Is that why my mate hasn't made a move in all this time?"

Xeal frowned as he used his dragon guidance skill to ask Watcher just that, and had a staring contest with Bīng while awaiting a response, which finally came a minute later.

"Xeal, this is why I didn't wish for all of them to be found. I had hoped that the coldness of Bīng, as you call her, would be enough to not send you to find the rest."

"Watcher, that isn't an answer!"

"I know. Just tell her that I grew tired of causing destruction simply by existing and doing what all living things instinctually do, namely procreating."

Xeal paused for a long moment as he let that answer sink in, before he spoke to Bīng once more.

"Watcher says that you are more or less right. Your very existences are destructive to everything around you and he chose to end the destruction that just doing what comes naturally for him causes."

Xeal could see tears almost form in Bīng's eyes as she frowned and worked to hold in her emotions, that he knew she rarely felt in any meaningful way as she responded.

"Is it so terrible to want to feel his embrace once more? I have waited so long and would even wait longer to have it, but to know that he doesn't feel the same way-"

"That isn't what he said," corrected Xeal. "He has no physical form because he knows if he did, he would be unable to resist the pull you and your sisters have on him. Now I will see about having Lingxin's brother come to visit you, as you decide what your feelings on this matter are."

With that, Xeal turned and led his group away while thinking over the situation that surrounded himself and all the phoenixes. His gut feeling was that they would each have the desire to create life as so much of it was being destroyed and he wondered just how that would play into events should they gain their freedom. Still, Xeal didn't discount the severity of the situation if that was really the case, as if anything was in tune with the world it was the ten of them. To investigate this further, Xeal sent a message to each of those marked by the phoenixes to check on them when they next got a chance.

With that taken care of, Xeal began leading his group through the mazelike area beneath the imperial palace, until they came out into an open area where they were instantly spotted by a pair of guards. Xeal felt pity for the guards as they froze mid-motion of pointing their spears at them when they saw the composition of the group. The poor tier-7 guards were face to face with two tier-8s and 11 tier-7s and had no hope to even slow them down if things turned violent. Xeal was just about to speak when one of the guards recognized him and seemed to realize that he wasn't about to die as he spoke cautiously.

"Master Bluefire? What is the meaning of your arrival with such company, if I may ask?"

"You may not, as we are not officially here. That said, we are going to meet with my brother-in-law and I would have Shen and Lina Chun summoned as well, if you two could head off to make the relevant parties aware."

Neither of the guards wasted a second as they hurried off and Xeal was sure that the whole palace would know they were there by the time his group arrived at the throne room. Especially as they were not hurrying, but instead walking at a purposeful pace that spoke of them belonging there as they passed one group of guards and ministers after another. Xeal could see a mix of many emotions on the faces of those whom they passed, which ranged from fear to hope, anger to joy and much more. Through all of this one thing was clear to Xeal. Things were not in a good spot at the current time and his arrival complicated everything.

When they arrived at the entrance to the throne room, Xeal just smiled at the crowd that had gathered to greet them. Standing there were over 50 guards and at least 100 government officials that would typically handle basic administrative work. At the sight of the guards keeping this group from approaching Xeal's group, it begged the question of what purpose the guards were there for as they stood aside and opened the doors to admit Xeal's group into the throne room. Unlike the last time that Xeal was in this room, he stood on no ceremony as he led his group in and stopped in the center of the long room that was packed. It seemed like every official that mattered who had been near enough to make it had hurried over, and if Xeal had wanted to he could have tried to have Queen Aila and Zylah clean house right then. However, Xeal still had a use for all the fools that had ruined the Huáng empire's chances of surviving the chaos that was upon them. So it was that after scanning the room and taking in the general attitude of those in attendance, Xeal started to speak.

"The Huáng empire is dead! At least the version of it that you all have known until this point, as I cannot save it as it was. However, I didn't believe that I could save it at all before recent events, so know that you have more hope than you did two weeks ago at the very least. Now the key to this is the acceptance of what is necessary and repudiation of many of the ways that you all came into the power that you have now. Emperor Huáng Jin, I ask you now, will you accept the changes that must be made to save your empire, even if it costs you your life, or will you hide here and wait for death to come for you?"

Xeal fixed Emperor Huáng Jin with a look that was meant to convey that if he refused, Xeal would simply walk away and leave him to his fate. After a long moment where Xeal was unsure of how the emperor would respond as this was a very different scenario than had been discussed prior to this meeting, the emperor stood up with a sword in hand and cut down the veil that hid him. There in front of the whole room, with nothing covering his face, was Emperor Huáng Jin, looking at all those present with pure determination as he spoke.

"Today I cast aside the veil that has hidden my face from all but my family and state that I will not hide from this fight. Nor will any minister who wishes to keep his head, as now is not a time to worry about power, position, or even tradition! It is a time to fight to survive and Xeal is right, our enemies made a mistake in this fight by attacking now, but if you all take your wealth and flee like I know most of you plan to, that hope will end and with it your lives will likely end as well!"

Xeal gave the room a long moment to settle after Emperor Huáng Jin finished delivering his answer. It was clear from the whispers that Xeal could hear that the room was divided over the developments of the last few moments. While some seemed ready to step up and follow the emperor's lead, most seemed to think that he had simply lost his mind and needed to be examined. It was the latter group that Xeal addressed as he next spoke.

"To all of you who believe that Emperor Huáng Jin's actions just now were foolish, or improper, know that they were not. He knows that whether in victory, or defeat, his days as emperor will likely end with this war, as will many of yours as ministers. He is also correct in assuming that your hope lies in the short window that you have before my kind reaches tier-7 en masse. After that, you will have lost any hope of making the changes that will be needed to gain the support that will be needed from my kind to turn the tide of events! Furthermore, I can promise you that any of you who run, plan to betray the Huáng empire, or refuse to accept the necessity of the changes to come will not live long!"

"Outrageous! Who are you to declare anything?! You-"

Before the minister who had about lost it could finish speaking, Xeal activated his lightning form and unleashed his aura on the whole room as he flash stepped in front of the minister and spoke once more.

"I am the key to the Huáng empire surviving and I will not save what it is currently. Had it not been for who the enemy is this time, I wouldn't even be willing to do more than save this city. Now, choose your path! Emperor Huáng Jin, I will await your answer in the garden where I first sat with Lingxin. Have Shen and Lina Chun join us there as well."

With that Xeal flash stepped out of the room and quickly found a deserted area near the gardens where he reequipped his gear and started to walk to the garden. Once he arrived at the table that he and Lingxin had first sat at, he just smiled as he took a seat and just thought about the path he had taken since that day. It had been over four years in ED since that day had come and gone, and he couldn't help but feel nostalgic as he remembered the caged bird that she had been then. As such, she had come alive from the simplest of his stories that he had shared with her as they chatted. As Xeal was thinking of this, he saw two guards leading Shen and Lina Chun over to him and a moment later they were seated across from him as they waited for him to speak. Finally, when Xeal decided that the others were going to be a while longer and they could handle a few things before they arrived, he spoke.

"I take it that Jingong is planning to fight till their last breath, at least at the top."

"Let's not pretend that there is anything resembling idealists above me in my guild," retorted Shen. "No, at this point we are all just arguing what the best way forward is, with Abysses End seemingly determined to turn this continent into a stronghold for themselves."

"Ah, so what is their offer?"

"Xeal, you know that I can't reveal that."

"No, but now I know that they have made one. Either way, I doubt that those at the top would ever accept terms that would force them into being a subordinate power. So, here is my message to them. If they win this fight, I will help them position themselves to be able to stabilize as a power which will compete with Abysses End at the very least."

"That speaks more of what you intend to do to harm Abysses End than what you will do to help us."

"Fair, but if you win this fight, it will position Jingong to take control of this continent in the same way I intend to hold Nium's. Believe me that while that alone will not return you to being a super guild, if the opportunity that it will present for expansion is taken, Jingong won't be far off from rising again."

"And what do you want for this," interjected Lina. "You never do anything for us out of the goodness of your heart."

"Jingong should never be the ones to say that. After all, they are even worse about such things. That said, my price is quite simple. I want them to replace Fire Oath in the trade deal that fell apart, only it will not be something that will ever be possible to break so long as FAE is able to hold up its end of things."

"Just how much help is FAE going to offer?" asked Shen.

"My main focus will be here as we will allow your members to attempt to reach tier-7 rather than be stuck on the frontlines. However, all of this hinges on other things changing and the Huáng empire accepting the reformations that need to happen to gain more support than just FAE and Jingong, as I will not simply throw credits away."

"Hmmm, I think there is a deal that can be made here. Now we just need to see if the Huáng empire can do its part."

"Grandfather, you are mistaken. The changes that Xeal speaks of would also be required of us, won't they."

"Lina, no guild should ever seek to deprive all other guilds of anything but scraps," commented Xeal. "If Jingong can't learn to share a country with other guilds like I have, it will find itself alone in the fight to come. The opportunity that will be created if the Huáng empire agrees to terms will be enough to quadruple the number of players that can be drawn into this fight."

"How will they get here?" asked Lina. "It's not like they can easily teleport over anymore."

"Oh, and why not?" questioned Xeal with a wide smile. "I mean, all that needs to happen is for the Huáng empire to activate a single teleportation hall to receive them."

As Lina realized the possibilities of doing just that and what it would mean if they did so, Emperor Huáng Jin came into view with Kate and the rest of Xeal's group besides Zylah. Xeal chuckled at her absence as he was sure she was playing games on the guards and officials, as they worried that she could be anywhere listening in. Still, the determined look on Emperor Huáng Jin's face made Xeal return to a serious mood as Kate, Queen Aila Lorafir and the emperor took the final three seats at the table. The looks on both Lina's and Shen's faces at seeing the emperor with no veil were ones of surprise as Emperor Huáng Jin spoke.

"Tell me what you need of me and I will see it done, even if I have to execute every minister in my nation."

"Executions are never good for morale," commented Kate. "No, what we need is for you to evacuate all of their loved ones, to include your own, to Nium. After that, you will declare that any minister who flees the war will have their families relegated to living as commoners in Nium and all their wealth stripped from them. Make sure Minister Fù spreads the idea to safeguard as much wealth as possible with their families, as they evacuate them as well."

"I believe that having them stay in my lands would be a better idea," commented Queen Aila Lorafir. "I fear that corruption would lead to issues if a house like the Mercers is allowed to influence the situation."

"Aila is right," agreed Xeal. "Though I fear overloading your capacity to offer aid and forcing you to deal with the issues they will cause, so I say we split the groups up and send the highest-risk ones to Anelqua and the rest to Hardt Burgh to stay with the beast-men."

"Is that it?" asked Emperor Huáng Jin.

"Not even close…"

Kate went on to detail every facet of the plan that Jingong and the Huáng empire needed to know for it to progress. Much of this was new to Xeal, as they had only been able to discuss things as they made their way from Bīng's prison to the point where they had run into the guards. Still, Xeal trusted it would achieve the needed results and position things to at least frustrate Abysses End and deny them complete control of the continent. Finally, after an hour of this, Emperor Huáng Jin agreed to terms and Shen and Lina left with a copy of the offer that Jingong would need to sign, as Xeal and his party escorted Emperor Huáng Jin to see Bīng.

This trip was a quiet one as Zylah rejoined them just after they entered the maze-like basement area. Xeal could tell that being the kleptomaniac that she was, she had enjoyed her time in the imperial palace a bit too much, as he wondered just what she had pocketed. Still, considering that she would be staying behind to guard Emperor Huáng Jin's life for the next few weeks at least, he wasn't going to begrudge her for it under the circumstances. Even if she took something that she really shouldn't, Xeal was confident that he could resolve the situation relatively easily. When they did finally reach Bīng's prison, they found the ice phoenix was still working through her feelings on Watcher's words when she noticed them. At first, she seemed annoyed before seeing Emperor Huáng Jin and realizing who he was as she smiled as she spoke.

"I see that you have cast off your covering. Now, why have you done so?"

"My empire is likely to fall and I am not willing to hide while it does. Besides, if I am not willing to do this much, how can I expect those beneath me to accept the changes that they must?"

"Very well. Now, how many concubines have you taken?"

"I don't see why-"

"Answer the questions I ask! If you try to avoid them, I will know and I will not tolerate it."

"55, with 71 children by my last count, none of whom I have named as my heir."

"You will send them all away to live their lives as commoners in 55 different countries. 100 gold per head and a single tier-6 guard who will become their new husband is all that they will take, besides the clothes on their back and items of sentimental value."

"And why would I agree to that?"

"Because you are going to become my consort and my children will rule your empire."

Xeal wanted to laugh at the look that Emperor Huáng Jin had on his face, as he processed what Bīng had declared as if he had no say in the matter. Though it was clear that Bīng was serious and wasn't going to take no for an answer and any argument would go poorly, so he spoke up.

"Bīng, what are you offering him in exchange for this?"

"You will use my next drop of blood to mark him and he will return here upon his death, and here he will remain until the situation that cost him his life has been resolved."

"What if he actually loves a few of his concubines?" interjected Queen Aila Lorafir. "I refuse to allow you to simply-"

"No," interrupted Emperor Huáng. "I do love them all, but not as I should. No, this is poetic in a sense, as none of those whom I chose had a choice either. So, I will accept this fate for what it is, so long as she agrees to bear me at least two sons."

"Fine, but it will be a daughter who rules," retorted Bīng with a smile. "After all, they will marry one of Xeal's children when the time is right for it."

"Bīng!" cautioned Xeal.

"What, with how many wives you have, you are going to have many between this world and your other world. For all I know, their partner will be one of your children from your reality. It is why it will be my daughter who rules, as she will only be holding the seat until one of your sons can claim her and if none of them can, well, I will be disappointed in your line."

"Ha, Hahahaha, oh Xeal, brother, she has you there, and

here I thought that Xin would be how your line ended up on my throne. I dare say that I like this better."

Xeal just sighed as he decided that this wasn't an issue worth getting entangled in at this point, as it would be decades before it mattered. Instead, he was focused on the pressing issue of finding 55 homes for all of Emperor Huáng Jin's concubines, which was going to be extremely difficult to pull off. Not to mention that just by the laws of averages, many of them would find themselves becoming refugees and even dying from the wars in other lands. It was with this thought and the fact that their children were all Lingxin's nieces and nephews that Xeal crafted his response as he spoke.

"No, I will not condemn family to the whims of fate like that. At the heart of my issues with the Huáng empire is the style of harems that are present. The emperor dissolving his own and declaring that the days of such practices are at an end is needed, but I cannot just allow my nieces and nephews to be scattered on the wind like that. Instead, I will shelter them in my lands and allow them to transition into the life of needing to stand on their own."

"No," responded Bīng. "They must be scattered such that they know that they need to adapt, or die. I would say that the same needs to be done with every such harem in the empire, but I doubt that there are enough men available to act as guards and new husbands to them. So, instead, I will just say that five times Jin's own must be sent away to obscure their identities further."

"Bīng!" shouted Xeal. "I am not negotiating this with you, I am telling you. If I determine that they are a cancer that needs to be cut out, I will send them to Cielo city and have the dragonoids train them as servants, or something, but they will not be scattered."

"Xeal, you believe that such a situation will lead to

anything good?" asked Bīng. "I dare say that you are a fool if you think those women can suddenly become friends, isn't that right, Jin!"

"Huh, some might, but most would more likely seek to kill the others and their children. It is part of why they are kept separate from each other. They are essentially pitted against one another in the pursuit of having their son be the next emperor. After all, after I took the throne all but my mother was scattered to various places where they will live their lives as their children are taken from them. Most of my half-brothers will be on the front lines of this war and almost all of my half-sisters warm a minister's bed, or worse."

"All I am hearing is that they are going to need time to work through the sudden change in their lives and I need to get ready to accept many more than just your concubines and children," retorted Xeal. "Make no mistake, they will know that they are commoners, which is fine as I need a good influx of such residents in my territory. Now, I will expect that every single minister will agree to sever their connection from their hidden concubines who wish to permanently accept a place in my territory as well. After all, they should be extremely concerned about what to do with them when you announce the end to the practice and the need for them to be publicly recognized if they are to continue to exist."

"Fine, but they must all accept that if they ever return to these lands, it will mean their death," replied Bīng. "I will not have them thinking that their sons can still become emperor as my daughter will have enough of an uphill battle when she sits upon the throne."

"As will Lingxin if she must act as our daughter's regent after my death," added Emperor Huáng Jin. "Now if that is all, I need to survive implementing these changes and you need to secure more allies. Thank you for leaving Zylah here to ensure that I at least survive until you return."

"Just don't send me a bill when you are missing any national treasures," quipped Xeal. "Zylah, please ensure that any minister that plans to revolt, or dispose of things they deem unsightly, is made an example of in the most poetic way you can imagine."

"Oh, you know just what to say to me," quipped Zylah with a broad smile. "I can see the faces of the poor fools now."

Xeal just smiled as he led the rest of his group away and an hour later, they were in Muthia with Mari added to the group and sitting across from Empress Sakurai Jingū as Kate went over the situation. It was clear that the focus on stabilizing the situation in the Huáng empire first wasn't what she wanted to hear, but she bore with it until Kate had finished sharing what was pertinent to Muthia. This was followed by a long silence before Empress Jingū spoke.

"This plan requires Muthia to suffer more than would be necessary, all to aid a nation that I frankly would love to see fall. I am aware that you have similar ties to them as you do to us and that you are cramming a ton of reforms down their throat, but how am I to sell such an alliance to my ministers while also naming you as my emergency heir?"

"The same way Emperor Huáng Jin is forcing the reforms on his people," responded Xeal. "By placing your neck on the chopping block and declaring it as what must be done to secure the aid needed to weather this storm."

"Oh, and just how do you see that playing out?" retorted Empress Jingū. "I am not such a pillar that I do not fear my ministers. It is why naming you as the emergency heir is so vital."

"Name Xeal as your heir until the end of this war, Mother," interjected Mari. "That will guard your life better than any guard could and give him the power to select any of your children, or grandchildren as emperor, or empress, once this war has ended."

"Mari, I do not want to be that close to becoming the emperor of Muthia, even if it would only be a temporary measure."

"Xeal, that could work," commented Kate. "Victor might need to be convinced, but possibly having Muthia as a subordinate to Nium for a few years would likely appeal to him rather well. Not to mention that it avoids one of Mari's siblings replacing Lady Sakurai and nullifying everything during the war."

"How about I just mark her and guard her life that way?" countered Xeal.

"Is that how you are protecting Mari's and Kuri's lives?" asked Empress Jingū.

"It is," answered Mari. "It is far more expensive for Xeal and nontransferable once done, meaning that if you survive the war, you will not be able to hand it over to your heir."

"Interesting and you are willing to do that for me now, but not before? Xeal, what changed?"

"The toll that the alliance will take on Muthia and my desire to not rule Muthia, even if it is in name only."

"You also have to take into account that if Mari, Enye, Lingxin, Dyllis and several others who he is guarding with the same resource die, he could run out," interjected Kate. "As such, he makes a point of holding a fair bit in reserve and only offers to use it when he feels it is necessary. While I agree that marking you is fine, I must insist that you realize that you will find yourself ruling from Nium until the war ends should assassins get to you here and your life will only be guarded by a feather."

"I see and just how many lives are currently being guarded with this resource?" inquired Empress Jingū.

"That is classified," replied Xeal. "It is enough for you to know that if they all died, I wouldn't be able to restore the protection."

"Huh, very well, I will see that my nation accepts these terms," stated Empress Jingū, as she held out her hand and Kate handed her the documents that had just finished being prepared.

The following hour was spent as Empress Jingū combed through the documents and asked one question after another as she proved that she was no fool. This prompted several more edits of the documents and rereads that uncovered more details that needed to be addressed, until Empress Jingū finally signed them. With that taken care of, Xeal smiled and was about to leave when Empress Jingū spoke once more.

"Now if you would be so kind as to explain what you will be doing to me in order to safeguard my life."

Xeal smiled as he pulled out the metal stamp that all who had arrived but Kate, Aila, Lucy and Takeshi had been marked by and explained what was needed. As Xeal showed the two-inch diameter circle which was filled with a yin and yang like symbol with a whirlpool in its center which blended the two sides together, Empress Jingū frowned. Though she held her silence until the end when she asked a simple question.

"Is there any other symbol that would work, as I am hesitant of having the mark of your house placed upon me."

Xeal frowned as he realized the issue as he reached out to Watcher for an answer.

"Watcher, is the pseudo mark design you gave me the only one that can be used?"

After a long moment Watcher replied while sounding slightly annoyed.

"Xeal, it is not, but it is the only one that I will teach you, as the others are far more involved and would require far more than a drop of yours and a phoenix's blood. They also serve a purpose for which you are not ready to use, as only those who have reached the peak of the mortal limits can handle them."

"Oh, now I think you are holding out on me. After all, you tell me that they exist and then refuse to teach me them, even when I reach that peak."

"You have no desire to rule, so you have no need of them. Besides, my great-grandchildren would certainly not let you using them slide."

Xeal just frowned as he shifted from the mental exchange back to reality and answered Empress Jingū.

"I am sorry, but it is the only symbol that I have the ability to use."

"So, there are others?"

"Not ones that serve strictly the same purpose."

Xeal could tell that Empress Jingū seemed annoyed at his answer as she paused before sighing and responding.

"Mari, if you would be so kind as to show me yours in the other room before I accept it."

"Very well, Mother."

With that the pair left the room and Takeshi turned to Xeal and spoke to him.

"Xeal-san, is there a reason that you have brought me to these talks today?"

"Takeshi-san, you are who will take over my position when I go dark. As such, you need to be intimately familiar with the core of this alliance. After all, you and Kate will be handling more than a few without me soon enough."

"Surely Kate-san can handle such things on her own."

"I need a conscience to accompany me," stated Kate. "If left alone, I tend to get a bit more cutthroat than is good long term, as shown by the situation surrounding Fire Oath and FAE at this point."

"Surely Geitir-san, or Casmir-san, could handle it as well."

"We did consider Geitir," replied Kate. "But, he still has issues from his time in Eternal Valhalla that have left their mark on him and he is too soft. Casmir is just not suitable to be considered a stand-in for Xeal in a negotiation."

"Just give up, Takeshi-san," interjected Lucy. "There really isn't anyone who makes any sense besides you, from mine and likely most of the guild's point of view either."

As Takeshi frowned, Empress Jingū and Mari returned and asked for Xeal to join them in the other room to place the mark on her. Xeal decided to use a drop of Eba the nature phoenix's blood to create the mark, and once it was done, he bid Empress Jingū farewell and returned to Nium. By this time it was already late night of day 158 and they still needed to meet with King Victor and finalize the formation of the alliance that would allow everything to start moving. With this, Xeal was just happy that the guards gave them no issues before escorting them to King Victor, who was sitting in his war room going over the latest reports from the battlefield when they entered. When the door closed, King Victor didn't even look up as he started to talk in a weary voice.

"Tell me that you have an army to drive Paidhia back while keeping Habia at bay."

"Tell me that you don't mind ruling a country of corpses when this war is over," retorted Xeal. "We both know that the battle lines will stay where they are for at least a few weeks at this point."

"Yes, thankfully the tier-7 members of your guild were enough to shift the tide of battle this time, so tell me what do you expect me to agree to?"

"My party and around 400 tier-7 members of my guild will be focused on the Huáng empire first and foremost, as it is the one in the direst of need. Muthia will require a few hundred of my tier-7 members to help hold the line there and you will be left with whatever that leaves behind. All of those numbers will grow over the next six months, which is when we expect the other guilds to start reaching tier-7 and our advantage will diminish. During that time, Nium will be focused on obtaining naval superiority with Odelia, Saphielle, Sylmare, Cremia and Itylara leading FAE's new fleet that is almost ready to launch."

"To think those five would become the key to Nium's victory. I must say that I am grateful that you have them under control, though they will be extremely hampered if their ship goes down. Are you sure that you want Nium's navy to simply hold down the areas they capture?"

"Yes, especially as I intend to claim every captured ship for FAE's new navy that is going to be crucial to winning the wars that come after these ones. Especially in both the Huáng and Muthia empires as I am expecting the result of the current fight to be close to a draw followed by a ceasefire if I am lucky."

"Be careful. Some might believe that your guild has become more pirate than anything else."

"I see no issue with that," interjected Kate. "That is so long as it is understood that only those who are in conflict with our interests need worry about us raiding them."

"We will limit ourselves to those who we are at war with," corrected Xeal. "As for the other details…"

The next hour was spent bringing King Victor up to speed on the current situation and negotiated terms, and obtaining his signature on the treaties that would make the alliance official. By the time that finally came to an end, Xeal was simply happy to return home and join the rest of his wives who were already asleep. As he wished to sit with them all for a bit in the morning, all of them were present and even Queen Aila Lorafir was spending the night with them as Xeal was happy to put day 158 behind him.

When Xeal opened his eyes on day 159, it was to the sight of all 11 of the women that he was committed to all being present. Most of whom were already up and about, as Eira and Mari snuggled into him as he smiled at them as he started his morning with catching up on all the kisses that had been missed over the past few weeks. Finally, with that done, Xeal took a deep breath as he looked at all of them and started to speak.

"Before I get into speaking on what I experienced in my tribulation, Aila, if you would ensure that we are free from all prying eyes."

As Queen Aila Lorafir activated her spell, Xeal turned on his enhanced senses and fought through the over stimulation to double check that nothing was within the barrier that had been erected. It was with this that Xeal got his first look at Gale, Aalin and Kate like this and he could see how the marks that were on them interacted with their bodies. This also highlighted the difference between Kate who had reached tier-7 and the other two who hadn't yet, as her energy was intertwined far more with that of the mark. At the same time, Xeal could tell that Freya, Levina and Bīng were paying attention as well and he just sighed as there was no real way to avoid them as he disabled his enhanced senses and spoke.

"Thank you, Aila. Now, what I am about to say is not to be shared and that goes for you too, Freya, Bīng and Levina. As Aila, Luna, Selene, Aalin, Gale and Kate are aware, I have the memories from a version of myself from 60 years after my kind first came to this world…"

Xeal explained the general state of ED and his memories

that he felt were pertinent for all of his wives to know. As he did so, he could tell that there were complicated emotions that were threatening to spill over for Enye, Lingxin, Eira, Dyllis and Mari. However, they all allowed him to finish before Dyllis was the first to respond, sounding like she was conflicted between being upset and relieved.

"Xeal, why is it that the five of us were the only ones who are just now learning of this?"

"Because he fears sharing it inside of this world too much," answered Kate. "He forced the five of us to learn about it in our reality and I expect that Aila extracted it out of him indirectly."

"No, I confronted him about his lack of desire to rule and he was honest with me about him viewing this life as a second chance of a sort. As far as I can tell, he is extremely guarded with it as had we not been under the same protection from spying eyes that we are now, I doubt he would have been honest with me."

"Either way, it isn't something that I should have kept from all of you for so long. It's just I never felt like it was time to share it and it never came up naturally, and I have begun fearing the answers to the how it is even possible."

"As you should," replied Dyllis. "Even with our world's time, magic can only stretch it, or speed it up. There is no way to go backwards and alter things that have already happened. Were it not for the fact that-"

"We believe him. You would think he is crazy," interjected Gale. "We are aware. Trust me, had I not known him since middle school, sorry, since I was like 12 in my reality and seen the sudden change that occurred on his 18th birthday, I would likely lean towards crazy as well."

"As would we," commented Luna.

"We mean having Gale to vouch for him," added Selene.

"Though we wish we knew him since he was 12 too."

"But we can't have everything we want."

"Even what our kind refers to as the main system's AI vouches for him," commented Kate.

"That is the entity that you speak to in the world where Austru is, correct?" ask Enye.

"Yes, it is very interested in Xeal and may have influenced events surrounding him accidentally when he first entered this world and saw his memories from the future," stated Kate.

"Is that why he has seemed to have nothing but good fortune since he came here?" asked Lingxin as she gave Xeal a hard look.

"No, that would be me following my memories. It simply left an echo, imprint, or whatever the right term is, in all of the inhabitants of this world before severing its connection to all of you. According to it, that is why it was easy for me to gain favor, or disdain, from the residents of this world at first."

"Was?" asked Mari. "You make it seem like you can't any longer."

"With each day, you all step further away from the you that you were when the main system could control your actions and who you were. That doesn't mean that you will ever break completely free from the you that it crafted, but it means that you could if you decided to. Also, for the record, I only found out about that when I was in the middle of my tier-6 ordeal and I had already accepted you all into my life completely by then."

"Oh, even me?" asked Queen Aila Lorafir.

"Aila, the moment I let you know about my past life I had accepted that you were going to be an important part of my life. Be that as a wife, mother-in-law, or simply an unshakable ally that I would be a fool to hide anything from."

"Alright," interjected Eira. "Let's put all of that to the side for now. Xeal, why was this pertinent to what you plan to share with us about your tribulation?"

"Because my tribulation was…"

Xeal went on to share everything about his tribulation, including the seduction attempts that he endured. He did his best to not leave a single emotion that he felt out until he got to the part where he was pitted against them and the system had pulled him out of it early. At this point he exhaled and closed off with his new skills and the changes to his elder dragon's mark, as well as his new title. Finally, he quieted down and waited for them to respond as the silence started to drag on, before Luna and Selene were the first to speak.

"Do you think the us you know from your last life influenced the versions of us there?"

"Yeah, you don't think that we would be so vicious now, do you?"

"Not to me," replied Xeal with a smile. "But I could see you being that way to anyone you remember and dislike from your time in Abysses End."

"I suppose that is fair."

"Yep, if we saw Harris again, we might just do that."

"I am more concerned with the way it ended," commented Kate. "Though I can see just how draining that had to be for you as well. Still, you need to move past your fear of betrayal and betraying others. It is going to happen at some point. You will likely not even realize it when it does, but you will forget something, or be put in a no-win situation like that again and you need to be able to act."

"No, we need to be able to act for him," stated Aalin. "Just as Luna and Selene are his hypocrites, we all need to be ready to bear this burden for him."

"Wouldn't that make us into what he hates though?" asked Dyllis.

"No," replied Gale. "Because he knows that we are doing it for him."

"Gale, Aalin, please don't," interjected Xeal. "I love all of you and Kate is right, to ask you to do that for me would feel like a betrayal as well. It would likely even eat at me worse than the one I suffered in my last life right before I found myself awaking in this one. I think that when the time comes that a betrayal is inevitable, I will choose all of you and let the rest of it sort itself out."

"That is fine," stated Mari. "But I wish to say one more thing. Aalin and Gale are right as far as one specific case is concerned. Should any who is allowed to join us as Xeal's wives betray us, the rest of us will be the ones to handle it. Xeal, I feel that I would not be here right now if you didn't have these complex emotions pulling at you and honestly, it makes your reaction to when we overloaded you make even more sense."

"Yes, this is enlightening on several levels of who you are," commented Queen Aila Lorafir. "It makes me love you more while also making me fear just how far you would go to avoid betraying us."

"Precisely," interjected Kate. "Xeal, we don't want you to destroy yourself for us!"

"Kate, Aila, Mari, you are missing one key factor. If one of you betrays me and the others, well, while it will destroy me in one aspect, it will free me in another. It is why I would have been fine at the end of the fight in my tribulation. I may rarely see the need to use it, but I still have the effect of my title, by the seat of your pants, from when I reached tier-6. Had those versions of yourselves decided to attack me when I left myself completely open to it, I would have used it, escaped and initiated a full-scale assault. Never think that I don't have it in me to respond to being truly betrayed by anyone, just know if that betrayal does come from within this group, I will cut out that cancer. Even if it rips me to pieces to do so, as I trust that the rest of you will be here to put me back together and if you're not, well then, I am likely the one who betrayed you and well-"

"Well nothing!" shouted Eira as she almost jumped to her feet and closed the distance to Xeal. "We will be the ones to handle any betrayal from within our ranks! That includes if you betray us! Xeal, you are our husband and I expect you to protect us from any external threats that will come for us, but you are not without your limits. That is where we come in. We will cover for your weakness and you will let us. Besides, I can't see any of us ever willingly betraying you. We all love you too much for that."

"We are just going to keep going in circles like this," stated Enye. "Xeal, no matter what you say, we are going to be there and all you will do by putting such a burden on yourself will be to harm all of us. So, let's just agree that we will work together if such a day ever comes. Though, I agree with Eira that such a day is unlikely to ever come."

As Xeal looked at Eira who was directly in front of him and Enye who was calmly looking at him, he couldn't help but smile as he shifted his focus to Aalin and Gale with his next words.

"Freya, Bīng, I have no idea just how far your influence on Aalin and Gale will extend if they reach tier-8, but know that should you ever abuse it, I will make it my life's purpose to destroy you."

"Xeal," mumbled Gale in surprise. "You don't-"

"Gale, I am well aware of the absurdity of what I am saying, but they both know that I mean it and nothing is impossible to destroy. It may just require that I embrace a path that would be better to never be explored."

"You would use Levina against them," commented Kate. "It's why you didn't mention her just now as she can't escape your control."

"No, only the void can erase that which can't die," stated Queen Aila Lorafir. "However, to wield it with enough power to be meaningful against a deity or primordial, risks, if not guarantees, one's own destruction as well."

Xeal just smiled as he didn't respond to either comment. Instead, he let out a deep breath as he spoke.

"I think I have had enough of this depressing topic for the day. Kate, Eira, is there anything you feel a need to share from your tribulations?"

"I already did," replied Eira. "When I said that mine cost me you and everyone else I loved, as I was forced to stand alone in the end. That is my greatest fear, being alone in this world as I was when Xeal came into my life!"

"Mine was also far less convoluted," added Kate. "I just had to deal with my father as an opponent in a series of schemes, only he also knew every move I was going to make before I made it."

"That doesn't sound less convoluted," retorted Gale. "If anything, that sounds like a true nightmare."

Xeal just smiled as the next hour was spent on Eira's and Kate's tribulations before the gathering came to an end and Xeal was left alone with Gale who was looking nervous as she spoke.

"Do you really think Freya would force me to do something that you would see as a betrayal?"

"If it suited her designs, but I don't intend to make things such that it would."

"There are times where I wonder if we all aren't making a mistake by letting all of these entities occupy real estate in our minds and bodies. Xeal, I really don't want to deal with

Freya if she could turn on us like that, even if it is only a minor possibility. Should I just die and lose the mark, or heck, restart?"

"Gale, that is the last thing any of us should purposely do. Like it or not, all that doing so would accomplish would be pissing them off to the point where they would be sure to target us. So, don't worry, I will know if Freya is the root cause if you ever suddenly change in ED and I will not see it as you betraying me. Heck, you could decide that you hate me and want to never see me again and so long as you told me it honestly and were civil about it, I wouldn't see that as a betrayal. A betrayal would be you joining Abysses End, or trying to cut Moyra off from the rest of us completely."

"Really, because I would see you deciding that you didn't love me anymore as a betrayal."

"That is fine, as I have no right not to love you after what you have given me and sacrificed to try and make this insane arrangement work. That goes for any woman that manages to join you and the others as my wives. All I ask from any of you is openness and understanding of why I can't give each of you the attention you deserve."

"Fine. Let's put that aside for now as I intend to get as much attention from you as I can right now, before I get none in this world for a very long time."

With that Xeal found his lips sealed as Gale pushed him back towards the bed.

A few hours later, Xeal and Gale separated, with Xeal headed to FAE's guild headquarters to handle as much paperwork as he possibly could before it was time to log off and Gale to do her final preparations to reach tier-7. As he worked through the mountain of paperwork that was waiting for him, Xeal kept track of the situations surrounding everything in ED and FAE. The situation in the Muthia empire was still stable as they focused on holding the line as more and more tier-7 members of FAE streamed in. Things in the Huáng empire were still in a precarious situation as NPC losses were increasing on all sides, and the counters that Xeal was working on were being put in place. Thankfully, FAE had successfully pushed Paidhia back to the border fort area where the ruins of the forts were still enough to create a stalemate, with what FAE was willing to do at this point.

By the end of day 159, Xeal was happy to see that the last of those who were part of the first 10,000 to attempt their tier-7 tribulations were done. The 1,869 that succeeded was almost double what Xeal had hoped for, as the next wave of 30,000 got ready to make their attempt. This would be the group that Gale, Aalin, Taya and Geitir would be part of, as they had been the ones running FAE during the first group's attempt. Still, Xeal was expecting about a ten percent pass rate as he knew that success rates were just going to drop with each wave, as hard mode was the easiest option available. While that would allow FAE to eventually see five percent of its current members reach tier-7, only one percent of all players would ever pass it if things were the same as in his last life.

Xeal had even remembered some guilds that ended up having no tier-7 members, as the few they did get left the guild, or they didn't want to deal with the attention that having one brought them. This was due to the focus that every major guild placed on recruiting, or ruining, any tier-7 player that wasn't part of one of them when it became clear just how few players could make it through their tribulation. Even FAE was already working to ensure that it was ready to secure any of them that they could. However, Xeal had created a way for any such guild, or player, to shift their operations to any of the countries that joined the alliance he was setting up. Xeal wondered what Jingong would do when they realized what they had signed for the latest agreement. Especially the clause of all tier-7 players who signed on to aid in the alliance's defense, gained FAE's and Jingong's protection from such aggressive recruitment tactics within the boundaries of the alliance.

It was things like this that made the alliance that Xeal was creating something far different than anything that had existed in his last life. While such an idea had been conceptualized by those who found themselves targeted by these aggressive recruitment tactics, they lacked any ability to implement it. Xeal believed that this, more than anything, had been what had led to so many of those who reached tier-8 staying hidden, as they would have been hunted even further. Even a talent like Frozen Sky, who was strong enough to prop up a guild against being exploited by super guilds, would have been targeted without the tens of thousands of tier-7s that he had behind him. While it wasn't guaranteed to work, Xeal hoped that this would create a new dynamic and an environment where the independent powerhouses became unofficial allies to FAE. Still, only time would tell.

With a stack of paperwork out of the way, treaties signed, thousands of NPCs and players getting ready for major migrations and pressure on all sides, Xeal called it a day and logged off. He knew that once he returned, that it would be time for him to really start taking care of the task that he needed to handle before he went full commando and practically lived behind the enemy lines. As things were currently shaping up, Xeal was only worried about having the misfortune of his group being discovered by a tier-8 entity. Though he also knew that he would need to risk just that with the missions his party would be undertaking.

(*****)

Morning May 9 to Evening May 13, 2268 & ED Year 6 Days 160-174.

Alex found himself sitting back in the nursery with all his kids playing, after participating in the morning kendo lesson on Saturday the 9th. He was happy to finally have his tribulation behind him as he just enjoyed being able to casually chat with the others. After being so guarded against accidentally revealing anything about his tribulation during his downtime, it was wonderful to not have to avoid any conversations. The contrast he felt between the past few days and now as he enjoyed his last morning with Sam and Nicole for a while was extreme. Though with both of them shifting their schedule slightly to reduce the chance of accidentally revealing anything about their tribulation while they were offline, it made him feel like they hadn't quite ended yet. So, Alex decided to stay offline for an extra hour to just be with both of them as they played with Ahsa and Moyra, who were both almost 11 months old and were both threatening to walk. Still, they were standing quite readily by pulling themselves up with anything they could as they watched how Evelyn, who was already walking, did it.

Alex just smiled at watching these little things that were all happening too quickly, as it seemed that they were watching Evelyn do everything and a month later they would be doing it as well. Andy was just a couple weeks behind Ahsa and Moyra as well, despite being almost a month younger than them as it seemed like he was both the first and last to do anything depending on how you looked at it. Still, nothing was more enjoyable for Alex than the babble that the four of them had all but mastered, though actual words were few and far between. In these moments, Alex could just feel the innocence that was so beautiful as they had no worry in the world beyond Daddy and their mommies not being around as much as they would like.

From what Julie said, each of them just lit up like nothing else when any of the six of them were around, though Ahsa and Moyra seemed to still like Kate the most for some reason. Though Sam teased that it was because Kate was the one they seemed to cheer up the most, due to the family issues that were still simmering between the Astors and her. While they had yet to make a move, no one thought that they had simply given up and the longer it took for them to act, the more on edge Kate seemed to get. Though the cutest thing was to see the pout when Kate was holding Aidan, Nadia, Evan, or Nova, rather than them like they had been all morning as Kate gave Ava and Mia a hand with post-feeding needs. Alex simply wished that these moments would never end at times, but as always, they did and Alex found himself needing to log in to ED once more.

Sunday to Wednesday passed much in the same fashion, only with the noted absence of both Sam and Nicole. Additionally, Harrison and an admin team headed to California for the second-to-last presentation at Alex's old high school. All things considered, this was a lighter visit as it was really just a precursor to the one that Alex had planned to close out the school year. They would also be focusing on filling up the summer intern positions that had been greatly increased from the year prior. This would involve them visiting every high school in the area over the next month to interview the applicants and would take up a significant amount of their time as they did so. While Alex would have rather that these interviews occurred in ED, due to the issues with moving about freely during war times, they had to compromise to hide just how freely FAE could still move.

When Xeal returned to ED on day 160, the first thing he did was verify that the situation was still stable as he planned out his next moves. It seemed that Abysses End was aware that they needed to keep pressing the attack from the reports that Xeal was reading, but the infusion of tier-7 forces was enough to at least slow their pace down at this point. However, Xeal felt like they were waiting for him to make a move personally, as it had already been leaked that he had returned as a tier-7 powerhouse. If Xeal was right, the moment he took the field that battle would be won, but three to four others would experience a sudden surge of forces. Particularly on the continents that he wasn't on and that would likely mean the border fort between Habia and Nium would fall before Xeal could return, if he didn't lay his own trap perfectly.

While the slowly encroaching doom for Nium pressed on, the Muthia empire and the Huáng empire was favorable to Abysses End currently, which was also perfect for Xeal. Put simply, it allowed him to continue to make moves that would flip the script on Abysses End and set the stage for their downfall. It was with this thought that Xeal summoned Lois and Sciencia Auger, and called Arnhylde and Lucida to join the group from the visit to the Huáng empire. Once they were all assembled and Arnhylde had confirmed that Matrikas the celestial phoenix was alone, they went to visit her.

When they arrived, the first thing that happened was Lois and Sciencia hurrying over to embrace their great-great-great-grandmother. This was followed by the three of them spending over 20 minutes catching up as they had never thought that they would get such an opportunity. Though eventually Matrikas adjusted her snow white hair as she turned her attention to Xeal and spoke.

"I must thank you for giving me a balm for my soul as I can feel the devastation that is coming. Now, Arnhylde was vague about why you wished to see me today. Tell me, have you decided to accept Lois or Sciencia as a bride, or perhaps even both?"

"No, I am here to make you an offer that may just save the Zapladal Theocracy from being twisted into a new form."

"Oh, and I suppose you would want to borrow our strength to fight a war on another continent now, in exchange for coming to our aid later. I am sorry, but such a deal isn't something that my descendants can weather. Though, if you were willing to give me a child, something might be arranged as even if you are hiding it with a skill, I can feel the power inside of you now."

"That is enough on that subject," interjected Kate. "Sorry, but Xeal is not interested and even if he was, he is not freely available to sow his oats wherever he pleases. As for what our offer is, it is simple. We want to set up a portal like the one here, that will connect to all other nations that we ally with for players to move about freely with. In return, FAE will come to your aid if and when your nation is attacked. Additionally, Queen Nora has consented to King Victor taking either Lois or Sciencia as a wife."

Xeal could see the look of surprise on both Lois's and Sciencia's faces as this was said, as they looked at Matrikas who seemed to be considering what was being offered. Finally with a sigh, she spoke in a slightly sad tone.

"I would be happy to agree to such terms and Jeren would likely support them as well, but ever since Lois and

Sciencia left, his authority has diminished. He has also entered the decline that takes all mortals and will likely not see another five years. So, you will need to convince the other factions who would push their own daughters to be the bridge between the nations."

"No, I need to restore Jeren," replied Xeal. "Huh, Kate, I am going to have to dip out for your trip to the Ivurith Empire and handle a few quests a bit earlier than I would have liked."

"Oh, are you going to seek out the waters of youth already?" asked Kate.

"Yes, and secure a few griffin eggs while I am at it as well. After all, having a few hundred, or even over a thousand hippogriffs could prove pivotal in the later stages of the wars."

"I take it that your information just happens to put them in the same spot?"

"Yah, but it is also in a level 200 to 250 area that will take me a week to complete both."

"Hold on, you expect us to just waltz into an area where the monsters will be over 40 levels higher than us?!" interjected Lucy. "Xeal, I know that you are good, but even you aren't that good, are you?"

"Lucy, you should be as well. The only reason that any of us had any issues with the level 209 monsters before reaching tier-7 was their reaction time. However, we will not be waltzing in. No, we need to sneak in as quickly and quietly as possible, else we will be overwhelmed."

"What about the rest of us that aren't fueled by gods, or primordials?" asked Alea. "I am sure that we can handle two, or even three, but I doubt that we have any hope once a fourth shows up."

"Alea, the level of danger that we will be in during this venture will be far less than we will once we really start playing our role during the war. It will also be a great training exercise as we are all used to the underground world a little too much at this point and this will take us high into the mountains instead."

"You're not one to communicate the true challenge of what you face," interjected Matrikas. "The waters of youth are never obtained easily and not even individuals like my champion Jeren, or the elf over there can simply just find such a substance at will."

"They are not me," retorted Xeal. "Matrikas, if I say I have a method, then I have one, or do you not believe in my abilities?"

At that the room grew quiet as even Queen Aila Lorafir seemed surprised by Xeal's declaration. After a long moment had passed, it was Eira who was the first to respond.

"If my husband says it is so, then it is so. Now let's get going."

"Right, let me just have Holly let Jewel know that we are going to be stopping by and have her meet us there," replied Xeal as he input a message.

"I thought you were going to be above ground," commented Kate. "Or is it that you need to head to Ethax before you reach your destination?"

"Kate, I will give you a full accounting later. Oh, and coordinate the assault to take the slime dungeon for Muthia at the same time. I am going to show up in a way that will really throw Abysses End for a loop."

"Xeal, what are you going to do?!" questioned Kate with a look of simmering anger. "We agreed that you would play out the stalemate long enough to set what we need into motion."

"Don't worry, my lightning form shouldn't be known to them yet, at least not enough to realize it is me fast enough to act. Holly says she will be there in 20 minutes. Kate, have Muthia ready to move in 12 hours."

Kate looked annoyed as she got to work while Xeal explained the plan to his party that would be accompanying him. 20 minutes later, Xeal smiled as he stepped through the gate once more as he, Eira, Lucy, Bula, Dafasli, Alea, Rina, Daisy and Violet prepared for their first expedition since reaching tier-7. All of them knew that this would be their life until the war ended, as they would rarely sleep in the same place twice outside the short breaks they would have when they returned to Nium. Xeal also knew that this was part of what had Kate so annoyed, as Xeal hadn't even said a proper goodbye to all of his wives as that was supposed to happen after another few weeks. During that time, Kate was working to organize a major offensive that would kick off with Xeal attacking a static point and creating as much chaos as possible. Xeal knew that him doing what he was about to put that in jeopardy, but any plan that couldn't be changed was worthless and he knew Kate would make the best of it.

With that thought, Xeal arrived in the cavern that served as Jewel's prison, which had been completely transformed since last Xeal saw it. Gone was the crystal dome. Instead there was ornate furniture that was covered in soft cushions as Jewel lounged about looking content as she spoke with Holly, while enjoying some chocolate-covered fruit. Xeal was sure that Holly had just delivered them as part of her greeting to the crystal phoenix that controlled the element that most considered earth. Though upon noticing Xeal and his group, Jewel's attention shifted as she spoke to him.

"So, you finally return to visit after all this time. I ought to ignore whatever request you have and just send you away."

"That is fine, as I don't have a request," retorted Xeal. "This was just the most convenient point for me to use to head for where I need to go."

"Hold on, you visit me for the first time in years and you don't even care if I am willing to cooperate with you!? I don't know whether to be offended, or impressed at your gall."

"Jewel, being offended is a choice, as is being impressed, so just be the one that will make you happier," quipped Xeal. "After all, I intend to just be happy that you and Holly seem to be getting along well enough."

"Yes, well, as I am sure you are aware already from the fact that you had Holly check up on me earlier, there is something that I do want. Yet I don't even have the beginning of options in regard to partners that make any sense beside you."

"That sounds like a real issue and if you would like to do something about it, I would speak with Holly and she is much more likely to have the time to remedy that issue than I will."

"Does that mean I can bring whoever I like here?" asked Holly, sounding slightly sarcastic. "I mean I enjoy delivering presents more than is likely healthy, but even I think that they should have a chance to get to know each other a little bit first."

"What about one of Mari's brothers?" suggested Daisy. "I mean that would possibly create a situation that is similar to what is going to happen in the Huáng empire."

"That would create a real mess," replied Holly. "Sorry, but ceremonies and public acknowledgement of all partners is very important to Muthia's imperial family."

"That they are," agreed Xeal. "Not to mention that I am sure Jewel would desire that her child be the next ruler of Muthia."

"Is that so wrong? It would be just ridiculous to expect my child to achieve anything less than ruling over other mortals."

"That actually wouldn't be that hard to achieve," interjected Lucy. "I mean, that is just having them perform great deeds and earn the favor of one ruler or another and seek them out to marry the next heir, or become the heir through the marriage. I could even introduce a few of the divine scions that have gathered already that might be a fit."

"Holly, feel free to discuss that further with Gale and Lucy as I want no part in it beyond their agreement of silence." Xeal shook his head before continuing. "This could quickly become a real mess if the gods start fighting over whose vessel gets to impregnate the phoenixes."

"Who says that I will allow one that has been tainted by a deity to even be my mate!"

"Jewel, don't look at it like that," commented Holly. "Look at it like which deity is ready to admit that they were wrong and is willing to bind themselves to you in such a way."

"There is also the question of if Freya will allow it," injected Bula, sounding slightly distant. "Especially as it would tie the new pantheon she is working to form to the primordials."

"She already is through me," replied Xeal. "This would just make the connection deeper, while also being such that she could place the focus on the 11 that have the power to control the rest."

At this Xeal suddenly got an idea that could solve several issues all at once, but it would require a lot of convincing and was likely to spark a war that could destroy all of ED. However, it could also bring about a new era that would be perfect to ensure a better balance in the late game that was so terrible for all but Abysses End in Xeal's last life. Still, that was years away from even being a possibility, as Xeal returned his thoughts to the present and spoke once more.

"Jewel, I will never force you to consider a divine scion as a mate, but I will ask you to not dismiss it out of hand. Holly, I am trusting you and Kate to handle the details of whoever you do bring down here as I don't want to know anything beyond that it is happening. Now, as much as I would love to stay and discuss the challenges of finding a mate when you are completely unable to leave this area, I have a timetable to keep."

As Jewel responded with a frown, Xeal waited for Holly to open the pathway into the slime dungeon that they had sealed off to avoid any unwanted visitors. Once that was done, Xeal and his party moved quickly as Holly sealed the entrance back up as they headed straight for the surface. As they did so, they avoided the parties of other players that were spread out all over the area as much as they could and when they couldn't they simply killed them. While Xeal felt bad for the mostly independent and low-skill players that he was doing this to, it was necessary as Abysses End had seized the dungeon over a year ago from Holly's guild Festive Spirit. They had declined the option of retaking it as Ethax had supported the move due to Festive Spirit's ties to the Muthia empire being revealed. After that, Abysses End had simply posted a few guards who would collect entry fees and control the number of players that were allowed in at any one point.

This would be how most lower-level clearable dungeons would be treated when the guild who controlled it didn't want it to actually be cleared. This included only letting players who were too weak to enter the dungeon accidentally, or purposely, unless they were members of the controlling guild there for a specific reason. This also meant that most of the players Xeal's party was killing would think that they were members of Abysses End at first and it would be difficult for Abysses End to deny it without losing face. Especially when the attackers entered from a lower area of the dungeon and not the main entrance, as this would mean that they had even more issues to deal with.

Though, none of that would matter once the day was over if Xeal had his way, as his party exited the dungeon wearing dark cloaks that completely hid their stats and appearances to any player under tier-7. The few dozen tier-6 guards and few hundred players there for the dungeon, or to sell goods, that were camped out at the entrance were all caught by surprise as the slaughter began. Xeal didn't even need to worry about their attacks giving them away, as Daisy and Violet activated a mass illusion spell that would be more than enough to mask their actions. While Xeal felt bad for the players who were just there to use the dungeon, he knew that it was necessary to send the message that he wanted. After all, Xeal was at war with Abysses End and all who would do business with them at this point and he wanted to make it clear that FAE would attack all those involved.

A bloody and profitable mess later and Xeal's party was on their way to the rear of the Ethax position that was heaviest along the Muthia border. Thankfully, Kate had sent Xeal a message saying that everything was good to go, as his party arrived at the staging point that they would use to perform their part an hour before everything was set to start. This point was just at the edge of the mountain range where Xeal planned to secure the needed griffin eggs and waters of youth over the next few weeks as well. As such, they had an excellent view of the defensive line's rear from the elevated position and would be perfect for what Xeal was planning to do. Though before that, it was time to let all of his stats return to their peak condition as he waited for Kate to give the go ahead. As they waited, Eira came over and sat on Xeal's lap as she started to talk with him.

"Are you really ready to spend so much time away from the others?"

"I will never be ready, but necessity is what it is."

"Right and how long do you think it will be before Daisy and Violet are sitting on either side of you while leaning on you at times like these?"

"Eira, I don't think of such things, especially when I have one of my wives sitting in my lap."

"Fine. Daisy, Violet, please come join us and yes Xeal, this has been cleared by all of us. Now that we are starting our lives behind enemy lines, they are allowed to make any pass at you that doesn't involve the removal of clothing. You have to do that, and yes, you are allowed to and for the record I hope you at least hold out a few months, but not longer, as the boost that they will give you is valuable enough for me to agree to them being part of this."

Xeal just frowned as Daisy and Violet sat next to him in a timid manner as they waited to hear his reply. A reply that Xeal took his sweet time in delivering as he looked for the right words to say in this situation, as he knew the whole party was listening in. As such, these words would likely have major ramifications on how things would be handled moving forward and could become a determining factor in the atmosphere and morale of the party. Finally, Xeal knew his answer and he made sure to look at every one of them before he responded.

"I want to make a few things clear. First, I will never shy away from comforting any of you in an appropriate manner. None of you should hold yourself back when you need someone to be there in the capacity of me being someone to care and I expect you all to be there when I need it as well. To say that our lives over the next few years won't be difficult and full of darkness would be a lie and if we let it consume us, we may very well become monsters ourselves. Daisy, Violet, I will not tell you to seek love elsewhere at this point, but please promise me that you will never take advantage of a moment of weakness where I need care, not lust. If you wish to join the ranks of my wives, I need to be able to trust you as I do Eira and we need to love each other in a way that is personal to us and is healthy. Bula, Dafasli, I see you both as well and while I will make no promises, I will try to not make the burden that your feelings create any heavier than it already is. Rina, Alea, Lucy, no just no. Under no circumstances are you three even allowed to entertain such notions. As far as I am concerned, the three of you may as well be men for the way I intend to see you in this party. Oh, how I wish Ignis or Amet could have tagged along for this mess. Still, if I can do anything to help, do not hesitate to ask as I can only be as good of a leader as you all enable me to be."

"Are you done?" replied Lucy. "Because give us a break. We all know what we have signed up for here. Yeah, it's going to suck, but that doesn't mean that we are all going to try to spend some time between the sheets with you."

"Speak for yourself," retorted Rina. "I for one appreciate him saying that, as Alea and I haven't completely ruled out such possibilities happening in the heat of the moment. Not that we are intending for it to happen, but as Bula knows all too well, sometimes we get so swept up in the events surrounding us that we say and do things that we shouldn't."

"Indeed. It is also good to know where we all stand and at the very least that our leader cares," added Bula. "If I had to guess, Xeal knew that you would be the only one to have any issue with what he just said."

"It's the charisma modifier," commented Xeal. "Lucy, as a cleric, you have a higher score and as a player, you're automatically more resistant to the passive effects of it. I am well aware that my words are not on the same level as the great orators of history, but it is enough that you can understand my meaning. Oh, and don't worry, you're the one that I am least worried about trying, or succeeding in finding their way into my heart and bed."

Xeal could see Lucy holding back a response as Violet spoke.

"Xeal, all we ask is to be seen and for you not to run from any feelings you may have for us. We already know what our feelings for you are and are willing to be a bit more patient for you to return them."

"Yes, as much as we would love to hold a wedding ceremony tomorrow, we know that is not how this will go," added Daisy.

"Darn right. After the amount of chasing I had to do once I had his affection, there is no way that I would be fine with that," commented Eira.

"Alright, alright, I think that is enough for now. Let's just focus on our current mission. Daisy, Violet, you two are key and the rest of you need to be ready to go as we won't be sticking around to see the results."

As Xeal finished speaking, silence overtook the group as Eira simply snuggled into him while Daisy and Violet each put an arm and two of their tails behind his back as they leaned against him. Xeal simply accepted their affection while not returning it fully as time passed, until it was finally time to move. At this, both Daisy and Violet kicked things off with creating an illusion of a massive storm that seemingly formed out of nowhere. Xeal knew that this would be instantly believed to simply be an illusion, but it was also on the scale that it could be seen as a tier-8 trump card spell. Such spells were usually governed by different rules than other spells and could take hours to prepare, unlike the standard short, medium, or long chant spells that most casters used.

As soon as this illusion was complete, Xeal shifted to his lightning form and used flash step to instantly arrive in the defensive lines' ranks. From there Xeal was on the clock as he constantly was on the move as he used the passive damage that just coming into contact with him would deal to disrupt the formation. At the same time, the assault from the Muthia side came in at full force as total chaos overtook the field of battle. While Xeal's actions wasn't creating a massive body count, effects like paralysis and reflexively attacking him was destroying the integrity of the defense. Especially as he was jumping around five times every second as he simply picked a new target and landed directly on top of them. The number of jumps was only possible due to every second feeling like four and two-thirds seconds to him currently.

Five minutes after Xeal's assault started, or what felt like 23 minutes and 20 seconds to Xeal, the defensive line had been breached and it was time for him to withdraw. Still, there was one thing left for him to do, so he flash stepped into the sky and unleashed all but the last 100 MP left in his MP pool to send a massive electrical attack down upon what seemed to be the leader of Abysses End's forces. With that done, Xeal didn't even take a second to admire his handiwork as he flash stepped back to the rest of his party and his lightning form ended.

As he was catching his breath, Daisy and Violet were making it seem as if the storm had ended and Xeal was already taking a meditative stance. As he did so, he enjoyed the fact that aura control reduced his recovery time for all his stats while meditating to 40 minutes instead of an hour. Once Xeal had recovered while Eira and Rina stood watch for anyone who had realized that they were here, the battle was already swinging Muthia's way. Additionally, Abysses End had not yet started a full-on assault elsewhere and from what Kate had gathered, the current theory was that Queen Aila Lorafir was behind the situation here. This had put them on high alert elsewhere as they once more were seeming to wait for Xeal to make a move, before picking where they should make a major push.

All this made Xeal smile as he signaled to have Daisy and Violet create the same illusion as before as he picked out his next targets. Among the sea of tier-6 and tier-5 players were several tier-7 NPCs that were acting mainly as support, or quick strike troops that were focused on closing any hole in the line before they became major issues. It was these NPCs that would be Xeal's next targets as the storm formed and he entered his lightning form once more. As he began his assault, he could tell that the players were already anticipating his arrival as they tensed up, but nothing else as they had no counter prepared. Had they understood the full nature of his ability, they may have tried tactics like creating a circle of lightning rods to catch him, but Xeal doubted that such tactics would do more than slow him down. His control over electricity was strong enough that it could cause it to ignore the ways it normally behaved as it bent to his will. Though Xeal wasn't foolish enough to not see the dangers of the force shields that were suddenly being erected randomly throughout the Ethax forces' lines.

With this adjustment noted, Xeal found himself having to perform shorter jumps and even jumping into the sky before going down to reach each of his targets. While he was still able to be effective, this time Xeal was sure that Abysses End would be even more organized against this phantom spell the next time. Still, Xeal had no intention of hiding that it was him the next time that he used this ability against Abysses End, and after killing four tier-7 NPC clerics the lines broke and Xeal ended his assault with another burst of electricity in the sky. Only this time it was aimed at a level 270 NPC that seemed to be leading the Ethax forces as they escaped. If Xeal had to place odds on it, he was sure that his attack had failed to kill the man, but the staff around him was likely not as lucky. With that thought, Xeal just sat as he focused on his breathing while he recovered.

While this was the first time he had killed a good NPC that was just doing their duty in this life, it wasn't the first time he had ever done so. No, Xeal had been in many battles and had the deaths of at least 20 such NPCs on his hands from his last life. However, Xeal could also tell that due to his position in this life, he would likely kill far more NPCs this time around and he began to mourn the lives he had just taken. He knew that their fate was to be processed and reabsorbed into the main system, as the resources used to animate them and make them a person were repurposed. This was why NPCs were so quickly removed, and in Xeal's last life it was commonly theorized that the wars and reduction in intelligent NPCs had served two purposes. First, to open more room for players to integrate into the economy and politics of ED and second, to reduce the cost of running ED's systems. The only exceptions that Xeal knew of were those who were selected by a deity to serve them even after death, like the fallen warriors in Freya's realm, Fólkvangr. Xeal wondered if he would be able to do something similar in the quest world once he completed his quest there.

As all of these thoughts crossed Xeal's mind, he could feel Eira as she sat on his lap and just held him close to her.

Xeal knew that she was well aware of his inner turmoil from how he was acting and at the same time she knew better than to say anything as words would do Xeal no good. No, he needed to simply accept that this was a situation with no good options as he focused on moving on and five minutes later, he decided it was time to do just that. While his MP pool was only around 11% of its max, the rest of his stats were fine and the longer they stayed the more likely that they would be discovered by the fleeing mass of players and NPCs. So it was that they slipped into the wild land map that was full of level 200 and up monsters, and was considered a forbidden zone by most NPCs.

The following five days were spent mainly avoiding battles as much as possible, while they relied on Xeal to handle the bulk of the frontline duties when they couldn't. Still, by the time they reached their first target on day 166, Xeal smiled as they approached what was nothing but a slow drip of water that seemed to be coming out of the top of a cave entrance. After letting a single drop fall in his mouth, Xeal spoke to the group.

"This is our first destination. As you see, that cave is sloped down and each drop is heading into the cave. If we follow the path, we should come upon a pool, or at least a puddle and that will be where we will find the waters of youth that we need."

"Hold on," stated Alea after tasting a drop like Xeal had. "There is nothing special about this water?"

"You're right and wrong. Much of how things work in this world has been shaped by the legends of mine. When it comes to the fountain of youth, the most famous would be Ponce de Leon's search for it that may have never actually happened, but you can find similar stories from many ancient cultures. Each is unique in some ways, but a spring, well, stream, or some form of water being the source is extremely common. As such, the key is that the waters of youth are simply hard to find, even seemingly impossible, but really you just need to find a source water point like this that pools and hope that it has matured. That it would likely take a thousand to ten thousand drops from that to make a single drop of the waters of youth and what we are going to likely find is a pool that seems like fouled water ahead. It will also likely be guarded by a cave monster of some sort that doesn't even realize what it is guarding.

"Once we take care of that, I will guide you on how to harvest what we are after as it will have settled to the bottom of the pool. Heck, if we are really lucky, it will have reached a point where the pool has overflowed over time and the waters of youth will be practically pure. Either way, we will need to be careful with how we handle the harvest, as the layer at which the fouled water and the waters of youth meet is extremely deadly. It is another reason why so few know about the secrets of these pools, as a single drop taken at once is enough to kill any but the hardiest if ingested."

"How do you know all this?" questioned Lucy. "Also, if it is such a great poison, wouldn't it be just as valuable as the waters of youth, if not more so?"

"No, it is more trouble to handle than it's worth, "replied Xeal. "It acts exactly the opposite to the waters of youth and ages anything that it comes in contact with before becoming inert. Only something that is extremely old, like the very rocks of this mountain, or is unaffected by age, won't interact with it and no, making a vessel out of this stone won't work. It's why a puddle is easiest to harvest and the most that has ever been reported being collected at any one time, as the wind takes care of this layer once the puddle reaches the point of overflowing."

"Xeal, if this layer will destroy anything that touches it, how are we to get past it if we find a pool like you hope?" asked Violet.

"That is simple," answered Rina. "We just keep feeding it until it becomes inert."

"No," replied Xeal. "Even if we think that it has reached such a point, that would be extremely foolish. We go around it. If we had Holly here with us, it would be extremely easy as she could simply have the stone tell her what we need to know. However, we will use poles to see at what depth the poison is and create a slanted hole about a quarter of an inch in diameter deeper than that to harvest. Anyhow, you will understand once we have found it and we get to work. Now let's follow this trail and see what we find."

Just like that, Xeal led his party into the cave as they advanced slowly while dealing with a few swarm-type monsters that were among the most frustrating foes to deal with. Especially the spiders that were all the size of gumballs and dealt stacking poison damage that threatened to kill its victims, even after the swarm was dealt with. While this was a major issue for most parties, Xeal just smiled as he had Alea, Daisy and Violet each hit him with a quick chant electrical spell as he acted like a human bug zapper. Next were the bat swarms that were at least manageable through melee attacks, if you could use them that was. Xeal, however, was almost useless during these fights as his advanced senses amplified the sonic assault that the bats were pelting his party with. These attacks dealt almost no damage, but they completely messed up one's balance over time and earmuffs were highly suggested once a fight with them began. However, even that didn't solve the issue for Xeal as he went to a knee and found himself focusing on ignoring the sensory input from his ears and just feeling the disturbances in the air from their wings. This only ended up with him knowing when to release small amounts of electricity that he was gathering from his elemental blades skill.

While Xeal could have likely used his aura control, or elemental filtered dragon's breath to handle the situation in a single go, he didn't. This was due to several factors, the chief amongst them being that Xeal didn't want to create a situation where other monsters were terrified and started to try to escape through the cave walls and cause a cave-in. Were this to occur, it could bury them alive, as well as the pool where the waters of youth were collected. So, like this, they continued to move forward until they reached the pool in question two hours after entering the cave.

The first thing that Xeal had noticed was the smell, as it would have been overpowering for those with normal senses of smell and for him it was almost debilitating. Luckily, stuffing wads of cotton in his nose made it bearable as he looked for the pool's guardian. Judging by the fact that the pool was five feet wide, Xeal was expecting something substantial. What he hadn't expected was for the whole top layer of the pool to move, as a giant slime that seemed to have absorbed most of the fouled water emerged. Xeal instantly looked at the level 250 monster and realized that the situation was worse than he feared, as they had yet to face anything over level 230. In that instance, Xeal shifted to his lightning form and flash stepped into the slime and focused on releasing electricity into it.

As Xeal did this, the others were unsure how to proceed, as the massive slime was well outside of anything that they had prepared for. While they had spells that were sure to harm it, they didn't dare have any of them act as the physical barrier needed to assault it. They had all expected Xeal to order them to withdraw, not enter it and start attacking it from within. So, as the steam began to rise from the slime, they were still unsure of what to do until Lucy took charge and started to give out orders.

"We can't let it fall back in the pool when it dies. If it does, the waters of youth will be mixed in with that filth and who knows how long it will take for them to re-separate! Alea, focus on creating a force shield to act as a lid. Daisy, Violet, hit it with anything you can that will push it backwards. If we can move it to the far side of the pool, it should solve any issues with the drainage from its body entering the pool. Finally, everyone do what you can to help with that goal, but don't touch it, or breathe in anything of the steam as it is likely highly toxic!"

With that they all shifted into action as Xeal paid attention to his MP pool as he struggled to ensure that he didn't cause the slime to explode. All he could think about was the possibility that the slime had taken on more than just the fouled water and also contained the poison. If it did, it would make sense of the feeling of danger that Xeal had felt from it as he made his rash decision to attack before it could. It was easily possible that a single attack could carry with it an instant death, even if it was blocked.

Two minutes after Xeal entered the slime, his MP pool was almost empty and the slime's health was still above 25% and he sighed as he started to activate his flash step to escape. This was easier said than done, as all Xeal could see was a few inches in front of himself and for a solid ten seconds Xeal worried that he had trapped himself inside of the slime as he could see nothing. It was just as he had about 15 seconds left on his lightning form that he saw a flash of light and jumped to it as he escaped the slime, to see Daisy and Violet sending one spell after another into it. Meanwhile, Alea had a force barrier over the now practically empty pool as everyone else was attacking the slime any way they could. Xeal quickly flash stepped to being next to the edge of the pool as he ended his lightning form and shot his normal dragon's breath attack off and the beam of blueish white light pierced straight through the slime. At the same time, it was pushed even deeper into the cave as Daisy's and Violet's attacks hit it simultaneously.

Unfortunately, Xeal could tell that they were losing ground as he summoned his electrical wyvern combat companion and Midnight. His wyvern was about the size of a black lab at this point and Midnight was the same as ever as he gave Xeal a look like this was all a major inconvenience. Still, he just smiled as he shouted out new orders.

"Daisy, Violet, Alea, hit me with all the electricity that you can! Lucy, toss a piece of parchment into the water that is left in the pool! If it doesn't disintegrate, Eira, take these and harvest as much of it as you can! Everyone else, focus on keeping the slime away from the pool. Now go!"

With that Xeal felt the electricity from Alea, Daisy and Violet, as his wyvern's electrical breath hit him as well. While the four of these combined was far less damage than he had been doing each second that he had been inside of the slime, it was enough to keep its health going down and that was enough for Xeal right now, as Lucy confirmed that the paper didn't dissolve and Eira grabbed the dozen bottles that Xeal had pulled out that would each hold a quarter of a gallon. 30 seconds later Eira called out from the bottom of the pool.

"Anyone have more bottles? That only got around half of what is down here!"

Xeal almost choked at what Eira had said. While he had hoped to find a small two or three-gallon pool of the waters of youth that had possibly run pure, six gallons was well beyond his most optimistic of expectations. With each gallon being enough to treat 291 years of aging, six gallons would handle 1,746 years of life and would be more than enough to keep Enye, Lingxin, Dyllis and Mari young well past when Xeal would die in reality. Heck, Xeal would have been happy if a single bottle had been filled as that would have been enough for almost 73 years and enough to ensure Jeren was returned to his prime. As Xeal was thinking about this, he frowned as he only had a few random containers that could be used and none of them were as large as the bottles he had given Eira.

In the end, between Xeal and everyone else, another two gallons were harvested, but that was it as Midnight turned his attention to the remaining few gallons in the pool. Before Eira could stop him, Midnight had started to lap it up and avoid any attempt to capture him. Xeal was about to unsummon him when he hesitated as he thought about the matagot's intelligence and just how old he must have been in reality. While Midnight had next to nothing in offensive abilities, he was completely focused on survival and prolonging his own existence.

While Xeal doubted that age mattered to a matagot, he did know that drinking the waters of youth could restore all aspects of one's condition, as in reality it was refreshing the cells in the body. It wouldn't turn an adult into a baby no matter how much you drank, but it would restore the elasticity of the brain to a certain extent. For players, this effect was basically wasted on them as their bodies were already eternal and their minds were based in reality, so all they got were a few free ability points in either constitution, SP, MP, or charisma stats. This was after they consumed enough of it to add a decade to an NPC's life and the points only lasted for a few years as well before being lost. Though they did stack and if Xeal used all that they had just harvested here, it could turn him into a true monster for the next few years of the war, but that would be shortsighted. Instead, he spoke up to his party as he gave out an order.

"Eira, give everyone but Lucy and I a large bottle to drink right now, to include yourself and pass Lucy and I two of the smaller ones."

"What!? Xeal, I don't want to be a little kitten again, I enjoy being your wife too much."

"Eira, just do it! You won't become a kitten, I promise!"

"Fine, but I am only drinking it after Daisy and Violet do."

Eira quickly got to work as she moved from one person to another and Xeal felt the short pauses in the spells that were entering him as each of them drank a bottle. As the effects took hold, Xeal smiled as each of the women reacted to the experience as all of their stats were restored to their peak conditions. As Xeal swallowed enough for about five years, his own stats returned to max, though the only other benefit that he got was a 25% boost to his recovery speed for the next month. This would take his 40 minutes and slim it down to 30 between fights, but right now all he cared about was the restoration of his MP pool as he returned to his lightning form. As he did this, Xeal flash stepped to right in front of the slime and pushed his arms inside much like Levina had done to him.

This caused the slime to start attacking him by extending part of its body out like a whip and swing violently at him. As each of these swings hit Xeal, he could see his MP drop slightly and the slime take damage, and Xeal just smiled knowing that this was nothing but his electrical form restoring itself much like it had been constantly doing when he had been inside of the slime earlier. Xeal was just happy that for whatever reason, the slime had no ranged attack as he watched its health drop below five percent as he yelled out in his distorted voice.

"Alea, separate me from everyone else with a force shield!"

As soon as he saw the shield go up, he increased his output as the final points of the slime's health disappeared and it exploded outward violently. As the sludge-like slime landed all around and destroyed anything that it touched while putting off a toxic gas, Xeal just increased his output of lightning to disintegrate every particle of its body. Just like the water version of the poison that he knew was the slime, the loot that was this sludge was better off being destroyed. As for the origin of that slime, Xeal felt like it would be better if he didn't look into it as such a monster should have not been there. With that thought came one of it being very possible that they had just harvested the hidden stash of whoever put that slime there, as it felt like it had been trained at some point to leave the waters of youth behind. This made Xeal wonder if the players who focused on harvesting waters of youth in his last life had developed similar methods, with the side hole method being the least efficient one that was leaked.

Either way, it was time to leave and Xeal didn't even bother looking at the just under five gallons that Eira handed him after he shifted back to a physical form and rejoined them. All he cared about was getting his gear on and putting a fair bit of distance between him and this cave, as depending on the exact situation, it would only be a few days at most before the master of the slime would return. Once they had reached the entrance, Xeal turned back around and shifted to his lightning form once more. This time he held nothing back as he unleashed a full-powered blast of electricity into the cave and controlled it such that it scorched every surface that it could, while going all the way to the deepest regions of it. As he returned to his normal form, he let out a sigh as Eira spoke.

"Xeal, what was the hurry to leave and that blast about?"

"I am about 70% sure that we just plundered a tier-8's hidden stash. My hope is that they are dead, but I am almost sure that slime was not native to that cave, or even wild. Also, I doubt even most tier-8s would have survived that fight, as I am pretty sure taking a single hit from that slime would have meant instant death from the same poison we needed to worry about when harvesting it normally. Though we did just learn a new way to harvest it and it is far more efficient than my method."

"Let's go back to that being a tier-8's stash part!" replied Lucy. "Just when did you realize that?"

"Right after I finished killing it and could focus on something beyond surviving. By that point there wasn't any going back. So, shall we head off to our next destination?"

"Wait, you still care about some griffin eggs when we could have a pissed-off tier-8 coming for us?!"

"Lucy, I destroyed every trace of the slime in there. Knowing that it contains that poison, would you hurry after us before knowing how we survived? Not to mention that if we found a way to harvest the slime's remains? Honestly, as long as we aren't right here when they get back, we should be relatively safe."

"Then let's get out of here!" retorted Lucy as she turned to leave and Xeal just smiled as he and the rest of his party followed after her.

The following two days was spent heading to what Xeal hoped would be a nesting area that had been known to be used year-round by griffins in Xeal's last life. As they arrived in the area, Xeal was able to spot what looked like three nesting mothers atop three separate peaks and as they watched throughout the day, three male griffins could be seen returning with fresh meat. Each of these griffins were between level 234 and 245, and each could easily accommodate two or three riders if Xeal were to tame them. Doing so was too tempting of a proposition, especially with another companion slot having opened up for players at tier-7, even if there was a high chance that it would end in failure. Griffins were proud and noble creatures who only ever recognized those who were able to defeat them as owners, and even then it was a rather tenuous situation. Xeal knew that if he were level 250, he would have no issues taming one, if not several, even without any of the skills that most beast tamers used, but he was over 30 levels below the weakest of them so he didn't like his chances.

However, Xeal was still planning to try to do just that as it would be the easiest way to secure their eggs. So, with his sights set on the weakest of the three mothers, Xeal separated from the rest of his party using his lightning form to flash step to the almost unclimbable peak. Once there, he hid in a nook just a bit from the top as he reequipped all of his gear and watched as the nesting mother fidgeted and looked around. Xeal knew that she could sense him, but not to the point that she was sure of where he was. As he got the last of his gear on, Xeal shifted his aura control to its active state and directed it at the female griffin, who instantly shifted to a defensive posture while calling out in what seemed like a desperate plea for help. Xeal wasn't about to simply allow that to continue as he pulled himself over the last ledge and the griffin quieted in confusion as she took in her tormenter.

Instantly her fear turned to rage as she attacked him, and Xeal avoided her as he saw the two eggs that were in her nest as he did so. When the next attack came, Xeal was quick to slide beneath her and next to her eggs as he held one of his swords to her belly, such that if she tried to slam down on him she would impale herself. This prompted her to take off and come around for a swooping attack as Xeal pocketed the eggs, and she screeched in fury as she entered into a diving attack. At this Xeal smiled as he returned to his lightning form and flash stepped to the next peak, leaving behind an enraged griffin as it searched for him.

As Xeal once more landed in an alcove, he resolved to deal with the annoyance of spending the skill points on the quick equip skill that he had been eying. After leveling it up to level four, he was left with only 11 unused class skill points and it allowed for him to set two full sets of armors and weapon sets, as well as a casual gear set to switch between. This bypassed the normal requirement of not being in combat and the slight delays that all clothing had if you didn't manually put them on, and instead allowed them to be instantly changed for 100 SP. There was even an advanced skill that he had unlocked if he wanted to spend the 50 class skill points for it when he had them, that would let him set as many presets as he liked. Xeal could see how some players who were hard on their equipment would love that skill, but for him it wasn't worth the points as the 70 points he had already invested were enough. With that thought, Xeal set his basic gear in it during the time the first female griffin was flying over and used the skill to reequip himself.

As the first griffin arrived, it made the new one take the same defensive stance that the first one had towards Xeal, only towards the first griffin. Xeal had picked a time slot when all three males would be out hunting to attack and when the second griffin was focused on the first, he hopped up and quickly went for the single egg in the nest. As he did this, the first griffin was shrieking as it alerted the second to the danger, only it was too late to do more than catch sight of Xeal as he stored the egg away and shifted to his lightning form as he escaped. By this point, the last griffin, which was also the most powerful at level 245, had noticed what had been going on and had taken note of Xeal's actions. So she didn't react to the two irate griffins headed her way, or Xeal, as she used her body to completely cover and guard her eggs while calling for help.

Seeing this, Xeal had to admire this griffin for its intelligence and willingness to leave itself in a vulnerable position to guard against him. Even as he put pressure on her with his aura, she just kept calling out as the other two griffins arrived and Xeal finally had all three together as he smiled. He wasted no time walking up to the mother who was guarding her eggs and dodging her one desperate attempt to peck at him with her beak and mounted her. At this she screeched in confusion, but didn't move for fear of exposing her eggs to danger as the other two started to swoop down at him. Xeal almost wanted to laugh as he dodged their attempts to attack him without angering the third griffin that still guarded her nest. Still, he knew that for them this was a traumatic moment and he needed to complete what he came here to do as he attempted to bind the third griffin to him.

Taken by surprise, the third griffin failed to resist until it was at a true disadvantage in the battle of wills and situations. Put simply, all Xeal had to do was remain atop the griffin for a solid five minutes and it would be considered bound to him in a manner that he could summon and dismiss it, like Midnight and his wyvern. While this would do little to actually tame it, he had Queen Aila Lorafir standing by with a few tier-7 members of FAE where he was going to send it to take care of that for him. As the screeching became more frantic, Xeal smiled as Lucy dropped down atop the weakest of the griffins.

Unlike most other members of FAE, Lucy had ignored

the companion settings completely as she found it too much of a hassle. So, she had all three of her slots open, two of which could be used on these griffins. As for how she had managed to get so far above the griffins, it had to do with the flight spell that Alea had taken as even now she was above them watching the scene play out. Had they tried to sneak up there before Xeal had begun his assault, they would have been seen instantly, but as Xeal had had their full attention, achieving this had been extremely easy. At the same time, this had finally pushed the griffin that Xeal was on to take to the sky as it exposed the three eggs it had been guarding. Though Xeal had little time to admire them as he found himself climbing quickly as he held on tightly. This was followed by the griffin going into a near vertical dive as it spun rapidly in an attempt to dislodge Xeal. However, Xeal just smiled as he held tightly to the area just below the griffin's wing joints and closed his eyes as he enjoyed the feeling of the wind on his face while laughing freely.

Meanwhile, Lucy was dealing with a similar situation as she screamed her lungs out and held on for dear life. Just as Xeal felt the griffin pull up, the last resistance to his bond ended and he wasted no time in exerting his control over the griffin as he dismissed it to the area that had been set aside for it and the others. As it vanished, Xeal shifted to his lightning form and used flash step to return to the peak where the second griffin stood over the three eggs, looking unsure of what to do. At the sight of Xeal, it began to screech as it looked for the third griffin frantically, and one flash step later Xeal was at the eggs and had ended his lightning form and activated the quick equip skill as he poked the griffin's underside with his blades.

As the griffin took off out of reflex more than anything, Xeal quickly secured the last three eggs, just in time to see a screaming Lucy whiz by on the back of the first griffin. Xeal was rather sure he heard a few curse words mixed in as he kept his focus on the second griffin who was looking at him in horror. It was at this moment that Alea sent up the signal that meant that one of the male griffins was returning and Xeal frowned as it was still too soon. Sighing, Xeal caught sight of the level 242 one that had been mated to the third griffin that he had already captured, as he returned to his lightning form and flash stepped to it. As Xeal's body came in contact with the griffin, it instantly started to spasm and fell into an uncontrolled dive. Xeal had to keep flash stepping to stay in contact as he allowed the griffin to fall a full 100 feet before returning to his physical form and gripping its back tightly. As he did this, he braced for impact as the griffin moved erratically as it attempted to correct its positioning and regain flight, but it was too late as it only managed to get two good flaps in before impact.

Xeal felt intense pain that radiated through his body and knew that the griffin was in even worse shape as it had rolled down the side of the mountain. Having lost a full quarter of his health despite being mostly shielded from the impacts by the griffin's body, even if the few that had hit home had been excruciating, Xeal was a bit slow in getting to his feet. Still, he was practically unharmed compared to the griffin, which was a mangled mess with shredded wings and legs that were bent at odd angles as its blood ran freely. Xeal could already see its natural recovery working to restore it, but that was barely keeping up with the bleeding damage as it lay on its side. While it still had over half of its health remaining, the fall had been such that even with video game logic being at play that it had gained the broken wings and legs statuses. Xeal wished that he could simply dissolve his last contract he had made to subjugate each of the griffins, but he would need to wait at least a week to be allowed to replace it. Put simply, the system wasn't about to let players simply buy and sell mounts and combat companions like that, unless they were a beast tamer and spent the hundred-plus skill points that were needed to unlock such a skill.

So, Xeal was left with only a single option for the griffin before him. He would need to break its will to resist completely. First, Xeal took out the three eggs he had stolen from its mate's nest and watched as it frantically struggled to move, only to worsen its condition as Xeal stored the eggs. At this same moment, Xeal unleashed his aura on the griffin while summoning the one he had already made into his mount. When it appeared, Xeal could see the drastic changes as Queen Aila Lorafir had really come through for him as it was harnessed and settled while looking utterly humiliated. As it realized that it had returned, it was quick to look around and was about to take off when it saw its mate and froze at the scene before it. Xeal pulled out one of the three eggs once more as he looked at his new mount, as he tried to impress on it the current situation as it looked distraught.

Xeal actually felt sad as he saw all of the fight leave it as it lowered itself such that it seemed to be inviting Xeal to ride it. He knew that Queen Aila Lorafir and his members had only had a few minutes to work with it, and now he had to wait an hour before dismissing it. This was due to the rapid summoning after dismissing it, but that was fine as he needed it for the rest of his plan. As Xeal stored the egg, he smiled at the good fortune that had been its mate being the one to return, as he sat on its back and looked at the crumpled mess of a griffin on the ground. As he sat there, he resisted the urge to stroke the back of the griffin's neck as he would eventually, due to it likely not wishing to be humiliated any further as he took out a collar. The collar had several copies of his crest on it and matched the one on his mount and Xeal looked at the male griffin as he pointed to one of them on both. After this, Xeal tossed the collar in front of the griffin and waited for it to make a decision.

If the griffin used its beak to throw or push the collar away, Xeal would know that it was refusing to be tamed and he would simply leave it there as he rejoined the others. If it accepted it, Xeal would place the collar which was enchanted to allow him to tighten it with a thought, so long as he was wearing the corresponding command item around his neck. While this would cause Xeal to have to use one of his magic item slots for the remainder of the journey, it would be well worth it if it accepted. Especially as an adult male griffin would allow the breeding of hippogriffs to be accelerated, to the point of having the first batch of mounts ready in a year rather than two. As Xeal thought about this, he could see the male griffin looking at the collar with indecision as he thought about what he would do. Finally, he took one look at his mate and gingerly picked up the collar with his beak and looked at Xeal.

Xeal held his excitement in check as he dismounted and slowly walked over to the griffin, as he was on guard against the griffin using deception to attack, even if it was unlikely. While griffins were intelligent enough to use it, they were normally too proud to, though Xeal had just stolen their eggs and was humiliating them, so he wasn't taking any chances. However, he needn't have worried as he easily fitted the collar on him and pulled out one of the smaller bottles of the waters of youth that only held around five years' worth of the miracle fluid, like he had used earlier. As Xeal opened it, both griffins honed in on it and the male didn't hesitate to open his mouth as Xeal poured it in and all of its wounds started to rapidly heal. At the same time, the female griffin was looking at Xeal expectantly and he just sighed as he took out a second bottle and fed it to her.

Suddenly both griffins seemed a lot less opposed to their situation as Xeal sat on the female's back and they rose into the air. As Xeal reassessed the current situation, he found that the other two griffins had returned with Daisy and Violet activating illusion spells to confuse them, as there were six Xeals moving around currently. Lucy had still yet to claim the first female griffin as she was still holding on while screaming as she tried to complete the process. It was then that the male griffin that Xeal had subdued let out a loud screech that caught the other four griffins' attention. Even the one trying to throw Lucy off stopped its erratic maneuvers to see what was going on, as Lucy finally got a second to catch her breath as she shot Xeal a dirty look. Xeal just held in a laugh as all four uncollared griffins flew over to the collared male as he entered a steep dive and landed not too far away. All but the one with Lucy on their back landed as screeching that sounded like an argument started between them.

Meanwhile, Xeal's attention was on the griffin that had returned to trying to shake Lucy off as she held on for her dear life. Though it seemed that she had at least managed to stop screaming and Xeal thought that perhaps she would actually start to make some progress on binding it to her. Even if it was a long shot, Xeal knew that it was worth trying as it would save a fair amount of experience needed to level it up. Finally, Xeal grew tired of waiting as he circled above and so he unleashed his full aura on the four wild griffins and jumped down into the middle of them. The two female griffins seemed to be ready for this, but their mates were feeling it for the first time as they tensed up and looked at Xeal in surprise. While Xeal could tell that his aura wasn't enough to subdue them on its own, it was enough that when he took a step forward, the griffins all stepped back unconsciously. At this Xeal just smiled as he pulled out the last collar that he had and tossed it in front of the mate of the one Lucy was dealing with.

As the confusion in the group reached a whole new level, Xeal pulled out the single egg from the other pair's nest and looked at them. Both looked like they wanted to attack him, but feared what would happen if he used their egg as a shield. As he did this, the female that had been acting as his mount landed and he walked over and placed the egg beneath her. This was followed by him taking out the two from the first nest and placing them there as well, to hopefully send the clear message that he only needed the one pair. As to what was actually understood Xeal was unsure, as all of the griffins tilted their heads as the one Lucy was clinging to finally landed, only to disappear as Lucy had finally succeeded in binding it. This caused the three wild griffins to shift their focus to Lucy who was still shaking as she panted for breath as she looked at Xeal before she started to shout at him.

"You! How dare you make me take part in such a plan when you know that I didn't want to!"

"Did you manage to pull it off?"

"Who cares! I never want to fly like that again, yet you want me to do it to one of these three, don't you?"

Xeal had to hold in a laugh at the looks all five griffins were giving her as he responded to her.

"If that one right there accepts that collar, I won't ask you to."

At that Lucy smiled as she looked at the mate to the one that she had just bound and put on what even Xeal felt was a slightly creepy smile as she pointed at the collar and spoke.

"Go on, take it, else I will attempt to bind the other male over there and you can be left with his mate!"

As she finished saying this, she pointed to the other male who looked confused as he shifted to be closer to his own mate and the male with the collar in front of him picked it up. At that Lucy started to walk forward as she took the collar and placed it around his neck and turned back to Xeal.

"There, can we go now, or do you plan on trying to capture those two as well?"

Xeal just smiled as he responded while returning all of the eggs to his inventory.

"Give me a second and tell me when you get the all clear and are about to summon your new mount."

"Oh, come on! You want me to bring that thing back here!?"

"It is a her, and yes, just focus on the other two for now."

As Xeal finished speaking, he put on the second collar's controlling accessory and waited. After a few tense minutes, Lucy sighed as she summoned her mount that looked disoriented and about ready to flee.

"There, are you happy now?"

"More or less."

As Xeal replied to Lucy, he pulled out the two empty small bottles before refilling them with one of the larger ones. As he did this, all six griffins took notice as the one Lucy had bound froze with its wings spread wide. Xeal simply walked over to the newly collared male after he finished filling the two small bottles. As Xeal held one of them out, he smiled as the griffin accepted it and he quickly turned his attention to Lucy's mount and repeated the scene before climbing onto his mount and speaking.

"Alright, mount up and fly over to the others."

Lucy just muttered to herself as she did as instructed and a few moments later they were all airborne, to include the two uncollared griffins. Xeal just smiled as they spent the next few days flying out of the wild lands in a route that would take them to Muthia-controlled territory. The whole time Xeal found himself with Eira riding with him as the others, doubled up as needed with Bula and Dafasli, dealt with a pair of makeshift saddles on the two uncollared griffins. By the time they landed, it was already day 171 and Xeal had reached level 201 shortly after they captured the griffins, that he was happy to hand off to the group of FAE players that had gathered to meet them. With the collars in place, Xeal gave the last two griffins small bottles of waters of youth as well, before he handed them over to the beast-taming-focused players, along with the eggs as he explained which ones went with each griffins. With that taken care of, Xeal spent the little time he had left before he would need to log off on making it back to his home in Nium. Once there, he smiled as he and Eira joined Mari, Lingxin, Enye and Dyllis in his bed.

On day 172, Xeal smiled as it was Lingxin's birthday and he was actually home for it, though all they got was an hour in the morning to be alone before they each had to return to their duties. Still, Xeal was happy to see that she had reached level 192 along with the rest of Xeal's wives. At their current pace, all four of them would be attempting to reach tier-7 at the same time as when Xeal expected the first non-FAE trained pro players would. Even so, Xeal wished that they could have just done as they had been expected to and evacuated to Cielo city, as it would be one less concern for him while he was operating behind enemy lines.

Speaking of enemy lines, they were ever encroaching as other than the border fort between Habia and Nium and the area Muthia had secured from Ethax, the enemies had gained on all fronts. This had created issues in the negotiations that Kate and Takeshi were leading as while they hadn't completely fallen apart, all of them were pushing for better conditions than FAE could offer. Xeal just sighed as he looked over the current situations across all of ED, as he was just relieved that the wars were still only on the three continents. However, FAE's current tier-7 players weren't going to be enough and it was clear from the 25,000 that had failed so far in the second group, that he hadn't found a way to get players past tier-7 without issues. Still, Xeal did take hope from seeing that Ignis, Amet, Aalin, Gale and Clara were all still active in their tribulations. If all of them passed, it would mean that if given the opportunities to grow, more players could achieve tier-7 and in turn tier-8.

With that thought, Xeal found day 172 coming to an end as he finished reading the reports surrounding the struggles of the war. Besides the theme of slowly losing ground day after day, Xeal found the lack of decisive battles strange. Even if Kate's theory of them waiting for Xeal to rear his head was correct, there should have been a major breakthrough somewhere. Instead, it was simply a slow and methodical advance and all Xeal could think of is that they thought that they would have better results when they had their members attempt to reach tier-7.

Day 173 saw Xeal return to the Zapladal Theocracy with Queen Aila Lorafir and the rest of the group from before his expedition into the mountains. There Matrikas and Jeren were awaiting him, as he smiled while pulling out a full bottle that would reverse the effects of over 70 years of aging and handed it to Jeren. At this both Matrikas and

Jeren looked surprised as Jeren spoke.

"To hand this to me without any deal in place is a foolish move."

"No, it is me saying that even without a deal in place, I would rather have you be the main voice for this country than an unknown. Besides, think of it as me mending the fence for refusing your granddaughters and being so ruthless in my approach with you."

"It is still a fool's move, but sometimes only a fool can win a battle because their opponent is expecting anything but one."

Xeal just smiled as they shifted to just what Xeal was hoping to accomplish, as Lois and Sciencia happily chatted with their grandfather until they came to an agreement. It was a rather simple arrangement as Xeal would set up a gate in the capital where any players with a special pass that FAE would issue could use the gate. These would come in different varieties, with the most common being the escape pass that would allow tier-5 players to leave a warring nation, but not return. While this would reduce the fighting force significantly inside of Nium, Muthia and the Huáng empire, it would also generate a good amount of quick gold to turn around and pay to bring in other players. All told, Xeal expected to make over a million gold like this as the casual players fled, while increasing the available resources for his own tier-5 guild members. With that the alliance had grown to four nations and four continents, which just left nine more continents to go before it could be considered complete.

The rest of day 173 was more paperwork for Xeal, as Kate refused to let him make an appearance in any of the other negotiations that she was working on. At the same time, players started to pass their tribulations as suddenly FAE had another 500 tier-7 members before he turned in for the night. When he awoke in the morning of day 174, that number was up to over 1,500 and climbing, as 26,000 had now failed. As the day continued, Xeal found himself dealing with aiding the work that was needed to assign them to their new duties, while preparing the next wave of 60,000 that were ready to make an attempt. This included several thousand that had already failed once and finally in the midafternoon, Xeal got word that both Aalin and Gale had been successful. However, neither was in any shape to do anything as they were recovering from releasing their latest seals. Along with this, Taya, Ignis, Amet, Clara and the rest of FAE's vice guild leaders successfully completed their tribulations. The day ended with 3,570 more members having reached tier-7 from the latest group of FAE players, with 26,430 failures.

This brought FAE's total tier-7 player base to 5,439 with a success rate of about 13.6%, which was much better than Xeal had hoped for, but was likely shocking to all the major powers who were watching FAE. Many were saying that it was the proof that Abysses End was right about FAE just having inflated levels, while others started adjusting their own projections and rethinking what was possible. Both were right from where Xeal was standing, as 20% had been what the first few waves of any major power had produced in his last life. FAE just didn't have that quality at the top of their ranks. However, it would likely still have over an eight percent success rate when the first million of its members finished their first attempts. Meanwhile, by that point even the most successful guilds only averaged a max of seven percent and it would just continue to decline as more and more players reached the second wall in ED.

Though, for Xeal to worry about any of this, FAE would need to weather the current storm first. With that thought he worked to redouble his efforts on ending the conflict in the Huáng empire in a draw as soon as possible. Though that would depend on many things, which included a whole lot of luck and the situations in Muthia and Nium remaining stable or in FAE's favor.

(*****)

Thanks!

Thank you to all of my patrons on Patreon, especially my knight-tier patrons Carl Benge, Alexander Casey Donnell, Timelesschief, Christof Köberlein, Benjamin Grey, Casey, Daniel Sifrit, Michael Jackson, Tim Bartlett, Jeffrey Iverson, James Vierra, David Peers, Kyle J Smith, Roman Smith, William J Dinwiddie II, Rick White, Ryan Harrington, Michael Mitchell, Stefan Zimmermann, Grantland Case, Francisco Brito, Peter Barton, Peter Hepp, Kore Rahl, Joel Stapleton, Lazai, Richard Schlak, Shard73, Blackpan2, Thomas Watret, Adamantine, William Adams, Matthew, Douglas Sokolowski, Edwin Courser, Sam Ellis, Andrew Eliason, Nick Stockfleth, DAvid Marksz, Fred Rankin, Georg Kranz, William Puryear, AR Schleicher, Angus Christopher, Roy Cales, JOHNNY SMILEY, Thomas Corbin, Spencer Ryan Crawford, Outwardwander, David Guilliams, Bern DG, Christopher Gross, Tony Fino, Ciellandros, David French, ABritishGuy, PeeM, F0ZYWOLF, Dan Dragonwolf, Marvin Wells, Dominic Q Roddan, Tanner Lovelace, Daniel Diaz, yo dude, Aimee Hebert, James A. Murphy, Mark reilly, Erebus Drakul Zaydow, tawshif tamjid, Kor Vang, nathrielos, James (Burnthemage), Fallen, Klaas Weibring, Shadowteck and michael berge.

(*****)

Afterword.

Thank you for reading Eternal Dominion book 19, Trials. I hope that you enjoyed it and will return for book 20 and beyond as the war arc really gets going!

Now onto me sharing a bit about other things going on and any news that I feel you all might want to know. First off, please, if you haven't done so yet, please either sign up for my mailing list to get the prelude novella in text form, or listen to it on Soundbooth Theater's website for free. You don't need a login or anything to listen on Soundbooth Theater's website and it is about an hour and a half long. It really isn't your typical prelude and I would say Alex/Xeal's story is only 25% of it, if even that. Rather you will get to see his friends, Takeshi, Kate and many others, as they experience events and fallout from Xeal's last login, much of which he was unaware of. Also, in case you missed it elsewhere, you can get all of the audiobooks on Soundbooth Theater's website for $4.99!

Next there is the fact that I really need all the help getting my story to those who will enjoy it, as Amazon seems to be playing with its algorithms. I can't say for sure, but I have been seeing major drops in new readers finding my books since February. To be clear, all of this was written on May 1, 2023 and I am hoping to change that before book 19 comes out, but I expect that I will still see my numbers way down. I am still more than fine, but if things continue to trend down like this, well, I might not be fine in another six months. Still, even if I have to eat the losses to finish Eternal Dominion, I will, and that includes the audiobooks, which might require me to switch to self-funding them. My commitment and my brand is to always finish what I start, as there is nothing I hate more when reading a story I love than it never being finished.

Alright, I will stop there before this becomes a rant that I really don't think anyone wants to read here. In other news, I really miss my wife! She has been out of town since March 20th and will only be getting back June 2nd... Hopefully this is a onetime thing and she is only gone for a week or two here or there, once she is done with the program she is in. Still, when you all read this, she will either be a day away from returning, or have already returned, so yay me! I am really looking forward to catching up on some snuggling and likely a fair bit of tickling her. I am also starting to get her to look at trying to address some of the areas that I haven't had the time to address, like how I am doing my advertising. Hopefully with some work she can find some solutions to the issues that I am seeing.

Now, finally, before we get back into the repetitive stuff that you should really read as it does change a bit from time to time, I would like to ask you all for help. As I said above, I need your help to make sure that by the time Eternal Dominion reaches its end next year, that I am not in the red each month. To be clear I am not asking any of you to over extend yourself, or even increase the money that you are spending on my books in any way. Especially with the world experiencing the insanity that it is right now. No, all I am asking is for you to talk about it and Kindle Unlimited to others, as you are my greatest marketer as you can sell more of my books simply by recommending it and sharing your honest feelings about it. It is why reviews are such a big deal and why I believe that I have seen the success that I have. Please don't go out of your way to share it, but if you see any of my posts on Facebook, or someone asks for recommendations and you think my book would be a fit mention it. Even just that can really make a difference and would mean the world to me, as I always smile when I see others sharing the joy my stories bring them.

Now onto the repetitive stuff. Did you know I have a newsletter and that by signing up you can get a free prelude novella for Eternal Dominion? Heck, it is really easy too. Just go to my website below and scroll to the bottom, where you will just need to put in your email address. Or you can go to https://BookHip.com/BAMDFBA, put in your email the single time and confirm it in your inbox to get the prelude and sign up for my newsletter in one go.

If you haven't already, go to https://soundbooththeater.com/team/bern-dean/ and listen to the free shorts that are available there. If you do it through a web browser you don't even need to create an account to do so, just select the listen now option. Zach and Annie have really gone above and beyond with their performances!

As always, if you feel I have forgotten something, feel free to reach out to me on Facebook through my page, or join my group. I am only one person and sending a message to my Facebook author page is the fastest way to get me to see it, as I don't get alerts on my personal page when non-friends message me for the first time. That said, I will not answer personal questions, like where I live, even in a general fashion. Please keep it to my story, or my writing process.

If you would like a weekly extra that focuses on looking at the supporting cast and is not plot necessary but is canon, I publish shorts on my Patreon. The first several of which are currently available to my $1 patrons, who will get another one every four weeks, while my $5 patrons get one each week. If you want to see what these are like, I have put a few up on my Facebook group as well now. I also now have a $5.50 tier for those who want to read the first 5 to 7 thousand words of the next book a week or so early, as that is when I have it back from the copy editor. To be clear, I delete the extended preview just before, or after, the book it is attached to is released. Some may ask why the extra 50 cents and to that I give two reasons. I have had some patrons tell me that they don't want the extended preview and it lets them ignore it. Also, it allows me to see just how much demand there is for extended previews.

https://www.facebook.com/groups/berndean
https://www.facebook.com/Author.Bern.Dean
https://www.patreon.com/berndean
https://www.Bernsbooks.com

Thank you again for reading my story and I hope you return for the next installment of Alex's tale. If you enjoy LitRPG and GameLit books, check out the following Facebook groups. Both are great and have helped me get my stories out to you!

LitRPG:

https://www.facebook.com/groups/LitRPG.books

GameLit:

https://www.facebook.com/groups/LitRPGsociety

Made in the USA
Monee, IL
01 July 2024

61040459R10152